I0662663

Killer Conference

by

Suzanne Rossi

The Snoop Group Series

This is a work of fiction. Names, characters, places, and incidents are either the product of the author's imagination or are used fictitiously, and any resemblance to actual persons living or dead, business establishments, events, or locales, is entirely coincidental.

Killer Conference

COPYRIGHT © 2016 by Suzanne Rossi

All rights reserved. No part of this book may be used or reproduced in any manner whatsoever without written permission of the author or The Wild Rose Press, Inc. except in the case of brief quotations embodied in critical articles or reviews.
Contact Information: info@thewildrosepress.com

Cover Art by *Kim Mendoza*

The Wild Rose Press, Inc.
PO Box 708
Adams Basin, NY 14410-0708
Visit us at www.thewildrosepress.com

Publishing History
First Crimson Rose Edition, 2016
Print ISBN 978-1-5092-1031-2
Digital ISBN 978-1-5092-1032-9

The Snoop Group Series
Published in the United States of America

Dedication

Critique groups can be a crucial asset to a writer. The premise is simple: a group of writers meet, read their latest efforts, and then discuss the pros and cons. What works, what doesn't, and most importantly, how to make whatever you've written better.

I've been fortunate to have many critique partners over the years—some good, some great, and a few quirky enough to make me laugh. I always gleaned something positive from the comments. And in most cases, those comments made for a much-improved finished manuscript.

So *KILLER CONFERENCE* is dedicated to all the hard-working, sincere, and, yes, occasionally quirky, men and women who have helped me on my way. I appreciate each and every one of you—especially those who made me laugh.

Chapter One

"Carmella Radcliff is a bitch. Everybody knows that. So stop crying and move on. Here, dry your eyes," Anne Jamieson said, handing Susan Lynch a cocktail napkin.

"But, she laughed at me. Said my plot was tired, my characters one-dimensional, my technique childish, and that the title was a silly cliché," Susan replied, wiping her eyes.

"Seems to me we said that about the title months ago."

"But I love that title. *Right as Rain* sounds so romantic."

Anne resisted heaving a sigh as she cast a glance around the spacious hotel bar from a table in the corner of the room. She willed the rest of their friends to arrive soon. Dealing with distraught, and as of yet unpublished, writers wasn't high on her list of fun things to do.

"Look, I told you not to send in the first two pages of your manuscript to be critiqued by her. She's the Simon Cowell of literary agents."

"But she's supposed to be the best."

"Says who? Personally, I wouldn't submit to her—if you'll pardon the cliché—come hell or high water. Send something to my agent."

"I...I did, but he rejected me," Susan sniveled.

"Then submit to someone else."

Anne wanted to scream with frustration. It wasn't the first time she'd had this conversation with her newest critique partner. Susan had a fantasy of her first book hitting the *New York Times* bestseller list. That was every writer's fantasy. The problem was Susan couldn't write for beans—at least not yet. She still had too much to learn. Even though Carmella had been nasty and insulting, she'd also been right. Susan wouldn't have had to go through this if she'd only listen to what her critique partners said.

Nancy Carlyle, another member of the critique group, walked up.

"Good grief, what's wrong with you?" she asked pulling out a chair and sinking into it.

"Susan submitted the first two pages of *Right as Rain* to Carmella Radcliff for the critique panel. She savaged it in front of a room full of people," Anne said, relieved reinforcements had arrived.

"That calls for sustenance. Why don't I get us something to drink?"

"Good idea," Anne replied, turning to the still weepy woman and patting her hand. "White wine all right with you, Susan?"

Nancy didn't wait for confirmation, but heaved her tall, lanky frame out of the chair and to the bar. Anne suspected her friend didn't really like Susan all that much, and this was her way of avoiding an unpleasant situation.

Anne didn't often attend conferences, but since this one, Sand and Sun, was sponsored by her Writers Association of America chapter, she made an exception. The affair was being held in San Sebastian,

Florida, her hometown, so she could attend the three-day meeting and avoid paying for hotel accommodations. Not that she needed a conference for the usual reasons. She was published with a major publishing house and had numerous books on the market. But several workshops dealt with marketing and promotion, along with the rise of technology and its effect on the industry. Plus, conferences offered an excellent opportunity to network. It seemed the publishing business changed on a daily basis. Keeping up with marketing trends was hard, especially when she was in full-fledged writing mode.

Nancy made her way back to the table as the fourth member of their group, Jennifer Swanson, arrived. Jen's blonde locks had gone through numerous changes. Right now, it was cut short and gelled into spikes. Her usual golden blonde color had been transformed into platinum. The changes gave her a gamin look, which worked well with her slender frame and medium height.

"Sorry, Jen. I just ordered wine for everyone."

"No problemo. I'll wait." She pulled out a chair and plopped into it. "What's wrong with you, Susan? Wait, let me guess. Carmella Radcliff, right? I heard she was being her usual self during a panel discussion. A lot of people were upset."

"Apparently so," Anne replied. "I can't imagine why anyone would set themselves up for a possible bad critique."

"Because it gives us hope," Susan told her. "We hope an agent or an editor will have something constructive to say and ask to see more."

"Well, far be it for me to crush hopes and dreams, but a public flogging in a crowded room isn't attractive." Anne brushed a lock of hair from her forehead. "Come on, Susan, buck up. It's not the end of the world. Didn't she rip everyone apart?"

"She wasn't complimentary to the others I heard. I left after she read mine. Wouldn't you know? I was the fifth one read. I guess that explains why she never even replied to my other submissions."

"What submissions?" Jen inquired casting a glance at Anne and Nancy.

"I've sent in several over the past year or so. I followed the guidelines for the first fifty pages and a synopsis. If I didn't hear back in three months, I sent an e-mail asking if she got it."

"Some agents state on their websites that if you don't hear anything in a month to assume they aren't interested," Nancy said.

"Personally, I think that's rude," Anne declared trying to take Susan's side. "A simple, 'Sorry, but I'm not interested' at least allows the author to submit elsewhere."

The waiter brought their wine. Susan gulped half of hers in one long swallow.

Jen ordered a glass for herself, and then snatched a handful of peanuts from the bowl on the table. She popped a couple into her mouth. "Carmella is worse than a bitch, but she only accepts the best to represent. I hear her sell rate is astronomical. I also heard a rumor she's an author, too. Uses a pseudonym."

"I take it she represents herself," Nancy said.

"Is that ethical?" Anne asked.

Jen shrugged. "I have no idea, but then I doubt ethics are a high priority for Carmella."

"I'm not sure I'd trust an agent who is also trying

to shop their own work around. You never know how hard they're working on your submissions," Nancy replied.

Susan drained her glass. "Well, I think someone should ram her head into a concrete wall until her brains fall out. Who does she think she is anyway? She could have said something nice like it needed more work. But no, she had to make fun of my miserable two pages in front of a hundred people."

The vehemence of the words surprised Anne. Susan was soft-spoken and timid about promoting herself. That did not, however, mean she took their comments without fuss.

I guess humiliation can turn us all into beasts. And she really doesn't take criticism well at all.

She laid her hand on Susan's arm. "Chalk it up to an unpleasant experience and let it go. At least all the critiques were anonymous, so nobody knows it was you."

"Oh, I put my name on it."

"For the love of God, why?" Nancy asked.

Jen shook her head and Nancy's tone suggested she was as exasperated with their partner as the rest of them.

"So that if someone said something nice, they'd know it was me," Susan replied with an earnest expression.

The usually outspoken Nancy sighed, no doubt because she was biting her tongue. Jen rolled her eyes and avoided looking at Susan.

"I had high hopes for good comments considering I'd pitched to her this morning." The earnest expression disappeared as Susan scowled. "Fat lot of good *that* did me."

Anne scanned the room. "Look, there's Howard Wright. He's the senior editor of the biggest romance publisher in the world. Why not go over, introduce yourself, offer to buy him a drink, and then discuss writing. Get his card, give him yours, and ask if you can submit?"

"Not right now. I'm too upset. Maybe tomorrow."

Anne sighed with irritation. This was so typical of Susan. Always finding an excuse. She, Nancy, and Jen along with a fifth member of the group, Rose Bennett, had spent the past six months critiquing together and mentoring Susan. So far, the poor woman hadn't learned much—or didn't want to. It was the ultimate frustration to give advice and have it ignored because the person on the receiving end thought he or she knew better.

Of course, it's up to the author on whether or not to take the suggestions, but when four people tell you the same thing, it's safe to assume they know what they're talking about. Anne didn't voice the thought. Susan probably wouldn't take it well at this moment anyway.

"Susan, I can't do it for you. If you don't make the effort, then you'll never become a published author," she said instead.

"That's easy for you to say," the woman shot back. "The three of you are already published. I'm still learning. I can't help it if I'm shy."

On those words, the waiter arrived with Jen's wine. Susan shoved her empty wine glass toward him.

"I'll take another."

As he nodded and left, Anne cast her gaze around

the table. Jen shrugged. Nancy sipped from her glass. They all knew Susan lacked initiative. She was one of those people who never quite rose above average— medium height, medium weight, medium brown hair, brown eyes, and a bland personality. Anne didn't want to be unkind, but Susan personified the word boring—a bit like her writing.

She immediately felt guilty for her unkind thoughts. She'd been working hard over the past year to control a tendency to be critical of others.

"So, what workshops did you all attend today?" Anne asked, changing the subject. It was better than listening to Susan complain. "Any of them good?"

They spent the next few minutes discussing the seminars. Rose, the last member of the group, walked into the room, waved, and joined them. Her slow, careful gait was an indication she'd just had a baby two weeks previously. On the plump side, she had light brown hair always in need of a trim, and her nail polish was frequently chipped.

"Rose, how are you feeling?" Nancy asked.

She cautiously lowered herself into a chair. "Not bad, considering. I'm tired and sore, but managing. Glad I'm only doing the Friday session."

"What do you want to drink?" Anne asked, signaling the waiter. "If we want refills, we'd better order them now. The place is filling up fast."

"A Bloody Mary," Rose ordered when the waiter arrived.

"Where are the kids?" Jen asked.

"With Jack."

"Your husband is actually taking care of the kids on a Friday?" Nancy said with raised eyebrows. Jack

Bennett was notorious for shirking child-raising duties. He was more into creating.

"I told him five kids, including a set of twins, under the age of eight is more than enough, and if he ever wants to have sex with me again he has to a) have the operation, and, b) deal with his offspring when I have writing-related work to do."

"Who's minding the store for him today?" Jen asked with a chuckle.

"Bennett Sporting Goods has a perfectly competent assistant manager," she declared. "I told Jack to let him manage. If I can compromise with cutting my conference attendance down to one day, he can do the same with the store."

"I don't see how you find time to write with your schedule," Susan murmured.

The wine and Rose's drink arrived. She stopped to take a sip. "Ah, after seven months on the wagon, this hits the spot. As for my schedule, if you want something badly enough, you find the time. By the way, I pitched *Only Hell is Hotter* to Regina Higgins of Spicy Hot Publishing. She requested a full."

"That's great, Rose! Maybe this time is the charm," Jen replied.

"Let's hope so. Anybody else have good news?"

"Not really," Susan answered. "Carmella Radcliff publicly ravaged me during the critique panel."

Anne sighed again. Leave it to Susan to turn the subject back onto herself. She ignored the little jab of guilt at the critical thought.

"Of course she did. That's her stock in trade. She's a total snake and ravages damn near everyone, so don't take it personally. I think she's nailed all of us at one time or another. I can't imagine why she was even asked to participate in the discussion. I'll bet she didn't request anything from anyone who pitched to her this weekend either. She just wanted a Florida vacation in March," Rose said in a soothing tone.

Before Susan could yet again lament her treatment, Anne again changed the subject.

"By the way, I saw Candace last Wednesday," Anne told them.

"How is she?" Nancy asked.

"Sober at last and doing pretty well for being in prison."

Candace Warren, a former member of the group, was currently doing two years at a minimum-security woman's prison facility on a charge of second-degree manslaughter. She'd killed Isadora Powell, another member of the group, for stealing, and then attempting to publish a book Candace had written. A good lawyer, and the fact she was in an alcoholic haze when she'd committed the murder, had bought her a favorable plea bargain.

"I can't believe Candace's sleazy ex-husband and his new wife tried to get a judge to give them the house and other assets," Jen muttered, finishing her wine.

"Once the settlement papers were signed, the house became Candace's. And since she turned everything over to her oldest son before she went to jail, Eric still has to make the payments. Serves him right," Nancy said.

"At any rate, she says to tell you all hello."

"I can't believe you guys investigated and solved a murder," Susan said. "I had just joined the chapter and thought you all had a lot of guts."

"Well, Dorie was a part of our group," Anne answered. She and the rest hadn't bothered to tell Susan they'd been suspects.

"So, what are we doing for dinner?" Jen tossed out. "I hear that Japanese steakhouse down the road is pretty good. It's not too far away."

"That works for me. I'll call Jack and let him know he has to make dinner for the kids, too," Rose said with a smug smile.

"No thanks," Susan replied. "I'm going home, but first I want to find that pasty-faced little troll and give her a piece of my mind."

"Susan, that's not a good idea," Jen said. "She can be damn vindictive."

"Oh, who cares?"

"Jen's right," Rose added. "You can't just waltz up to her and tell her she's a bitch. Besides, she already knows it."

"I saw her schedule when I pitched to an editor this morning. Her last appointment is at four-twenty." Susan checked her watch. "It's four twenty-five. If I go now, I can tackle her as she leaves the room."

"You pitched to Carmella *and* to an editor?" Jen asked.

"Of course! I have more chances that way. And both requested partials for your information," she said with a sniff as if to say 'so there.' "I'll see you all later."

"Two glasses of wine seems to have strengthened her spine. Someone should go with her," Anne commented as Susan left the bar with a determined look and her fists clenched.

Nancy shook her head. "Why?"

"What if she says something insulting to Carmella?"

"Carmella will wipe the floor with her. Besides, we all know Susan won't say a word, even if she does find the little weasel. She'll chicken out. Let her be," Jen replied, finishing her wine. "She's entitled to her two cents worth, provided she musters up the courage to express it."

"Wonder if she's telling the truth about Carmella requesting a partial manuscript," Nancy said with a frown.

Anne sighed. Susan was a nice, if sometimes irritating, person, but not fitting in well with the group. She wanted feedback, but argued and tried to justify her writing when the comments were negative.

The group had broken up for a few months after Dorie's murder and Candace's arrest. Gradually, they had gotten back together. Adding Susan to the circle had been a mistake. But dumping her without hurting her feelings would be tough. And who else in the Southeast Florida chapter of the WAA could they ask to join them? Experienced writers were already involved in their own critique groups, and Anne wasn't sure she could handle another newbie like Susan. She didn't mind mentoring, but why bother if the writer refused to listen to advice? Jen's voice brought Anne out of her thoughts.

"Think we should make a reservation at the restaurant?"

"Sounds reasonable to me. Some of the attendees may decide to go there," Nancy said. She pulled her phone out of her purse. "I'll pull up the website and call."

"I'll give Jack a buzz with the bad news," Rose said with a chuckle.

"Oh, there's Rebecca Larson from Tampa. Haven't seen her in ages. I'll be right back." Jen left the table to talk with the other author seated at the bar.

Meanwhile, Anne listened to two conversations as she finishing her wine. Attendees were on their own tonight, but tomorrow evening finished up with a big dinner in which the winners of the chapter's annual writing competition were announced. The conference officially ended Sunday at noon with breakfast, a speaker, an auction, and a panel discussion followed by a bunch of appreciation speeches. She wasn't sure yet if she'd attend. On the other hand, she didn't have anything better to do either. Luckily, the kids were spending spring break this week with her ex-husband in Orlando.

"Hello, I'd like to make a reservation for four tonight... Six-thirty..."

"Jack, everything all right? I'll be back later. I'm going out to dinner with the group..."

"On second thought, make that reservation for five. We might have another coming after all..."

"The baby's easy. I left several bottles in the fridge, and Graham can have a toddler meal. The jars are in the cupboard. Just heat it up along with some veggies and fruit. Order in pizza for everyone else..."

"Carlyle... C-a-r-l-y-l-e. See you later."

"Jack, this isn't rocket science. You'll do fine. I should be home by nine... See ya."

Both women hung up at the same time.

"We're set for six-thirty. Maybe Susan will change her mind and come with us."

"Maybe," Anne said, but secretly hoped she wouldn't. She couldn't take much more of the woman's whining. "How did Jack take the news?"

"I think it's been an eventful day," Rose replied. "But he didn't say too much. He'd better get used to it because that's the way it's going to be from now on."

Anne glanced at her watch. It was four-thirty-five. Carmella's last pitch should be over. Would Susan confront the woman?

She pushed her chair back and rose. "You know, I think I'm going to look for Susan. Maybe head off a nasty confrontation."

Nancy sighed and shook her head. "Oh, all right, do what you have to do, but she's probably nowhere close to Carmella."

Knowing full well Nancy considered her a fussbudget, Anne left and followed a wide corridor to the meeting room where editors and agents had listened to pitches all day. As she rounded a corner, an incredible scene was taking place between Carmella and Susan. Carmella's face was beet red and Susan was sobbing. The two women stood near a display table heaped with freebies from various authors.

"You dumbass! If you can't take criticism, then get out of the business," Carmella shouted. "Your writing sucks. I told it like it was. Live with it. And I rescind the request for the partial I asked for when you pitched earlier. You pitch a whole lot better than you write. Why should I waste my time on you?"

"You arrogant toad! You didn't need to go on and on, picking on every little detail in two stinking pages. It was humiliating and just plain mean," Susan shot back through her sobs, taking a step forward, her hands clenched.

Carmella shoved her out of the way. "Don't crowd me!"

Susan yelled something incoherent and shoved the agent hard in the chest. Carmella staggered back, and catching her heel on the edge of the table cover, toppled like an imploded building into the display. The table collapsed under her hefty frame.

Carmella lay amid the wreckage screaming and thrashing like a beached whale—an apt description for the five-foot, close to two-hundred pound woman. Several people stood nearby either staring in shock or laughing. More attendees crowded the doorway of the nearby bookstore for a good look.

Susan turned and ran full force into Anne.

"Susan!" She grabbed her friend's arm.

Susan wrenched herself free and pushed her away. "Leave me alone, dammit."

Without another word, she whipped around the corner and disappeared. Anne turned her attention to the thrashing woman trying to get up from the debris.

"I'll sue! I'll own this stinking chapter and WAA! Get me the hell out of here!"

Several people rushed forward including Anne.

"I'm so sorry," one woman said, reaching for Carmella's hand.

Terry Whiting, the conference chair, also ran up to help. Between them, they finally got the agent back on her feet. She swayed for a moment smoothing her clothes until taking a deep breath and glared at Terry.

"I'm suing. I also want the cops called. She assaulted me. That crazy bitch needs to be put away."

"Actually, you shoved her first," Anne said in a

calm tone resisting the urge to giggle. Seeing the tubby agent with her skirt bunched up around her thighs *had* been funny.

"Who the hell are you? Butt out. She invaded my space."

"But she didn't touch you. You shoved her first. I saw it."

Carmella's face turned redder. "I said butt out, you asshole!"

Anne shrugged and moved away. Let Terry take care of the irate woman. She needed to find Susan. But her newest critique partner was nowhere in the hallway or any of the meeting rooms off of it. Perhaps she'd gone home. Anne had had enough of dealing with Susan today, so decided not to search. A phone call later tonight or tomorrow would suffice. At least the whole nasty affair was over.

Anne made her way back to the bar.

"Did you find her?" Rose asked.

"I'll say. You're not going to believe this." She told them of the confrontation.

"How long did Carmela flop?" Jen asked popping more peanuts into her mouth.

"Not long. Terry, another lady, and I finally helped her up. She was screaming she'd sue Susan, the conference, the chapter, and everyone within hearing range before I left. I have to say, it was entertaining. A lot of people were laughing. Probably the highlight of their day. Sure was mine."

"Who'd have thought Susan had the guts to do any more than blubber?" Nancy asked.

Anne searched for the waiter in the growing crowd, caught his eye, held up her glass, and pointed to the rest of them at the table.

"I don't know about anybody else, but I'm having a real problem with Susan," she said.

"How so?" Rose asked.

Anne explained her thoughts to the other three. "I'm just not sure I can deal with her anymore."

"Me neither," Nancy added. "I tried to take in consideration she's new to the writing game, but after six months, she just doesn't get it, nor does she even try."

"She *does* tend to get huffy whenever we say something that isn't a glowing testimonial to her efforts. And glowing testimonials are few and far between for her," Rose added.

"Her plots begin just fine. In fact, they're kind of intriguing, but then she thinks she's got to make things more complex and goes off on a tangent until the original story is totally lost," Anne commented.

"And don't forget that lame story about finding true love in a commune for God's sake," Nancy reminded them. "It was too recent to be called a historical romance, and too old to be labeled contemporary. She got damn defensive about it."

Jen rolled her eyes again, her favorite way of showing exasperation. "Sometimes I think she's read Dorie's bio and is determined to do the same—minus the getting killed part, of course."

"Isadora Powell's rise to fame and the bestseller list was a one in a million shot. Normal writers don't have that kind of luck," Anne said.

"Is Susan that delusional?" Rose wondered.

"I'm beginning to think she is," Nancy answered with a sigh. "I miss Candace. She wasn't a great writer, but at least she took what we suggested in stride and tried to put it to good use. Susan ignores us for the most part. I think it's time to part company."

"But how do we do that without hurting her feelings?" Jen asked as the waiter brought another round of drinks.

"Sometimes feelings just have to be hurt. I hate to do it, but one person with her attitude can bring down the entire group. We should have jettisoned Dorie ages before Candace did it for us," Anne told them.

"So, are we all agreed? Susan goes?" Rose said.

They looked at each other, sipped from their glasses, and nodded.

"How and when do we give her the bad news?" Jen inquired.

"I'm all for an e-mail saying the group dynamic isn't working and for all concerned we think it best if she finds other people to work with," Nancy suggested.

"That's pretty cold," Rose said with a frown.

"But effective and there's no misunderstanding," Anne replied. "Any way we do it, we'll end up as bad guys."

"I'll do it. I'm usually the bad guy during critique group anyway," Nancy volunteered.

Jen shook her head. "I vote we give her one last meeting, and if she argues with us, tell her the truth right then and there—face-to-face."

"She'll probably cry. She always cries," Anne muttered. She never knew how to react to tears.

"Then she cries, but it'll be over," Rose said.

"Hi everyone, how did your day go?"

Anne looked up to see the conference chair, Terry Whiting, standing next to them. The chapter president,

Fran Harrison was right behind her.

"A lovely conference, Terry. Congratulations. How's Carmella?"

"I don't know. When someone suggested that calling the cops wasn't a good idea, especially if she started it, she told us all to fuck off before stomping away. And thanks, Anne for telling us she *did* start the shoving match. Several others present confirmed it."

"Think she'll sue like she threatened?"

Terry shook her head. "I doubt it. The story will make the rounds for a few months, and then die away, but a lawsuit would keep it alive for ages. Carmella's not that dumb. I'm sorry we invited her."

"Susan is your critique partner," Fran said. "You should have done something to stop her."

Jen shoved the bowl of nuts toward the woman. "Chill out, Fran. Take a seat, order a glass of wine, and have a couple of peanuts."

The chapter president stepped back with a scowl. "Are you trying to be funny?"

Without another word, she whirled and left the table.

"Funny?" Jen questioned with raised eyebrows.

"Where is Carmella now?" Nancy asked.

Terry shrugged. "I have no idea and really don't care. I helped pick up the remains of the goodie table and came in here for a drink. God knows I need one."

The subject of Carmella, along with Susan and her imminent departure from the group, fell by the wayside to be replaced with chatter about the conference and various workshops before Terry left. Over the next hour, writers came to the table, talked for a few minutes, then moved on.

Jen looked at her watch. "It's almost six. I say we settle up here and head for the restaurant."

Anne removed a couple of bills from her wallet and pushed her chair back. Susan's absence concerned her. "This should take care of my and Susan's portion of the bill. I think I'll hit the restroom, but first, I want to take a quick look around and see if I can find Susan."

"For Pete's sake, why?" Nancy asked.

"She was awfully upset. If she's still around, maybe I can help. In spite of everything, I feel sorry for her. Should we meet in the lobby?"

"Sounds good, but don't look too long. It's Friday night in season. Traffic will be heavy," Rose said.

Winter in South Florida was a nightmare of temporary residents—called snowbirds by locals—tourists, and traffic.

Anne left the bar heading for the lobby. Susan was nowhere in sight. The main hallway to the conference meeting rooms was nearly deserted. In her anger and embarrassment, Susan had probably gone home. She turned toward the main floor ladies' room. The line was out the door. It seemed like a lot of people were hitting the restroom before heading out to dinner or home.

"Damn," she muttered.

She'd been in this hotel for meetings off and on over the years and knew another restroom was located on the mezzanine level. With the corridor in front of the elevators crowded, Anne took the stairs, found the facility, and pushed the door open. The lights were off. By reflex, she flipped the nearby switch and entered a stall. While washing her hands, a strange feeling that she wasn't alone crept over her.

She turned. The rest of the stall doors were open

with the exception of the last. A pair of sturdy shoes showed through the bottom. Walking slowly, Anne approached. Total silence reigned, further enhancing the uneasiness.

She hesitated, and then said, "Hello, are you all right?"

Silence. The hair on her arms stood at attention. A shiver worked its way up her spine.

"Hello?" she asked again in a breathy voice with the same results. Then she remembered the lights.

Who the hell goes to the bathroom in total darkness?

Swallowing hard, she knocked on the stall door. It wasn't latched and swung open.

Carmella Radcliff sat slouched on the toilet, her head against the back wall. Her purse still hung by the strap from her shoulder. It dangled past the porcelain bowl.

But Anne only saw the knife embedded in the woman's chest. She screamed and jumped back.

Chapter Two

Anne's breath caught in her throat as nausea churned her stomach. She clapped a hand over her mouth and backed up until the vanity counter stopped her motion. The horrible vision of her, Nancy, and Candace finding Isadora Powell's body flashed through her mind.

God, not again!

She whirled, ran for the door, jerked it open, and then rushed out on shaking legs.

Help. I need to find help.

Too impatient to wait for an elevator, she ran for the stairs, her heart pounding in heavy, rapid thuds. Clutching the handrail, Anne stumbled down the steps. At the bottom, she paused trying to bring her ragged breaths under control, then ran into the lobby and up to the front desk.

"Help! There's a body in the mezzanine ladies' room," she said with a gasp.

"Excuse me?" the woman manning the area said staring with wide eyes.

"I said there's a dead woman in the restroom on the mezzanine level."

"Is this some kind of a joke?"

Anne wanted to slap her silly. "Of course, it's not a joke. Call the police!"

The woman, identified as Angel by her nametag,

lifted a phone and punched in a couple of buttons. "Security? I have a lady here who says someone needs help in the mezzanine ladies' room. Please go check it out."

"Take my word for it, she's beyond help. Call the police!"

"Ma'am, perhaps she's just passed out. Let us handle it."

Nausea welled into her throat before she could explain about the knife. "I'm going to be sick!"

Anne took off out the front entrance, raced around the corner, and threw up in the bushes. Once again, the nightmare scene at Dorie's came to mind. She'd hurled then, too.

Finished, she wiped her mouth with a tissue and hurried back inside, only to run headlong into Nancy, Jen, and Rose.

"Good God, what's wrong with you?" Nancy asked.

"It's Carmella Radcliff. She's dead. Up in the ladies' room," she replied in a breathy voice.

"What? Are you sure?" Rose said in a high-pitched tone.

"Oh, yeah." She told them what she'd seen.

"Come on, sit down," Jen ordered, steering her toward the sofa in the lobby.

The phone rang at the front desk. The clerk answered, listened for a moment, and commented, "Oh my God!"

She hung up and immediately dialed again. "Hello, nine-one-one, this is Angel Simpson at the San Sebastian Inn on State Road Fifteen. We have a body in one of the restrooms. According to our security guard, she's been stabbed... One of our guests found her... Yes, of course... right away." She hung up and stared across the space to where Anne and the others sat. "The police are on their way. They said for you to stay where you are until they arrive."

She dialed again and spoke with whoever answered. "Cops are on the way. Don't let anyone in."

The woman sent Anne a stern look.

"Why is she staring at you like that?" Rose asked in a low tone.

"I wasn't too coherent when I told her. She thought I was joking."

"Oh, for crying out loud, who jokes about something like this?" Nancy asked.

"You really have to stop finding bodies, Anne," Jen declared.

"Tell me! I should have just waited in line, but no, I had to go up to the john on the mezzanine."

She swallowed and proceeded to tear the tattered tissue into narrow strips. *Why me?*

With her friends by her side, she gradually calmed as more security personnel rushed past the front desk.

"I wonder who did it," Rose mused.

"Just what I need, another mystery," Nancy muttered. "Why does this shit always happen when I'm on deadline?"

Anne's throat was desert dry. She rose from her seat. "I need a bottle of water or something. I'll be right back."

She took three steps when the desk clerk called out, "The police said to stay put, ma'am."

"All she wants is some water," Nancy told her with a glare. "Why don't you do something constructive and get her one instead of just staring?"

The woman hesitated before disappearing into a back room. She returned a few seconds later with a bottle and set it on the counter.

"Here. I think it best if she stays right where she is."

Nancy stomped over and snatched it off the granite. "Thanks loads." She returned and handed the bottle to Anne. "Officious bitch."

Anne had known Nancy for what—twelve or thirteen years? They'd been critique partners for almost as long. Other partners had come and gone, but Nancy had developed into a good friend. Quiet as a rule, when she did speak it was often sharp and pithy.

"She's probably unnerved, too," Anne replied, holding the cold bottle against her hot cheeks.

"Hotels hate it when something bad happens on the premises," Jen said. "Gives them all the wrong publicity."

Anne unscrewed the top and drank. The cool water helped lubricate her mouth and throat. Why was it that one's mouth and throat got dry during a time of crisis? The fear factor? Maybe.

People came and went in the lobby, but no one appeared to know what had taken place on the mezzanine. A security guard stood off to the side near them.

Good grief, is he standing guard over me*?*

"I guess I should cancel the reservation," Nancy said.

"Good idea. I don't think we'll be eating any time soon," Rose concurred.

Nancy moved off to make the call while the rest of

them waited. Then, three police cars and an ambulance pulled up out front, followed by an unmarked car. Anne breathed a sigh of relief. Finally—someone who was really in charge.

Then that breath caught in her throat. Detective Gil Collins emerged from the unmarked car.

Gil! The lead detective on Dorie's murder case eight months ago and the man with whom Anne had hoped to start a relationship. But her frequent lies had destroyed their fragile bond of trust. She hadn't seen or heard from him since after Candace's arrest.

Swell, I find another body and it looks like this will be Gil's case. Wonder what he'll think of that?

He entered, glanced her way, raised his eyebrows, and then made his way to the front desk where he held a brief conversation with the clerk. The rest of the police and paramedics entered. Gil directed them upstairs before turning his attention to the women.

He walked over and stopped in front of Anne, neither frowning nor smiling. "Hello, Anne, ladies'. I see we meet again under deadly circumstances."

"Hello, Gil. Yes, so it would seem." Was this the best she could think of saying to a man she hadn't seen in months and missed dreadfully?

"Stay here. I'll be back in a few minutes."

She nodded and he walked toward the elevators on the far side of the lobby.

"Looks like your detective is on this case, too," Nancy said.

"He's not my detective," Anne automatically answered. "After the last time we talked, I doubt he's very happy to see me. Did you notice? His face was completely devoid of any expression."

25

"I watched his eyes," Rose said. "They didn't look *dis*interested."

"Besides, he's trained not to show emotion. Rose is right. He'll be back in your loving arms soon," Jen added.

Heat flooded Anne's face and her ears burned. "Will you get serious? This is just another case. The fact *we're* involved again probably has him reaching for an antacid."

She wasn't about to admit her heart had gone pitty-pat at the mere sight of him. Almost made her forget about why he was here. It was so high school.

They all fidgeted as they waited. Nancy paced— ten feet one way, and then back again until Anne wanted to scream. The repetitive motion was getting on her nerves. Rose sat on the sofa fiddling with the strap of her purse. Jen slouched in one of the chairs as she drummed her fingers on its arm. Those actions bugged her, too. She kept taking tiny sips of water. Twenty minutes passed. Finally, Gil returned.

"Want to tell me what happened?" Staring at Anne, he pulled out a notebook and pen.

"The usual. I found a body," she said.

He shot her a stern glance as if to say, this isn't funny. "Do you know the victim?"

"Not really. I've met her a few times. Her name's Carmella Radcliff. She's an agent with Summers Literary Agency in New York."

"Know why she's in San Sebastian?"

"This is our annual writers conference. She came to hear pitches from prospective clients."

"Pitches?" he asked with a quizzical expression.

"An author who seeks representation from an agent

will schedule an appointment to tell that agent about her book. Sometimes writers prefer to talk directly to an editor. It's called a pitch," Jen told him.

"Did any of you pitch to this woman?"

Anne shook her head. "No. We all have agents."

"I don't," Rose volunteered. "But she'd be the last person I'd pitch to."

His eyebrows rose and his tone sharpened. "And why is that?"

"I pitched to her once before. She wasn't too nice and I didn't feel any kind of bond."

"Okay, now take it from the beginning. What happened?"

Anne recited her ordeal. "I just didn't think anything was out of the ordinary until I saw her feet under the stall door. I mean, who goes to the bathroom in total darkness? Even if it's an emergency, you take time to turn on the lights."

"So you have no idea who'd want to harm Ms. Radcliff?"

Anne looked at her friends who avoided eye contact. Should she mention Susan's confrontation with Carmella? In view of her last experience with Gil and dead bodies, that sounded like a good idea. Besides, if she didn't, someone else certainly would. Before she could say anything Nancy made a comment.

"Carmella took pitches most of the day, so she wasn't out roaming the hallways. Maybe it was someone who wanted to rob her and followed her to the ladies' room."

"Maybe," he replied writing in the notebook. "What were you doing say an hour prior to finding the body?"

"Sitting in the bar, having a couple of drinks and discussing the day," Anne said.

"That's SOP at conferences," Jen informed him. "We all go to different workshops, and then compare notes later."

"So who's in charge of this conference?"

"Our chapter president is Fran Harrison. The conference chair is Terry Whiting," Anne said.

"I'll need to inform and talk to both of them. Anyone have a number where I can reach them."

"I do." Nancy scrolled down her cell phone and gave him the numbers.

"I'll be back. Stay here." He moved toward the front entrance to call.

"What have I gotten myself into now?" Anne said with a groan.

"Well, at least you'll get to see Gil again," Jen replied.

"And this time, you can't possibly be a suspect," Rose added.

"Big deal. He hasn't bothered to call since Candace was sent away." She paused. "Actually, I could be a suspect. I had words with Carmella after she fell."

"But you were with us after that," Rose said.

"Are we going to offer our services to help solve the murder again?" Jen asked.

"Yeah, like he's gonna jump at that chance," Nancy drawled. She paused for a moment. Then a look of consternation crept onto her face. "I wonder where Susan is."

Anne bit her lip, wondering the same thing.

Rose sucked in a deep breath. "My God, you don't think…"

"Nancy! You don't really believe…" Jen echoed at the same time.

"All I'm saying is that there were a lot of witnesses to the fight she and Carmella had. What if she didn't go home, but hung around, followed the bitch into the john, and nailed her?"

"I can't see Susan having the guts. She was publicly humiliated by the critique, but watching Carmella flounder in the debris of a display table more than made up for it," Anne said. "Besides, where would she get a knife?"

"Yeah, well none of us thought Candace could brain Dorie with a Campbell either," Nancy replied mentioning a prestigious writing award. While not large, the statuette was heavy, making it an excellent blunt instrument.

Her friend had a point. Candace had been pushed beyond the limit by the betrayal of a so-called friend. Yet alcohol had played a major role in Candace's actions. Susan had been angry, but certainly not drunk.

"We should tell Gil," Anne commented.

"What do we tell him?" Rose said. "We haven't seen Susan since she left the bar."

"We don't need to tell him," Jen answered. "Like Nancy said, there were a lot of witnesses. Someone will bring it up."

Jen's words echoed her thoughts of a few minutes ago. Not sharing information is what had destroyed the relationship between her and Gil in the first place. Plus all the lies. Anne didn't want a repeat of that.

"I vote we tell him." Her stomach growled, a reminder dinner was long overdue. "I wonder how much longer we have to stay. I'm starving."

She hoped her statement hadn't sounded crass given the circumstances.

"I guess we could grab a bite in the hotel dining room," Rose said.

"Not if lunch was any indication of their culinary skills," Nancy said.

Anne agreed. The luncheon provided by the conference consisted of dried out salmon in some kind of glue-like sauce.

"There's always Rafferty's," Jen said, suggesting a chain restaurant not far away.

Rafferty's. They'd spent more time there while investigating Dorie's murder than at their own homes.

"It's season and likely to be packed," Rose said. "Let's just keep it simple and eat here. How bad can it be?"

She liked Rose's suggestion. Besides, if they ate here at the hotel, she might see Gil again.

She was about to comment when a voice said, "Glad you guys are still around. I take it you're all going out to dinner. Mind if I come along?"

"Susan!" Jen said with a gasp.

"What's with all the cop cars and the ambulance?"

"What are you doing here?" Nancy demanded. "We thought you went home."

Susan shrugged. "I planned to, but needed some time to myself first."

Anne cleared her throat. Time to get some answers. "I only saw the last part of your fight with Carmella. What led up to it?"

Her eyes hardened. "I cornered her in the pitch room. Told her I found her comments hurtful and insulting, and that alienating a potential bestselling author was not smart."

"Bet that went over big," Nancy said in a sarcastic tone.

Sarcasm, however, was lost on Susan. "She laughed, said if that was the best I could do then the bestseller list wasn't on my horizon. Then, she called me a few more names and flipped me the bird as she turned and walked away. I was crying, but went after her. She stopped by that display table of goodies and told me to stop following her or she'd call security. I don't know what came over me. I called her a toad. She shoved me and I shoved her back—hard. She rammed into the table. It collapsed and I walked away." She shook her head. "I was so mad I could have killed her."

Her last sentence sent a chill down Anne's spine. She looked up to find Gil standing at the edge of the group, obviously taking in all they said.

"You could have killed who?" Gil asked.

"What?" Susan answered.

"Who was it you could have killed?" he repeated.

"Oh, this really obnoxious agent."

"Carmella Radcliff?"

She shot Gil a strange look. "Yes. Who are you? An author? Did she piss you off, too?"

"I'm Detective Gil Collins of the San Sebastian Police Department. Who are you?"

Susan's eyes widened as she glanced through the entrance to the ménage of official cars and trucks out front.

"The police? What's going on?"

"It seems someone killed Carmella in the mezzanine ladies' room. I found the body," Anne told her.

"Oh, my God!"

"You said you pushed her into a display table earlier?" Gil asked.

Susan shifted from foot to foot and stared at the floor.

"Let's start with your name, address, and phone number."

"Uh, Susan. Susan Lynch. I live at 10359 Harrow Place in San Sebastian. My phone number is 555-200-1000."

Gil wrote, and then lifted his head. "Now, suppose you tell me again about the confrontation you had with the deceased."

Susan repeated the story again with frequent lip biting and refusal to make eye contact with any of them.

"What's a goodie table?" he asked with the same puzzled expression as earlier when asking about pitches.

"It's a table where authors display promotional material. It's free to whoever wants it," Rose said.

"It's a very effective way to get your name and books out there," Jen added. "I've picked up free books from future *New York Times* bestsellers at conferences. My first book is due out soon, and I hope to have several copies at the national Writers Association of America's annual conference in August. I'll also make up a basket for the literacy raffle. Maybe I'll include some chocolate—or coffee. Writers exist on coffee and chocolate…"

Gil held up his hand. "Thank you, Mrs. Swanson."

Anne glanced at Nancy, who shrugged. Jen babbled constantly, but babbled more when nervous.

She supposed being involved in another murder qualified as a nervous situation.

Given her past with Gil, Anne thought this was the time to tell him of her involvement.

"I saw the tail end of the argument. Susan left immediately and Carmella wasn't hurt."

"Thank you." He turned his attention back to Susan. "And where did you go when you left Ms. Radcliff?"

"I…I was going to go home, but was too upset, so I found a quiet nook and tried to get myself together."

"And where was this nook? Did anyone see you?"

"It was just a little area with a chair and a table outside the business center. I don't recall seeing anyone, so I guess no one saw me either."

"And how long were you there?"

"I'm not sure—ten or fifteen minutes, maybe."

"Where were you for the past hour?" Gil asked writing in his notebook.

"I went for a walk."

"Where?" he insisted.

Susan shrugged. "Out in the little garden area, then I found an out-of-the-way table near the pool."

"Anybody see you there?"

"I don't remember seeing many people about. The sun was going down and the air was getting cool. I guess most people had gone inside."

"I see. What was the fight about? I've heard Ms. Radcliff was… abrasive."

Susan launched into an explanation of her day and Carmella's character.

Anne looked at the others. Jen, for once, was silent. *Keep quiet, Susan. Don't tell him how angry you were with the woman.*

But her friend didn't keep quiet. She gave Gil and everyone else an earful of her opinion of Carmella. Finally, she reached the end of her rant.

"Exactly how angry were you, Ms. Lynch?"

His soft tone scared Anne. She'd heard it before—usually prior to being asked to go police headquarters for questioning.

Before Susan or anyone could say another word, Terry Whiting rushed up closely followed by Fran Harrison. They introduced themselves to Gil.

"I can't believe this!" Terry said, worry emanating from her face. "Who could have done such a thing?"

Fran wrung her hands. "And everything was going so well, too. My God, this could be a disaster. What editor or agent will want to come next year?"

Anne considered the comment in poor taste. Worrying about a conference a year from now sounded callous and cold. She didn't like Fran much. Opinionated and forceful were the first adjectives that came to mind. Her harsh words in the bar earlier still had Anne wanting to smack her. Like she could have stopped Susan from doing anything!

"Fran, this is a business. It's their job to come to conferences," she said.

Fran glared, but made no comment.

"Who found her?" Terry asked. "I hope it wasn't an attendee."

"I found her," Anne said.

Fran's right eyebrow rose and her lip curled slightly. "You? You found Dorie, too, didn't you? Are you some kind of dead body magnet?"

"That was uncalled for," Nancy replied in an angry

tone. "I was with Anne when we found Dorie. It was not a pleasant experience."

"And your critique partner killed her!"

"Ladies, if you don't mind, I have work to do," Gil exclaimed. He turned to Terry. "You're the conference chair?"

"Yes, that's right."

"How many people are at this conference?"

"Fran and I were just going over the figures when you called. At last count, we had two hundred-twelve attendees total. Not all are here for both days. Some just came for today's session, while others will attend only tomorrow's. I'd say we had maybe a hundred and thirty or forty who opted to attend both sessions. Sunday is a come-if-you-want-to kind of a deal."

The women went on to tell Gil how the conference operated and the schedules for pitch sessions and workshops. Terry promised to have all pertinent information to him as soon as possible.

It gave Anne time to think. To kill someone in a restroom was bizarre. It suggested the killer wanted a face-to-face confrontation with Carmella. Perhaps to tell her off, or to demand an apology, or to stick a knife in her.

Did Susan lie? Could she have waited for Carmella to pick herself up from the remains of the goodie table, and then followed her to the restroom? But where had the knife come from?

Anne wished she'd paid closer attention to the murder weapon. Had the hilt been wood? Porcelain? Plastic? She closed her eyes to focus. It was hard. All she recalled was the body and the way it had sprawled back over the flushing mechanism. Blood had stained the pink blouse from the point of entry to the waistband of her skirt. Not a lot, but enough to let someone know she was dead. And the knife had been positioned just under the breastbone in close proximity to the heart.

Wood. She was almost certain the handle was wood. And big—a hunting knife, maybe. Anne had never seen a hunting knife and had no clue what they look like. But who the hell carried a knife to a conference? The answer was obvious—someone who intended to kill. *Which makes this premeditated.*

Anne heaved a sigh and opened her eyes. She wanted to talk this over with the rest of the group—sans Susan if possible. Surely, the woman realized she'd given Gil a whale of a motive for murder.

Her stomach grumbled again. "Excuse me, Gil, but are you finished with us. I'm starving and it's after seven."

He closed his notebook. "Yes, for the moment. Anne, I'll need you to come down to the station to give your statement soon. Sleep on it. You might remember more. How about tomorrow at ten?"

"I'd planned to be here tomorrow. There are a couple of workshops I need to attend."

"Could you come in later this evening, say after dinner? I may not be there, but you can talk to whoever is available."

"That's fine."

His gaze swept to Susan. "I'll need you to come in, too, Ms. Lynch."

"Tonight?"

"The sooner the better. Get it over with," he said with a smile.

Anne remembered that soothing smile, guaranteed

to put you at ease before he lowered the hammer.

"Sure, I guess so."

Anne glanced at Susan. Her expression showed worry. *It should. She vented to the wrong person.*

"Where are we going to eat?" Susan asked in a subdued tone.

"Here at the hotel dining room," Rose answered.

"We usually go to Rafferty's during times of crisis, but decided to keep it simple," Jen added.

Gil smiled again as he extended a hand to help Anne rise from the sofa. Her skin tingled at his touch. Maybe he remembered Rafferty's, too. But intuition told her Gil would not be leaving the hotel anytime soon.

"Yes, we decided to stay, in case you need to talk to one of us again. I'm sure the food in the dining room isn't as bad as what comes out for the conference. Besides, I'm not sure how much I can eat." She hoped her desire to see and talk to him again wasn't too obvious.

Before any of them could move, the paramedics brought a woman on a gurney off the elevator and wheeled her toward the entrance. Her head and shoulders were propped up. An oxygen mask covered her face. Her hand movements indicated agitation as if trying to talk through the plastic shield.

As they passed the seating area, the woman suddenly sat up, pulled the mask away, pointed a finger at Anne, and screamed.

"That's her! That's the woman I saw running from the john and down the stairs! There's your killer!"

Chapter Three

Anne closed her eyes, groaned, and heaved a deep breath. She opened them and stared at the distraught woman whose pointing finger shook as her eyes bulged.

"I saw her! She ran out of the restroom and down the stairs. I thought about it for a couple of minutes, then decided her behavior was suspicious. So naturally, I went in, looked around, found the body, screamed, and ran out as fast as I could. I bowled headlong into a security guard. I tell you, I was terrified she'd come back to get me, too. I almost fainted. I still feel very shaky." The woman sobbed and flopped back onto the gurney. "This has all been so traumatic."

Gil approached and spoke to her in a soft tone. Anne didn't hear what he said, but the woman reacted.

"Nonsense! She ran! Arrest her now!"

"Who is this stupid cow?" Nancy asked in a loud voice. It carried across the room.

The woman sat up again to glare. "Cow? How dare you."

"Lighten up, lady," Rose said. "She didn't kill anyone. She reported it to the front desk."

"Ha!"

"It's not smart to go around pointing fingers and making unsubstantiated accusations until you know the facts," Jen added with a righteous expression.

"I know what I saw! And I saw her running away.

She must have done it." She flopped back for the second time with a ragged sigh.

"Like I said, a stupid cow," Nancy repeated with clenched fists.

Anne took a step toward her friend. Nancy's temper, something she'd worked hard to control over the years, showed signs of blossoming into full bloom.

The woman struggled to sit up. "Why, you...you..."

Nancy took two paces forward. Anne followed quickly, ready to step in if needed.

"Oh my," Susan murmured.

Gil held up a hand. "Ladies! Do you mind dispensing with the drama? Let me handle this."

Nancy backed down. "Are we free to go? I'm hungry."

"Yes, you can go. And do not, I repeat, do *not* discuss the details of this with anyone else. Understood?"

The five of them nodded, and hustled out of the lobby.

"What? You're going to let her go? What kind of a cop are you? Or do you think I'm..." Distance finally cut off the woman's outraged voice.

"I don't believe this," Anne said with a groan.

Rose waved her hand. "Don't pay any attention to her. She loved being the center of attention."

"Who is she?" Susan asked.

"I have no idea," Rose replied.

"Are you sure you're okay?" Jen asked Anne.

No, she wasn't okay, but wanted to keep her composure in front of her friends. She was supposed to be the logical, organized member of the group. Even though their personalities complimented one another, she'd often wished for Jen's gift of gab, Rose's thoughtfulness, and Nancy's sarcasm in dealing with difficult situations or people.

"Yes, I'm fine. Let's get something to eat. Why don't you guys go on ahead? I'll be along in a moment."

Anne turned and walked toward the ladies room. She hesitated a brief moment before opening the door.

Another woman looked up and smiled as she washed her hands. Not wanting to make small talk, Anne entered a stall. A few seconds later, she heard the lady leave and inhaled a deep breath before taking a few minutes to compose herself. Apparently, word on the murder hadn't been officially released yet.

The encounter with the hysterical woman had more of an impact than finding the body. Would people think she'd killed Carmella? Anne had barely known her and didn't have an axe to grind. *Just because I didn't like her, doesn't mean I killed her.*

The last murder she'd investigated had disrupted her life more than anyone knew. Now, months after Isadora Powell's death, Anne was just beginning to get back on track.

Her new novel, written during the investigation, had been flat out rejected by her agent. He'd said it wasn't new or fresh, and advised her to revise as soon as possible. Otherwise, he'd never be able to sell it.

So Anne had worked to revise. Three weeks ago, she'd resubmitted. As of this morning, she hadn't heard back. Anxiety, coupled with the basic insecurity many writers—even successful ones—have about their work, had given her more than one sleepless night.

Anne exited the restroom and headed for the dining room.

The facility was busy. She recognized many in the crowd as chapter members and conference attendees.

Anne wormed her way inside through a standing crowd to the hostess stand. Her friends waved from a circular booth in the corner. She hurried across the room. As she passed tables, the occupants spoke in hushed whispers while casting furtive glances in her direction.

Great. Thanks to that silly blabbermouth, the whole conference probably knows about Carmella and thinks I did it.

She finally reached her friends and slid in next to Jen.

"How did you get a table so fast?"

"Most of the diners are small groups. I told them we had six and this spot was open," Nancy replied. "Are you sure you're okay?"

"As okay as can be expected. You won't believe the looks I got. I know everybody thinks I'm a cold-blooded killer."

"Well, at least we won't have to obey Gil's warning about discussing the case. That asshole in the lobby let everyone know. A brass band would have been more subtle," Rose said.

"I can't believe I found another body. This is getting to be a very unpleasant habit."

"Well, at least this time it's not a member of the group," Jen said.

"Yeah, but I'm sure the list of suspects will turn out to be just as long and distinguished as that for Dorie," Rose drawled. "I wonder who did it."

"The police are going to think it was me, aren't they?" Susan asked in a tremulous voice.

"Probably," Nancy said. "But I'm sure she must have had words with others throughout the day."

"Could be an old lover who followed her here or just happened to be here at the same time," Jen mused.

"Very coincidental," Nancy said.

"But not illogical. Maybe it was an attendee—one of Camilla's clients. What if she dropped this person or withheld funds or something?" Jen continued. "Or if she had dirt on somebody and they didn't want it known, kinda like before."

"I doubt if Carmella was blackmailing people like Dorie," Rose added.

"Blackmail?" Susan asked in a squeaky tone.

Nancy waved a hand. "It's too complicated to explain."

Susan's face turned sulky, obviously unhappy she wasn't privy to the total story.

"Maybe not for money, but I'll bet she could do a mean emotional blackmail on someone," Anne suggested.

"How?" Jen inquired. "And where's our waiter? I need a drink."

As if hearing her, a young man appeared at the table and took five orders for white wine. They all spent some time checking over the menu. It gave Anne a chance to clear her head. By the time their drinks arrived, along with a bowl of rolls, they'd made up their minds and ordered.

"What do you mean by emotional blackmail?" Jen asked when the server had left, bringing the conversation back to Carmella.

"I'm not sure, but maybe instead of money, she wanted some kind of favor."

"Like what?" Rose said.

Anne fiddled with the napkin on her lap. It was cloth. She couldn't shred it. Shredding paper in times of nervousness was a habit she'd developed while in college. It was one she was trying to break. She picked up a roll and tore off several small hunks.

She pulled her mind back to the conversation. "I don't know. Maybe a published author pitched to her and she said she'd read the full manuscript in exchange for the writer helping her land another author. One she knew she could sell."

"You mean like stealing a client from another agent?" Rose asked.

"More or less."

"But is that a killing offense?" Jen replied.

"On the surface, I'd say no."

Nancy sipped her wine with a thoughtful expression. "Unless, the author did as told, got the other writer to sign with Carmella, and then Carmella in turn, rejected the original author. Does that make sense?"

Susan frowned. "I'm getting confused by all the authors."

"I've heard rumors that Carmella was an author herself. Lord, you don't suppose she pulled an Isadora Powell and submitted someone else's book as her own, do you?" Nancy asked, her gaze darting around the table.

The mere thought of that scenario appearing again made Anne's stomach cramp.

"If that's the case, this profession is doomed," Rose said. "I mean, who's going to submit to a third party like an agent, if the possibility of being screwed is there?"

"Well, we're living, breathing proof it happens in critique groups, too," Anne answered.

"Someone submitted another author's work as her own?" Susan asked.

Too late, Anne realized they were discussing something Susan knew little about—a fact she'd like to keep that way.

She shrugged. "Yes, but it's too long to go into now."

Susan once again shot them all a look that said she didn't like being left out of the loop, buttered a roll, and nibbled. "I can't imagine what I'd do if someone did that to me. Kind of makes self-publishing more attractive. I might go that route. I think my writing is pretty good."

Anne cast her gaze at her friends. Jen rolled her eyes. Nancy's eyebrows rose. Rose sipped from her glass to avoid eye contact.

The troublesome woman caught their expressions and glared. "What? You don't think I can do it?"

"I'd be very careful with doing something that," Anne suggested. "A lot of authors make the mistake of publishing before they're ready. I've read plenty of garbage."

"So have I, but I think I can hold my own."

Nancy stared, and then bit her lip as if holding in unkind words. Anne was impressed. Nancy wasn't always so reticent.

It was time to change the subject.

"I just hope nobody takes that idiot in the lobby seriously," she muttered remembering the covert glances from other diners.

Rose waved a hand. "Don't worry. She may have embarrassed you, but she made a fool out of herself."

"And besides, you reported it to the front desk before security even got to her," Jen said.

"Yeah, but she could have said she'd seen someone running from the scene while I was out barfing in the bushes."

"Plus you have absolutely no motive for offing Carmella Radcliff. A few words in the hallway don't count. Besides, you weren't angry," Nancy declared.

"Unless, of course, you submitted to her," Susan said with an innocent look.

Anne wanted to smack her. That was another thing about Susan that irked her—she frequently used innuendo in subtle ways, then acted upset when someone called her on it.

"I have an agent. And even if I didn't, she'd be the last person I'd want representing me."

Susan's eyes opened wide and she placed a hand over her heart. "Oh, don't be offended. I'm just thinking out loud—like a book plot or something. You know, author gets dumped by agent of long standing, submits to another agent who ridicules and rejects her, and in revenge, author kills second agent—or something like that. And your last story was initially rejected by your present agent."

Anne didn't buy the backhanded apology or the disingenuous expression.

"Keep your thoughts to yourself," Nancy stated in a hard tone.

Susan sent Nancy a hurt look, put the roll down on a plate, and wiped her hands on her napkin. "I didn't mean anything by it. Really."

The obvious attempt at garnering sympathy fell flat. No one patted Susan's arm or said they believed her. Her days as a critique partner grew shorter.

Funny, why hadn't they realized before how manipulative she was? What was it called? Passive-aggressive? Getting people to do things you want by making them feel sorry for you or guilty for rejecting your suggestions.

The waiter arrived with their food and another round of drinks. As he served them, Anne secretly watched Susan. The woman kept her eyes on her plate. A furrow developed on her forehead. *She's worried, and she has every right to be. Popping off to Gil that way wasn't smart.*

She barely tasted her bourbon-glazed pork chop, not with the images of Carmella and Dorie still stuck in her mind.

She also kept looking toward the entrance of the restaurant. Would Gil come? He'd seemed pleasant enough in the lobby, but would he—could he—involve the group again?

Are you kidding? After the lies we told to cover our asses during Dorie's investigation? Should I take a chance and call him? Maybe he'll be at the conference tomorrow. I could accidentally on purpose run into him.

If she were honest, she'd admit seeing him again had awakened how attractive she found the detective. Eight months hadn't changed anything. The important point was, however, was he ready to forgive and trust?

"I wonder how the conference will go tomorrow," she announced. "I may even go on Sunday morning.

Anyone else interested?"

"Not me," Rose said. "Jack has to be brought along on taking his share of kid responsibility slowly. One full day and evening is all he can handle just now."

"I think I will. Carl and I don't have any Sunday plans," Jen replied. "He won't mind if I spend an extra day here."

Susan nodded. "Oh, I'll come. I don't want to miss the editor/agent panel discussion."

Nancy stared at Anne with a knowing look. "Even though I'm on deadline, I don't have anything better to do, so I guess I can go."

Divorced many years ago, Nancy devoted ninety percent of her time to writing. Over the years, it had paid off.

"Breakfast begins at seven on Sunday," Anne answered. "We could meet here in the lobby."

They finished eating, paid, and left.

Nancy pulled her aside. "You hate those Sunday morning self-congratulatory, bullshit speeches. Why do you want to go?"

Anne shrugged. "I found the body. It makes sense for me to ask questions."

"And if you're asking questions, then perhaps Gil Collins will be doing the same. Right?"

She nodded and sighed. "Yeah."

"Are you thinking of trying to talk him into letting us help again, in spite of what happened the last time?"

"The thought crossed my mind."

Nancy rubbed her forehead. "I kinda thought that was the plan. Think he'll go for it?"

"I have no idea. I'll try to tackle him with the question tomorrow. I mean, he's sure to be here, if for no other reason than to question anyone who had contact with Carmella today and maybe last night."

"Aren't you supposed to go give your statement tonight?"

"Yes, but that's no guarantee Gil will take it."

"I guess it can't hurt to ask, but be prepared for a resounding no. I'll see you tomorrow."

Anne followed slowly down the glass-enclosed hallway leading to the lobby, the darkness hiding the lush greenery outside. She alternated between excitement at the hope of working with Gil again, and dread at what he would do and say. Would he brush her off? Possibly, but he'd be polite about it. Since none of them were suspects this time, he might see his way clear to them gathering information.

On the other hand, he might not. Besides, I don't even know if he'll be at the conference tomorrow.

However, a large part of her hoped he showed.

She paused as she passed the bar area. It was fairly full. Suddenly, she didn't want to go to either the police station or home. She craved company.

Anne entered the darkened lounge. The first person she saw was Wendy Travers, the committee member responsible for inviting editors and agents. She sat alone at a table near the doorway, a glass of wine in front of her. The poor woman looked miserable.

"Hi, Wendy. May I join you?"

"Yeah, sure," she answered in a lackluster tone.

"You look the way I feel," Anne said taking a seat.

"I swear to God, if I'd known these editors and agents were going to cause me this much grief, I'd have never volunteered. And now Carmella Radcliff has been murdered. I'm as low as I can get." Wendy took a large gulp of wine.

"I hear you." A waiter arrived to take Anne's order for a diet soda. "Sometimes editors and agents can be a bunch of prima donnas."

"Tell me! It started last night. Fran, Terry, Liz Howard, who's working with the hotel, and I all have rooms here in case something came up. That way we could deal with any problems."

"I take it something came up."

"The first person I ran into was Alan Grayson," she said, naming a well-known agent. "He was not a happy camper. Said if he knew Carmella was going to be here, he'd have never accepted the invitation. I guess they don't get along. At any rate, he informed me he'd be leaving in the morning. I had to mollify him and stroke his ego by saying he was fully booked with pitch appointments and that I'd had to turn people down who requested him. That seemed to please him and he said he'd stay. He didn't want to disappoint."

"Was what you told him true?"

"No. He had plenty of spaces left. Carmella garnered the most requests. I figured it would be late afternoon before he realized what was what."

"And if he threatened to leave again, you could always tell him his Saturday line-up was full."

Wendy nodded. "Something like that. In the end, he stalked off saying he was tired and hungry."

Anne's soda arrived. She pulled the paper off the straw, suppressing the urge to tear it into tiny pieces, stuck the straw into the glass, took a long draw, and focused on her friend again. "It's hard babysitting a bunch of editors and agents, but I think you're doing a good job."

Her friend made a face. "I had two editors call me last week demanding a change in their air reservations. Seems they didn't like the discount airline we were using and wanted a legacy carrier where they could rack up frequent flier points. Plus, they also wanted first class. When I told them they could use whatever airline they wanted, but anything over the amount allotted for their tickets was on their dime, they got testy. Said they wouldn't come. I had to run it by our treasurer and Terry. It was too late to find replacement editors, so we caved. The bitches flew first class."

"Prima donnas," Anne murmured again.

"And then to top it all off, Fran gets a call around midnight because of an argument in the bar. She goes down to see what it's all about. Seems Carmella got into it with someone. So Fran calls me. I show up and find Carmella three sheets to the wind. Just what I needed, a hung over agent for the next day. Between the two of us, we got her up to her room."

"Any idea who she argued with?"

"No, but the bartender thought it was someone involved with the conference. He said they talked in low tones until tempers rose. Then it got nasty with a lot of name-calling. When he tried to intervene, Carmella told him to fuck off. That's when he called the hotel manager. When he arrived, Carmella told *him* to fuck off, too. *Then* the manager called Fran." She glanced at her watch. "It's almost ten. I've got to get some rest. I'm sorry you had to be the one to find Carmella. No offense, but better you than me."

"None taken," she replied as Wendy paid the bill and left.

The bar crowd thinned. Anne finished her soda, left

some bills on the table, and departed. She still didn't want to go home. Unfortunately, Gil hadn't put in an appearance.

Even though it was late, she went to the police station. Maybe Gil was there. She'd give her statement, and if luck was with her, they could chat.

****

Anne arrived at the hotel for the Saturday session a few minutes after eight. Even from the lobby, the buzz of conversation emanating from the ballroom at the back of the hotel reached her ears telling her breakfast was in full swing. She met Nancy in the hallway. There was no sign of Jen or Susan.

"How did it go last night? Did you give your statement to Gil?"

"Gil wasn't around. I talked to another detective."

"Did Susan show up?"

"Not while I was there." Anne paused as a couple of attendees walked past, glanced at her, and then put their heads together to whisper. "I guess we should move on."

"Sounds like a full crowd," Nancy said.

"I'm not surprised. Probably more people than they thought are attending. Let's hurry while the food's still available."

"Why? The food sucks."

"Last night's wasn't too bad."

"That was a real dining room, this is conference fare."

They entered the room and headed straight for the buffet. Anne chose bacon, scrambled eggs, and a bagel. Nancy moved toward a breakfast burrito and a Danish. They both poured a glass of orange juice, and then found space at a table for ten, greeting the people they knew.

Nancy was right about the food. The bacon was greasy, the eggs cold, and the bagel tough.

"So, Anne, is it true you found Carmella Radcliff?" one of the women asked.

Anne nodded and sipped her juice, discreetly spitting a pit into her napkin. "Yeah, not the best way to finish off the day."

"Her performance at the critique yesterday was embarrassing, not only for her, but for everybody," another lady said. "Gives agents a bad image."

Anne didn't recognize her, but her nametag read Jackie Simmons and she was an agent from the Coyne & Company Literary Agency in New York.

"She was certainly abrasive," Peg Wheeler, a chapter member declared.

"I don't understand why some people feel the need to be so nasty," the first woman said.

"Insecurity, maybe?" Peg suggested.

"What on earth did she have to be insecure about?" Nancy asked. "She was a successful agent who represented several big name authors—not just in romance, but in the mystery and thriller genres, too."

Jackie shrugged. "Who knows, but the New York rumor mill was churning that the last few authors she sold didn't make earn-out. Not good for the author, the agent, or the publisher."

Anne pushed the remains of dry scrambled eggs around the edge of her plate. Earn-out, also known as sell-through, was the industry phrase for not producing enough in sales to pay back the expenses laid out by the publisher. It happened more than everyone concerned admitted, and publishers did not like losing money. More than one author had been dropped when they couldn't produce the desired revenue. And an agent representing several dropped authors could also find him or herself *persona non grata* at the publishing house door.

Then Anne remembered a snippet of conversation from the day before. "I heard she was also an author."

"She was," the agent said. "Wrote mysteries under the name Regina Day. I read one. It was pretty good."

"Kinda makes you wonder if she was ready to drop being an agent," the first lady added.

"Not likely," Jackie said with a snort. "She made a lot of money on her clients. I heard her talking yesterday that Brad Kilgore's newest thriller got an advance well into six figures, and even though she'd have to split with the agency, that still represents a lot of bucks," Jackie informed them as she glanced at her watch. "Oops, I'd better run. My first appointment is in fifteen minutes. I'm taking over half of what would have been Carmella's pitches today. Alan Grayson and others are doing the other half. Gonna be a busy day. Too bad. I was hoping to get in a little beach time this afternoon."

She rose, tossed her napkin on the table, picked up her large tote bag, and hurried from the room. Her departure signaled it was time to leave.

"Which workshops are you attending?" Nancy asked as they left the table.

"I think I'll check out the one on self-publishing. I'm not interested in going that route, but I should keep up on the possibilities."

Anne didn't want to admit that if her agent rejected

the revised manuscript again, the possibility loomed on the horizon.

"I might as well join you. The other tracks don't sound like anything new."

"Have you seen Jen or Susan?"

"Nope, but I'm sure they're around somewhere."

The two women made their way to the meeting room. Close to fifty people were already seated. Susan waved from the third row.

"Anne, Nancy, come sit with me. Still a couple of chairs available."

They threaded their way through the crowd and sidled past the knees of those already seated to sit next to Susan.

"How are you feeling this morning?" Anne asked.

"Better." She pitched her voice low. "Wish I could say I was sorry that bitch is dead, but I'm not."

"Did you go to the police station last night? I didn't see you there when I went to make my statement."

Susan shook her head. "No, I went home first to talk to my husband. He didn't like the sound of things, so he called our lawyer. I went in early this morning with both of them and talked to the detective."

"Probably a good move, since you couldn't produce a witness who saw you after the fight with Carmella," Nancy said.

Susan shot her an irritated glance. "I'm sure there must be somebody who saw me and hasn't realized it yet."

"Well, I wouldn't worry too much," Anne replied as the speaker walked up to the podium. "I'm sure there are surveillance cameras all over this hotel."

Susan gave her a startled look, but before she could

answer, the workshop began.

Anne kept her eyes open for any sign of Gil Collins. If he was there, he was staying out of sight.

As soon as the seminar ended, Susan rose. "I'll see you all later," she said and rushed from the room.

"Where's she going in such a hurry?" Anne asked.

"Who knows," Nancy replied. "Do you want to attend any more workshops?"

"Not really."

Standing in the hallway a few moments later, Jen joined them.

"Hi," Jen said. "How's your day going so far?"

Nancy shrugged. "As good as can be expected, I guess. I'm not really getting much from the workshops. Where have you been?"

"I got here early, took one look at the buffet, and headed for the restaurant. Then I went to the workshop on self-editing. It was so-so."

They discussed the speakers for a few minutes until Anne finally asked, "Jen, did you see Susan? She was with us in here and took off like a rabbit as soon as it ended."

"I saw her a few minutes ago. She was on her cell," Jen offered. "I didn't feel like talking, so I avoided her."

Anne could relate to that. She let her mind wander as her friends flipped through the program. *Is Gil here? Is he talking to people? Will he want to talk to me again? Or will he want to avoid me and assign that task to someone else? Surely, he can't consider me a suspect. I had no beef with Carmella.*

She hated to admit how much she wanted to see him. Just a few brief minutes yesterday had reawakened the interest. Could she convince him she deserved a second chance?

He was hurt and disappointed by my lies and deceit when Dorie was killed. How do I make him believe I'll never do that again?

Anne's mind went into fantasy mode, conjuring up scenes of her and Gil dining at an intimate restaurant, dancing, making love. All trust was restored and the relationship was moving on to higher ground when Jen nudged her.

"You looked like you were on a far away planet. Were you with Gil?"

"Just thinking, that's all."

"Where are you heading next?" Nancy asked.

She shrugged and opened her program. "I have no clue. This seminar on paranormal settings might be fun."

The three of them weighed the merits of various workshops before deciding to attend separate seminars. They parted ways.

Anne walked slowly toward the meeting room, and then changed direction to head for the lobby. Perhaps a quiet hour of being alone would help her out of this funk.

She sank into the plush cushions of a sofa and leaned her head back closing her eyes. Why was she here? Why even bother to attend workshops? If she'd stayed at home, she would have never found Carmella.

Damnation! Why does this stuff always happen to me?

The list of clients and potential clients the agent pissed off over the years was no doubt long. Anybody attending the conference could have had a prior run-in with Carmella. Did someone who'd had an issue with the woman bide their time to let the grudge build?

"Hello, Anne," a familiar voice said.

She opened her eyes and stared at Gil Collins.

Chapter Four

"Gil, how nice to see you." Anne flinched inwardly. Why did her mind always revert to banalities when she was with him? *Nice to see you?* She struggled to sit upright on the cushy sofa. "I mean, how goes the investigation?"

"We're making progress. May I buy you a cup of coffee?"

"Sure. I was just thinking about that myself."

He smiled and extended his hand to help her up. She accepted and like last night, a warm glow spread from her hand throughout the rest of her body.

A simple touch and he makes me feel safe, protected.

They walked across the lobby and down the corridor to the dining room. Today, the glass enclosed hallway showed the ferns, Mexican petunias, and sago palms reminding them they were in tropical Florida. The breakfast buffet was still set up in the dining area.

"Have you eaten already?" he asked.

"A very bad breakfast in the ballroom."

"Join me. I've been running on coffee since seven this morning. I could use some fuel."

"I'd love to."

The hostess showed them to a table for two. Then they made their way to the buffet. The spread here was ten times better than the one in the ballroom. Anne selected bacon, a freshly made waffle from the hot station, and a glass of orange juice, this time minus the pit.

Seated at the table, she bit into the perfectly cooked bacon as Gil attacked his pancakes. A waitress stopped by to fill their coffee cups to the brim. As she sipped, she looked at him through her lashes.

His light brown hair was touched with gray, and the crinkles around his blue eyes indicated he knew how to laugh. So what if his ears stuck out a tad? It was just a part of him. Of medium height and weight, he was definitely not the hunky hero of most romance novels, but Anne found his average looks appealing. She had from the first day she'd met him.

"So, explain to me again about conferences," he said.

Dragging herself out of her daydream, she put her cup down and poured syrup over her waffle. "Conferences offer workshops on a variety of subjects and genres. They also offer the opportunity for unpublished authors to have a one-on-one with an editor or an agent to pitch their stories. In addition, it's a good venue for networking with published authors. Panel discussions are crucial. An author gets to hear the inside scoop on the latest industry trends from editors, agents, and best-selling writers."

"I suppose I can see why someone who isn't published would attend, but why you? You have an agent and a publisher, don't you?"

"Yes, but it's a good idea to attend one every once in a while to keep up with what's going on. To be honest, I prefer to attend a conference held every year in Atlanta, but since my chapter is sponsoring this one,

I decided to support them. It's been a while since I've attended. Wish I'd had the sense to stay at home, considering."

He didn't reply, but forked a chunk of pancake into his mouth, and then sipped from his coffee cup.

"How are the editors and agents chosen to come?" he asked.

"A conference committee is formed and the work divided. For instance, there's a committee to select workshops, one to come up with a keynote speaker—ours this year is Deborah Worth. She writes contemporary romance and is on the *New York Times* bestseller list. Another committee selects editors and agents. Then there are committees that deal with hotel accommodations, including the food, which I have to discuss with someone." She finished with a laugh.

"So, someone from your group extends an invitation to various speakers and such to come to the party?"

"More or less."

"How do you know who to invite?"

"I was on the workshop committee six or seven conferences ago. The chapter president usually makes an announcement on the chapter president's link saying we're taking applications for workshops. That in turn is forwarded to the chapter online information loop. Then established authors send in a presentation and the committee decides. Editors and agents are contacted directly with an invitation."

"Do many refuse?"

"Some. They might have a conflict or might not be actively acquiring at the moment. And before any invitation is extended, the committee makes sure they're open to new material."

"And did Ms. Radcliff meet the criteria?"

"I have no idea. To be honest, I understood Carmella wasn't all that interested in new authors. She preferred to stick by her tried and true clients, yet I heard she did ask for material here." She sipped more coffee, and then lowered the cup to the saucer. "Gil, why are you asking me all this? Fran or Terry could give you the same information."

He smiled. "Maybe I just wanted to hear the sound of your voice again."

Warmth that had nothing to do with coffee washed over her. She leaned forward. "I've missed you."

"I've missed you, too, Anne."

"Look, I know I did things eight months ago that destroyed what we could have had together. What I did was wrong. I know that, but is it possible to wipe the slate clean and start over?" Anne held her breath. She wasn't sure she could take another rejection.

"I don't know, but maybe the fact that we've been thrown together again under similar circumstances is an act of fate."

She exhaled. Fate. Maybe that *was* the answer.

"You...you don't suspect me of killing Carmella, do you?" Her voice had a slight tremor.

Gil shook his head. "No, but your friend Susan Lynch is on the list."

"Poor Susan. She's impatient with learning the process and the craft. We're about to dump her from our critique group. Even so, I don't see her killing anyone."

"None of you saw Candace Warren killing anyone, either."

She bit her lip. "That's true, but Candace had...extenuating circumstances. Gil, even though we screwed up royally last time, would you consider letting us help again?"

He didn't answer for a long moment, but stared into her eyes. She had no clue what he was thinking.

"I'm not sure I trust any of you yet."

"I can understand that. It took a long time for all of us to trust each other again. Too many secrets, too many lies, but we can listen to conversations and ask questions, make comments that will evoke an answer. And this time, I promise if I find out my mother killed Carmella Radcliff, I'll tell you."

He chuckled. "I don't think you'll have to do that." He sobered. "All right, ask your questions. Who had a grudge against the woman? Did anyone else have an altercation with her—that kind of stuff? Meet me in the bar around three o'clock. Make sure the others are with you, so I only have to listen once."

"Rose isn't attending the session today, but Nancy and Jen are here. What about Susan?"

He shook his head. "Leave her out of it."

"Got it."

He smiled. "Eat up. Your waffle is getting cold."

Anne happily ate the remains of her now cold waffle. It didn't matter. This was the first step to getting back on track to a relationship that had been terminated by her own stupidity. Gil was willing to let them help again.

It's a start.

****

All thoughts of attending any further workshops vanished. Anne sat in the lobby making a list of questions to ask of editors and agents. They'd be the best source of information on Carmella.

Gil had left as soon as they finished breakfast.

"I'm reviewing surveillance tapes, and before you ask, you can see them only if I see someone or something suspicious. Okay?"

She'd nodded. "I understand. In the meantime, I'll make casual conversation with people."

Anne put the pad of paper down and pulled her cell from her purse, then speed dialed a number.

"Rose, I don't suppose there's any chance of you coming here today, is there?"

"Are you kidding?" her friend said with a snort. "Jack practically fled the house at seven-thirty this morning. I think yesterday was an eye-opening experience for him. Working at the store probably sounded like heaven on earth. Why do you ask?"

Anne explained the situation. "I thought maybe you could talk to people and get their reactions. I'm hoping to grab Nancy and Jen between workshops in a few minutes to do the same."

"So, Gil is letting us help? I'm surprised considering the Dorie fiasco. At least you'll get to see him."

"He still doesn't trust us completely, but I'm hoping to change that."

"You know, I might be of some help after all," Rose said slowly. "I can make a few phone calls. Not everyone is attending the conference. I'll make it sound like I'm spreading the news about Carmella, or gossip, if you will. Oh! I'll call Alice Kartchman. Since we write the same genre, she and I became friendly after the ordeal with Dorie. And Alice is very much in touch with the publishing world. I swear she has an insight into the business that is a sheer gift. She might know something we don't."

Alice Kartchman, a very successful erotic romance author, lived in New York City. If there were rumors flying around, she'd know about them.

"Good idea. Call me when you know something. I've gotta go. The last morning workshop just let out. We have a half-hour break until lunch and the keynote. I'll talk to you later."

She hung up and went in search of Nancy and Jen, finally finding them in the bookstore.

"Hi, how did the paranormal workshop go?" Jen asked.

"I don't know. I didn't go." She filled them in on her activities and on Gil's okay to ask questions. "I think we should all sit at different tables for lunch. Try to find one with an editor or agent."

"Or a disgruntled author who also got slammed at the critique panel yesterday by Carmella," Nancy added.

"Good point," Jen replied. "I heard Caroline Houseman was in tears and that Joyce Watson was so mad she got up and left the room. And Joyce is a good writer. I've seen some of her stuff during those informal critique sessions during chapter meetings."

They left the bookstore and wandered into the ballroom. Anne counted twenty-two round tables of ten set up. The head table would be made up of Fran, Terry, the keynote speaker, and the rest of the chapter board members. Some attendees had already found seats. At least one editor, agent, or bestselling author was assigned to a specific table, giving writers the opportunity to chat outside of the workshop or pitch room.

"Okay, find someone and take a seat," Anne said.

Nancy went to the left. Jen took the right hand side of the room. Anne strolled down the middle until finding a place card with Jackie Simmons' name on it. Jackie had mentioned this morning that she was taking part of the list of hopefuls designated for Carmella. She might have something to say. Anne pulled out the chair next to the name card and sat. She scanned the room. Nancy had maneuvered herself into a seat near the head table. Jen was chatting with Howard Wright at a table not far away.

Good, we're all in place. I hope we can get something concrete to give Gil.

Sometimes, people were hesitant to talk to the police, but would discuss things with a civilian, so to speak. Plus, she wanted to do as much as possible to clear even the smallest hint of suspicion she had killed Carmella from people's minds. That idiot's accusations from yesterday had some attendees looking at Anne in a strange way. Never again did she want to be in the position of suspect.

Another woman walked up and claimed the chair on the other side of Jackie's, then gave Anne a calculating glance.

Anne stared back, wondering if the woman was trying to figure out a way to cut her out of any conversation. *Nope, not gonna happen, sweetie.*

Much to her consternation, the accusatory nitwit from yesterday walked by, started to pull out a chair, saw Anne, sniffed, and walked on with her nose in the air. Thank goodness. She didn't want to deal with an idiot over lunch.

Anne chuckled. The obnoxious woman plunked her butt in a chair at Jen's table. With Jen there, she'd never get a word in.

The room filled rapidly. More writers joined them and the conversation centered on general chitchat. The final unassigned chair was taken. Only Jackie was missing. Anne spooned dressing on the salad in front of her and nibbled. Not bad, and experience had taught her that this may be the best tasting item on the menu. She ate it all. Waiters moved amongst the crowd removing the salad plates and replacing them with the entrée. She stared at a chicken breast with some kind of cream sauce poured over it, green beans, and rice pilaf— typical conference fare. Anne cut off a piece and popped it into her mouth. On the dry side. And the sauce was too thick, but still edible. *Better than yesterday, at least.*

Finally, Jackie arrived and took her seat. "Hi. Sorry I'm late. Got caught up in a conversation and couldn't get away. Did I miss anything?"

"Not at all," the lady on her other side gushed. "I was hoping to talk to you about my pitch from earlier. I do think ten minutes is too short a time to get the message across, don't you? And I'm sure I made no sense whatsoever. I always get so nervous. I want to go into further detail about my work. Now, the heroine…"

"Excuse me, but could you please pass the salad dressing?" Jackie asked interrupting her.

When the woman turned to reach for the container, Anne jumped in.

"So, you must be swamped what with taking over Carmella's appointments and all. How's that going?

Have you heard anything that sounds exciting?"

"Actually, yes. One lady had a very interesting story about shape-shifters. She was supposed to pitch to Carmella. Knowing Carmella, she'd have brushed the woman off. I can't figure out how she kept getting invited to these conferences. To the best of my knowledge, she wasn't acquiring. Oh, thank you." Jackie accepted the dressing from the pushy woman and spooned some over the lettuce while still chatting with Anne. "And I had another great sounding story from a woman just before we broke for lunch. In fact, she's the reason I was late. I had to know more about it."

"Well, in that case, I'm sure you won't mind hearing more about my book, too," the insistent woman said glaring at Anne.

Anne wasn't about to let her horn in and rushed to continue. "Let me say that on behalf of the Southeast Florida Writers chapter, thank you for taking on such a load. I just hope the good pitches outnumber the really awful ones. I'm sure you've heard more than your fair share of those this weekend."

Jackie looked at her, grinned and made a slight inclination of her head to the woman on her other side.

"You have no idea."

The other writer leaned forward. "Now, about my heroine. She's a soft, gentle creature who is secretly in love with the hero, a very macho type who…"

"Didn't you say this morning that you found Carmella?" Jackie asked, totally ignoring the yammering from her right.

Anne shuddered. "Yes. It was not the most pleasant experience in my life."

"Well, I don't know what I would have done if it

had been me. Imagine walking into the restroom, flipping on the lights, and finding her. What made you open the stall door?"

"I just had this creepy feeling I wasn't alone. Then I saw her feet under the door. I knocked, it swung open, and…there she was. All I could think was to get the hell out."

"I would have run out screaming." Jackie turned her attention to the main course.

"I'm sure the publishing world is stunned," Anne replied.

Jackie ate a morsel of chicken, made a face, and pushed the plate away. "I'm sure they are. Funny, but there's this rumor going around that Carmella was about to quit being an agent and go to writing full time, but, like I said this morning, I don't buy that. She made too much money being an agent."

"Even so, she'd represent herself, no doubt. I mean, she had all the contacts. Is that ethical?"

"Now, about my book," the woman said in a louder voice.

Again, Jackie ignored her. "Carmella didn't concern herself with ethics. If she saw an author she wanted, she'd go after them regardless of whether or not they already had an agent. I know for a fact that she snatched at least two clients away from Alan Grayson in the past year." She lowered her voice. "He told me this morning he hoped Carmella Radcliff was burning in hell. He hated her guts."

Anne contemplated this information. Could Alan Grayson have followed Carmella into the ladies restroom and stuck a knife in her chest? It took a certain amount of strength to stab a person. And according to

Wendy last night, he'd been highly upset about her even being here.

"Now, I'd like to get back to my story," Miss Persistent began.

Jackie looked at her watch. "Goodness, would you look at the time? I'd love to stay for the keynote address, but I have to go to my room and check e-mail. Plus, I have several missed calls to return. It was nice chatting with you both. See you later."

She pushed back her chair, rose, and wound her way through the tables to the doors where she disappeared.

The other woman gazed with a stunned expression at the now empty doorway. Others at the table glanced at each other, too. So much for a chance to chat with an agent over lunch. Not a very nice thing to do, but then maybe Jackie had had enough of pushy authors.

That's got to be the shortest conference luncheon on record. She spent a whole ten minutes at the table.

The woman glared at Anne over the empty space. "If you hadn't monopolized the conversation, I would have had a chance to discuss my book with her."

"You already pitched. Did she request anything?"

"The first three chapters and a synopsis, but it deserves a full submission. In fact, I think I'll send that in anyway. My heroine is wonderful. She's young, impressionable, mad about the hero, and just waiting for him to see her qualities so he can confess his undying love and take care of her forever. He's a take-charge man who is used to making all the decisions. I just know she'd love it, but you had to keep talking."

A virginal, submissive heroine and an uber-alpha hero? Unless a publishing house dealt with sweet romances or was Christian based, Anne couldn't think of anyone who published that type of writing anymore. And the plot was outdated. Many readers wanted more action, a stronger heroine, and of course, more sex. Plus, ignoring the request guidelines was a big no-no.

"If I were you, I'd send in exactly what the agent asked for, nothing more."

"Nonsense. A writer has to strike while the iron is hot and take a chance."

Anne groaned inwardly at the tired cliché and wondered if this was indicative of the woman's writing style.

"My book is fantastic—a bestseller," the obnoxious woman barreled on. "Maybe I'll go to her room. That's it. I can tell her all about it and we won't be interrupted."

She rose, glared once more at Anne, and stalked away.

"Boy, have I got a critique partner for you," she muttered under her breath. "She's delusional, too."

"Good afternoon, ladies and gentlemen. Welcome to Southeast Florida's Sand and Sun Conference."

Anne turned her attention to the podium at the head table and Fran, chapter president. Out of the corner of her eye, she saw Alan Grayson sidle out of the room. Making a snap decision, she followed. She didn't want to listen to either Fran or the keynote speaker anyway.

In the hallway, she spotted Alan on his cell turn a corner. She followed. He stopped near the now resurrected goodie table. She sauntered up, pretending to look at the material presented while keeping her ears tuned to the one-sided conversation.

"Yeah, I've heard some good pitches, but the

majority are nothing special...I'll send most to an assistant to deal with the 'thanks, but no thanks' e-mail...Not that I know of...Nobody's going to miss Carmella Radcliff, especially Jack Summers."

Anne's attention sharpened. Jack Summers was the urbane owner and head agent for Summers Literary Agency—Carmella's boss. She'd met him several times at conferences over the years.

"They've got some kind of dinner tonight, but I think I'll ditch it and go find a good restaurant. The food here sucks...I'm on an afternoon plane Sunday...Right, see you Monday."

He hung up and glanced at Anne. The eye contact was an invitation to speak.

"Mr. Grayson, isn't it? I'm Anne Jamieson and on behalf of the Southeast Florida chapter, I want to thank you for stepping up and taking over Carmella's appointments. I'm sure it made your day all that much busier."

"So I work a little longer. I don't mind. That's what I get paid for, and I think several agents and editors split up the rest."

"Certainly was shocking about Carmella."

He shrugged. "To be honest, I'm surprised someone didn't kill her a long time ago. She wasn't the most pleasant person to ever come down the pike."

"I know. I've dealt with her a couple of times. Still..."

Grayson made a face. "Somehow, getting offed in a john sounds like poetic justice to me. I heard the woman who found her almost fainted and had hysterics."

"Uh, yeah, I guess I would have, too." Anne didn't

think he needed to know she was really the one who had discovered the body. The fainting, hysterical woman he mentioned had to be the flake on the gurney. "I was chatting with a friend who said Carmella was about to give up being an agent and work full time on her own novels."

"I wouldn't know. I didn't concern myself with Carmella Radcliff's activities," he replied giving her a sharp glance.

"Well, maybe now those authors she snatched from you will return."

His eyes narrowed. "I don't know what you're talking about. Now, if you'll excuse me, I have some business to take care of. Good day."

Alan Grayson turned on his heel and strode away.

He might say he doesn't know what I'm talking about, but his body language sure does.

Anne wandered into the bar and ordered a glass of white wine. Grayson was not particularly tall or athletic looking, but he certainly had enough strength to jam a knife into Carmella's chest. So far, he also has the strongest motive. If Carmella was hijacking his clients, especially bestsellers, then that represented a fair chunk of change he no longer collected in commissions.

I wonder how many other agents she victimized.

She reached into her carryall and extracted the conference program. Turning to the biography section, she scanned the names of attending agents. Besides, Grayson, Carmella, and Jackie, there were two others. Both were from small agencies and not likely to be considered poachable by Carmella. The editors ranged from large, traditional publishers to small e-publishers and print on demand houses.

I wonder who Carmella had the argument with the other night. And who's to say it was an editor, agent, or author? Could have simply been an attendee. Maybe someone had the bad luck, not to mention judgment, to pitch uninvited in a bar when the agent was half-loaded.

She could just imagine how Carmella would react to something like that.

The name of a workshop presenter caught her attention—Beth Hardaway. Wasn't there something about Beth and Carmella a few years ago? She'd have to find her and ask.

As she sipped her wine, Iona Smalls, an editor with a medium-sized publishing house wandered into the bar area.

"Iona, how nice to see you. It's been a long time. Have a seat."

"Anne, how are you?" she replied with a smile, sliding onto the next stool and ordering a glass of wine. "Shocking about Carmella. I heard you found her."

Anne shuddered and gave her the basics keeping Gil's warning in mind. "It was traumatic to say the least."

"Can't say I'm surprised, though. Carmella was as cold as a witch's tit in a brass bra. She was mean, calculating, and greedy."

"I guess as an editor you must have had to deal with her on a regular basis."

Iona snorted. "Are you kidding? She never sent anything my way. Didn't have the nerve."

"Why not?"

"About seven or eight years ago, she tried to muscle in on one of my clients in the bar during a conference. Had the nerve to plunk herself down at our table while I was off to the ladies room. When I got back, there she was, singing her own praises and bad-mouthing me. I told her to take her fat ass out of my sight before I smacked her in the mouth. She left and I kept the client."

Anne was confused. Why would Iona be upset about an agent talking with an author? "Why was she hassling your author? Didn't she already have an agent?"

Iona stared at her over the rim of her wine glass. "Honey, *I* was her agent. I started out at the Ferguson Agency. Switched to being an editor about five years ago. I thought you knew."

"No, this is the first I've heard of it. So you knew Carmella up close and personal, too. I understand Alan Grayson hated her guts."

She rolled her eyes. "I'll say. That all started when she dumped an author. Alan picked her up and her next book made the *USA Today* bestseller list. Carmella accused him of poaching and said she'd get even. She glommed onto three of his clients in the past year. He was not a happy camper and threatened to sue. I don't know who was in charge of lining up editors and agents for this conference, but inviting the two of them was not a good move."

"I thought I'd find you here," Nancy said sliding onto the other vacant stool next to Anne. "Hi, Iona, long time between conferences."

"Hey, Nancy, and you're so right. Is the keynote done?"

"Just about. I couldn't take much more. Really boring. When it's over, Fran will make a few announcements, so I slipped away. I see you did the same."

"I've heard so many keynotes over the years, I can't tell the difference between the subject matters." The editor glanced at her watch and downed her wine in several gulps. "Damn, would you look at the time? Guess that means I have to go back to work soon, but first I have to freshen up. I'll see you tonight at dinner."

"Where's Jen?" Anne asked as Iona slapped some money onto the bar and exited.

"Probably still working the room if the speech is over. You know Jen, talk, talk, talk."

"She may talk a lot, but she also listens." Anne gave Nancy the rundown of the last forty minutes.

"Hmmm, that's interesting. Alan Grayson could be the best suspect. It takes a lot of strength to stick a knife in someone's chest—all that bone and muscle. Would a woman have it?" Nancy said.

"If she was mad enough. Remember Dorie? We had her ex-husband all set up as the killer. None of us suspected Candace. She's on the slender side. However, she was drunk and infuriated. I've heard that strong emotions can give a normal person superhuman strengths."

"So, what do we do now?"

"Go find people to talk to, I guess." Anne took a ten out of her wallet and laid it on the bar. "That should cover my wine. I think I'll hit the restroom, and then try to find Beth Hardaway. Let's meet back here at three. Gil said he'd join us."

Anne left the bar and walked down the hallway to the ladies room. There she paused a moment, her hand on the door, ready to push it open.

"Oh, for Pete's sake, open the damned door, dummy," she mumbled under her breath. "You're not likely to find another body."

She shoved hard and walked in. She was alone. A few minutes later, she exited. A quick glance at her watch showed it was only twelve forty-five. That gave her about fifteen minutes or so until the ballroom emptied.

The stairs to the mezzanine were not far away. Curious, Anne climbed and turned toward the scene of the crime. Yellow tape crisscrossed the restroom door. Knowing better than to disturb it, she walked on until finding a sign that read "Business Center" on a closed door.

Susan had said that after the fight with Carmella she'd spent the time in a nook near the business center. She walked a few steps further down the hall until finding it—a small alcove with an end table and a chair.

But Susan never mentioned the nook was on the mezzanine. Had she seen the instigator of her humiliation enter the restroom? How hard would it be to slip in and kill Carmella?

Anne swallowed hard. If she found the little alcove by the business center, then certainly Gil had also. Then from behind her came the sound of soft footsteps, as if someone tiptoed over the carpet. The hair on her arms rose and her heartbeats suddenly intensified.

With a gasp, she whirled.

Chapter Five

Anne stared at the hysterical woman who'd accused her of killing Carmella yesterday.

The woman also gasped and took a step backward. "Stay where you are. Don't come near me!"

"Oh, for crying out loud, get a grip. What are you doing here?" Anne's momentary fear had turned to irritation.

"I saw you on the stairs and decided to follow. Criminals always return to the scene of the crime."

She wanted to bitch slap this moron in the worst way. "First of all, I don't like being followed. And secondly, I did not kill Carmella Radcliff. I found the body."

"*I* found the body—right after you hightailed it out of the restroom. I can't figure out why that idiot cop didn't arrest you."

"Because he knows I didn't do it." Anne paused. "And why were you up here in the first place?"

"One of the workshops was held in a room down the hall. I had to go and this was the closest bathroom."

"And no one else saw you? If a workshop had just let out, then a bunch of people must have been here."

"I didn't leave right away. I read the program to see where I wanted to go the next day. And I don't need to explain my whereabouts to you!"

"Maybe you had a tiff with Carmella. Maybe *you*

pitched to her and she called your story shit. *Maybe* you saw her enter the john, followed, and killed her."

The woman's face turned white as her jaw dropped. "You're insane. I never even talked to her—ever."

Anne lifted her chin and strode past the irritating lunatic who squeaked like a cornered rabbit and flattened her body again the wall.

Turning, she fired a last salvo. "And if I see you again within ten feet of me, I'm calling the cops. It's called stalking."

Anne walked down the stairs as regal as a queen with her head held high. *If she's so scared of me, why the hell did she follow me up the stairs?*

Her pace slowed, stopping as she reached the foot of the steps. A good question. Why did she follow? Could she have had a confrontation with Carmella? *I need to find out who she is.*

As Anne entered the lobby seating area, she spotted Beth Hardaway sitting on the sofa.

"Hi, Beth, how are you?" She didn't wait for an invitation, but sat next to the author.

"Anne, hi. I'm fine. How about you? Is it true you found Carmella's body?"

She gave a fake shiver. "I'm afraid so. Scared the crap out of me. I wonder who killed her."

"I'm sure the police have a long list of suspects."

Anne fingered her skirt, making pleats. "I wonder where she started. Was she always with Summers?"

"Hell, no. She began at a small agency in Chicago and worked her way on up to larger places until she hit New York and met Jack Summers. Rumor has it she slept her way into that job."

Anne pictured the rotund Carmella and her boss thrashing around between the sheets. It was not a pleasant image.

"I'd think Jack would be more discriminating. Physically, Carmella was no prize."

"She didn't always look like a bowling ball with legs. Fifteen years ago, she wasn't bad."

"I never had much in the line of dealing with her. Did you?"

Beth nodded. "She was my agent for a while. She dumped me five years ago when two of my books didn't earn out."

"I heard she had a habit of doing that. Not every book is a winner in that department. Happened to me a couple of times. I can see a publishing house not renewing a contract, but if my agent dumped me just like that, I'd be pissed."

"I was. She and I got into a heated discussion at Nationals a few months later. She said I was a washed up flash in the pan—talk about clichés—and I told her she wouldn't know a good story if it up and bit her in the ass. Luckily, I nailed down my present agent and things have been profitable for all concerned."

"Good for you."

"I'll tell you this, I won't miss her. She had this reputation as being the best, but if she was, she'd have seen the flaws in my stories and caught them before submitting to a publisher. I think she just skimmed the manuscripts and sent them on. As it was, I had to work like hell to revise and they still came up short. When she first started in the business, she often sold to small publishers who didn't hand out big advances, hence the earn-out not taking as long."

"So she got a rep as being a super-agent when it wasn't quite earned."

"Exactly. She could point to how quickly her clients began to collect royalties. A total sleazebag."

Anne's accusatory stalker walked past where they were seated, but didn't look their way. *Speaking of bitches...*

"Do you have any idea who that woman is?" she asked.

Beth glanced over as the woman stopped at the front desk. "Oh God, let the earth open and swallow me now. Her name is Joan Quaylen and she's a monstrous pain in the ass. Thinks she'd God's gift to writing and doesn't hesitate to tell you so. Take it from me, she ain't, which explains why she's still unpublished. I read a couple of her things for contests I had judged. Since contest judges and entrants are anonymous, she had the audacity to have the coordinator forward an e-mail to me saying I was being very short-sighted."

"I had a run in with her yesterday. She apparently found Carmella's body after I did and made a huge production out of it. Even accused me of being the killer."

"That doesn't surprise me. She's a drama queen." Beth chuckled. "About a year ago, I was at a conference when she and Carmella got into it."

I knew it! "Really? What happened?"

"She kept pestering Carmella about some proposal she'd sent in months before. You know, 'Have you read it yet? What do think? How much can you get for it?' That kind of stuff. She also had the bad taste to do it in a crowded bar. Carmella told her the writing sucked and to get off her back."

"Bet that didn't go down well."

"Old Joanie was livid, not to mention humiliated. Said she hoped Carmella fell down a manhole."

Was this a motive for murder? *She could have been watching to see who discovered the body, and then when I bolted, waited for security to let them believe she found it. And Carmella had argued with someone Thursday night. Could it have been Joan Quaylen?*

In the past couple of hours she'd found several suspects. Terry Whiting walked past, a cell clapped to her ear.

"Oh, Beth, please excuse me, but I have to talk to Terry. Are you giving a workshop today?"

She nodded. "At three."

Nuts, the same time she was due to meet with Gil.

"I'll try to make it." She hated lying, but had to say something.

Anne rose and hurried after the conference chair. She caught up as the phone conversation ended.

"Hi, Terry. How's everything going?"

Terry rolled her eyes. "If I'd known being a conference chair was this aggravating, I'd have never raised my hand. All these nitpicking details are driving me crazy, not to mention this business with Carmella. Some people are demanding their money back, saying we provided lax security."

"I'd say that was more the hotel's problem. Funny, I was talking to Wendy last night in the bar and she basically said the same thing about the job being a pain. I don't think she ever wants to see another editor or agent again. By the way, is it true Carmella had some kind of argument with an attendee the other night?"

"That's what I heard. For once, Fran couldn't

demand I take care of something. I'd turned my phone off and was relaxing in a warm bathtub with a glass of wine."

"I have a question. Could I see a list of the pitches Carmella took yesterday?"

The woman shot a keen glance toward her. "Are you playing detective? Fran said you would."

Anne gritted her teeth. "I'm just curious. Maybe she argued with an author she rejected. I know quite a few of the attendees. I thought maybe I could help."

Terry frowned. "I guess it's all right." Her phone rang again. "Damn. Check with Patty Morrison. She's coordinating the pitches. Tell her I said it's okay. Hello?"

"Thanks."

Patty Morrison would likely be near the pitch room. With Carmella's death, other agents were doing double duty. Patty liked to micro-manage, so instead of letting her volunteers keep the sessions on time, she would take over.

Anne's assumption was right. As she approached the sign-in table, Patty was flitting around like a nervous butterfly, constantly giving orders and making comments. When she stopped to take a breath, Anne broke in.

"Hi, Patty. How's it going?"

"Are you kidding? I'm up to my eyeballs with long winded authors and one less agent."

"Well, you're doing a wonderful job. I was just talking to Terry and she said I could take a look at Carmella's schedule from yesterday."

"Why?"

Anne shrugged. "Why not? She may have had a

beef with somebody she rejected."

Another author walked up to sign in for her pitch. Patty immediately turned her attention to the newcomer.

"And who are you here to see?" The woman gave a name and a time. "I think he's about ready. Let me check. Dee, keep a close watch on your times. I don't want to fall behind. Now where was I? Oh yes, the list. If Terry okayed it, I guess it's all right." She walked to the end of the table and opened a folder. "Here's a copy. Go ahead and take it. I made several. I had to give the original to the police."

Anne accepted the sheet of paper as another author arrived, and then spotted Caroline Houseman exiting the pitch room.

"Caroline! Wait up." She walked over to the woman. "How did your pitch go?"

"Pretty good, actually. I pitched to Iona Smalls. She requested the first one-hundred pages and a synopsis. Typical response, but I'm keeping my fingers crossed. How are you doing? I wouldn't have come within a thousand miles of this place if I'd have found Carmella."

"I'm surprised I'm here, too," she replied with another forced shiver. "But if I'd stayed at home, all I'd do is think. Better off among friends and fellow writers. So far, not too many people are sorry about Carmella. I heard she put on quite a nasty show at the critique panel yesterday."

Caroline heaved a huge sigh. "I hate to speak badly of the dead, but that woman was a bitch through and through. She didn't like anything presented. Tore Susan Lynch a new one and called my stuff awful. 'Gilded garbage' was the exact wording, I believe. I almost cried. Pissed me off—and I'm pretty thick-skinned about criticism. Told her off later, too."

"Oh really? What was her reaction?"

"She scowled and said not to give up my day job."

"Ouch. When was this?"

"I'm not sure, but we were standing in the line for the ladies room around five or so."

Before Anne could ask another question, Joyce Watson emerged from the pitch room with a grin on her face.

"Hi Anne, Caro."

"How'd your pitch go?" Anne asked.

"Fantastic! Betty Holliday with that new publisher of inspirational romances requested a full. Shame that nasty little troll, Carmella Radcliff, isn't here to know. She had me so angry yesterday at the critique that I walked out. I mentioned her comments to Betty who said Carmella deserved what she got."

"No one deserves to be murdered," Anne replied. "But I get where she's coming from. What did Carmella say to make you so upset?"

Joyce waved her hand in the air. "Oh, called it twaddle and said she quit listening to the moderator reading it after the first paragraph. Wish I'd had the guts to do what Susan Lynch did. I saw the whole thing and almost died laughing." She checked her watch. "You know, I think I might find a quiet spot, pull out my tablet, and see where I can tighten up my story. Talk to you all later."

As she walked away, Caroline also looked at the time. "I'd better scoot, too. I want to hit the bookstore before the next workshop. Nice talking to you, Anne.

Have a good one."

Anne retraced her steps to the lobby. *So Caroline had words with Carmella in line at the ladies room, and probably heard her announce she was finding another restroom. Did she follow and renew the argument? Plus, for someone who had been reduced to tears, she told me about it in a remarkably calm voice. Same with Joyce. She could have followed the agent, too.*

She sighed. She just didn't see the women as killers. But then, she hadn't seen Candace in that light either. Once again seated, she read the list of names. Some she knew, some she didn't. Somehow, she didn't think this was going to help much.

And none of the names she knew on the list sounded capable of premeditation. No, the murderer had calculated, waited, and then taken a chance. Nothing spur of the moment about it.

Susan's name, however, popped out at her. She'd pitched to Carmella at nine o'clock that morning. The critique panel had taken place at three o'clock. And she'd heard the agent rescind the request during the argument. Could that have been the catalyst?

Jen walked up and plopped herself into a chair. "Whew, what a boring lunch. I'd have thought Deborah Worth would have had something better to say other than how she made it to the best seller list and how much money she got in advances."

"You're kidding! She actually talked about her finances?"

"Didn't you hear her?"

Anne shook her head. "Nope, I skipped the speeches."

"Wish I had. And none of the workshops sound all

that interesting this afternoon."

"Did you talk to anybody? I saw you sat at Howard Wright's table."

"Had a nice discussion with him. I also learned that Carmella hadn't sold a story to him in a couple of years. Last fall, she cornered Howard at some conference and tried to twist his arm to buy some property she was hustling. When he told her to go through the usual channels, she got pissed, called him a few names, and told him she'd never submit a client's work to him again."

"He probably heaved a sigh of relief," Anne said in a dry tone.

Jen grinned. "He didn't sound too unhappy about the prospect. Maybe she was pushing her own story. Wouldn't put it past her."

"I noticed that nasty woman who accused me of killing Carmella sat at your table."

Jen made a face. "Pushy broad. Kept trying to monopolize the conversation with how good her book was. Howard didn't look impressed. I just chattered over her. I also got reprimanded by Fran."

"About what?"

"After the speeches, she overheard me talking to a couple of women who'd pitched with Carmella. I was asking how their sessions went and such. She pulled me aside and told me to shut up about Carmella and that we—meaning us, I guess—keep the hell out of the investigation. Claimed a bunch of amateurs nosing around asking questions was a bad image to produce for the attendees."

"Interfering twit."

"That's kinda what she called you, too, only her

terminology was more crude. Said you had to be the center of attention, and meddle in things that don't concern you."

"Bitch," Anne muttered. Across the lobby, she saw the object of her derision striding in their direction. "Oh, swell. Speak of the devil, here she comes."

Fran approached and stopped with her hands fisted on her hips. She glared at both of them.

"I've been looking for you," she said to Anne.

"Well, you found me. What do you want?"

"For starters, butt out of the police investigation. I don't care what you did with Dorie's murder, but this one is off limits. Is that understood? You don't have the expertise to play Jessica Fletcher."

"Excuse me?"

"I said back off!"

Anne took a deep breath to help curb the seething anger swelling in her chest. It didn't work.

"Make me."

Fran's eyes went wide. "What?"

"I said, 'Make me.' Let's get something straight, Fran. I will help the police in any way possible. You have no authority to tell me otherwise. I found the body, so that gives me a leg up in wanting to know what happened."

"You always seem to find a dead body," the chapter president snapped. "Half the chapter members were certain you'd killed Dorie. This kind of thing hurts every one of them. Maybe you should consider rethinking your membership."

"Maybe you should consider dropping dead. We have as much right to speculate as the next person."

"By the way, didn't you have a run in with the late,

unlamented Carmella at the national conference last summer? I'd be interested to know where you were when the murder occurred," Jen said with a smug expression.

Fran sucked in a deep breath as her eyes opened wide. "I never spoke to the woman while she was here. How dare you try to make me look bad! I had no reason to kill anyone. And if you tell anyone I did, I'll sue your ass off! Just remember what I said. Keep out of it!"

She whirled and stalked away.

"Jen, are you serious? She had a beef with Carmella?"

"She was talking about it at one of the meetings. It had to do with a submission. Fran was livid when the committee invited Carmella to the conference. Tried to get them to rescind the invitation, but they refused. Wendy told me that at the last meeting. Said Fran had the nerve to suggest Wendy invited Carmella just to get an 'in' with her for a pitch. Wendy told Fran to cram it. Although it's true, Carmella's acceptance to attend *would* spur a lot of authors to sign up for the conference just to get a chance to pitch to her. "

"Fran's another possible suspect. I'd like to know where she was when the murder occurred, too."

"I can ask around. If nothing else, it'll piss Fran off."

"Jen, I love you, but you aren't the most subtle of people," Anne said.

"Part of my charm," she replied with a grin. "People sometimes find my questions so outrageous they answer without thinking."

Her friend had a point. "Well, at least try to be circumspect with it, okay?" She glanced around the lobby. "Wonder where Nancy is?"

"Haven't seen her in a while. Maybe she's in a workshop." Jen rose. "I'll go see if I can find her."

"We're due to meet Gil in the bar at three," she reminded her.

"I'll be there."

"Also haven't seen Susan since this morning, either."

"She was at lunch. I saw her sitting at a table with an editor from a small press, can't remember her name, and that woman who gave a workshop on self-publishing."

"Maybe she's avoiding us. We didn't give her a whole lot of sympathy about her run-in with Carmella."

Jen shrugged. "At least we didn't have to listen to her moan and groan."

"She could have seen the writing on the wall and realized we want to dump her from the group."

"Maybe. I'll see you soon."

Jen left, leaving Anne alone again. She was contemplating her next move when Jackie Simmons, the agent she'd spoken with at breakfast, walked up and plopped into a chair with a huge sigh.

"Would you believe I actually have twenty minutes to call my own?"

"And how did that happen?" Anne asked.

"I have no clue and wasn't about to ask that pompous schedule coordinator why. She'd have found a way to keep me busy."

Anne almost laughed, but managed to suppress the urge. "Patty is very organized. Anally so. More than I ever was. She can't stand a vacuum. Hope you avoided that obnoxious woman from the lunch table. After you left, she said she was going to find you and pitch again—in your room if necessary."

Jackie groaned and grimaced. "Her pitch was awful. A tired plot and totally uninteresting characters. I requested the usual just to shut her up, but I'll bet she sends a full, not the three chapters."

"That's exactly what she said she'd do. I take it she didn't find you."

"I lied about going to my room. I have everything I need on my phone, so I found a quiet area out by the pool, checked my e-mail, and made a few calls. I'm sorry I left in such a rush. I guess I disappointed the rest of the ladies at the table, but I didn't have the best of mornings."

"Jackie, you said Carmella was an author. Did she represent herself?"

"I would imagine so. In Carmella's mind, she was the best, therefore…"

"Seems to me, Jack Summers would object. I mean, if she sold a book, would she report it to the agency?"

The agent shrugged. "Maybe not. She wouldn't have to split any of the commission that way. And she certainly wouldn't demand a fee from herself. Carmella was a conniver of the first degree, and not above screwing others."

"I talked with Alan Grayson. He denied Carmella raided his authors."

"Of course, he would. But I can tell you, it happened. I also heard she made promises to some author about representation if the author could get a couple of other authors to sign with her."

Good grief, the group had bounced that theory

around last night at dinner.

"That almost sounds like extortion. Wonder if it's true."

"I have no idea." Jackie glanced at her watch. "No offense, but I think I'll spend the next ten minutes outside. It's so warm; I can't pass up the poolside relaxation. Doesn't look like I'll get to the beach after all. Too bad, I was looking forward to it."

She rose and walked away once again leaving Anne alone. The suspicious desk clerk from yesterday kept staring at her as if wondering whom Anne was going to kill next.

A brief walk for some fresh air sounded like a good idea. Maybe it would help her think and try to disseminate all the information she'd picked up. She exited the lobby and strolled along the pathways of a small garden. The warm sunshine was a pleasant change from the cold temps in the meeting rooms. Why did hotels always keep the temperature in conference rooms on a par with meat lockers?

She tried to organize her thoughts as she wound through the flowers and greenery. The suspect list was growing by the minute—Caroline, Joyce, that nitwit Joan Quaylen, Beth Hardaway, Fran, Alan Grayson, and of course, Susan. Caroline, Joyce, and Beth were long shots, but the others? She wasn't sure.

Maybe I suspect Fran and Susan for personal reasons. Grayson's hatred of Carmella sends him to the top of the heap. The knife was the key. Anyone could have brought one and carried it in a purse or tote bag. Had Carmella really pissed someone off that morning?

"Or the night before," she muttered out loud remembering Wendy's information about an argument in the bar on Thursday.

Half an hour later, her walk over, Anne entered the lounge and chose a table for six off in the corner. She ordered a glass of wine and jotted notes about the conversations she'd had with people.

A few minutes later, Gil arrived and pulled out a chair next to her. When the waiter brought her wine, Gil ordered coffee.

"Hi, you're early," she said.

"I've been looking for you. Figured this was the best guess. You people spend a lot of time in bars."

Anne shrugged. "No place better in the world to network."

"How come you're not at a workshop?"

"Not really interested in any at the moment. Had a run-in earlier with that silly Joan Quaylen—the woman who accused me of killing Carmella."

"I know. She found me and said you threatened her."

Anne choked as she sipped from her wine glass. "I was pissed and told her to stop following me or I'd report her as a stalker. I was on the mezzanine when she crept up behind me. Scared me to death."

His coffee arrived and he blew on the contents before sipping. "Why were you on the mezzanine?"

"Just looking around. Wanted to see things for myself. I didn't disturb anything."

"Nothing to disturb now. Scene's been released." He paused. "I supposed you checked out your friend's story about sitting near the business center."

She nodded. "She could easily have seen Carmella enter the restroom."

"And followed her inside."

"What about surveillance tapes? How goes the viewing?"

"The recent recession has hit everyone hard. To cut costs, the hotel also cut down on security and the working cameras. They exist in the parking lot, the lobby, the little boutique, the souvenir shop, and the elevator lobbies on each floor. Those in the hallways, stairwells, or the elevators are strictly for show. Not enough personnel to man the video screens."

"Thereby giving guests a false sense of security. So, you have no tape of anyone coming or going to the mezzanine ladies room."

"Nope. According to the manager, very few events are held on the mezzanine. No need for cameras. We're lucky the one by the elevators worked. Doesn't make my job any easier."

Anne fiddled with the stem of her glass before taking a small drink. She'd love to see those tapes and wanted to frame her request in the right way. But before she could ask, Gil broke into her thoughts.

He heaved a deep sigh. "Anne, would you like to have dinner with me tonight? Just the two of us. Alone. No dead bodies, no investigation. Just us."

Chapter Six

Anne's heart did one of those stutter steps at Gil's words. Dinner? Alone? Just the two of them? Forget the conference banquet!

She reached out and laid her hand on his arm. "I'd love that."

Gil smiled and covered her hand with his. "There's a nice restaurant over on Park Street called Corey's. It's small, intimate, and I hear the food's great. Is seven-thirty all right with you?"

Small and intimate? Sounded perfect. "It's fine."

He patted her hand, and then released it. The warmth lingered on her fingers. They trembled slightly as she curled them around the stem of her glass.

She stared into the yellowish-white depths of the wine. *Maybe this is the new beginning I've hoped for all these months.*

Her mind immediately foraged in her closet, choosing clothes. She wanted to look fabulous for him.

"Looks like your friends are here," Gil said.

Anne looked up and saw Nancy and Jen hovering near the doorway. She beckoned them over.

"Are we interrupting something?" Nancy asked.

"No, of course not. We agreed to meet Gil here at three. It's a little early, but have a seat."

"Thank you for coming," he said as the women pulled out their chairs and sat. The waiter appeared a few seconds later to take their wine orders.

"Where's Mrs. Bennett?" he continued.

"She just came for the Friday session," Jen answered. "She had a baby a couple of weeks ago and didn't want to overwhelm her husband with babysitting chores."

"Isn't she the one with a lot of kids?"

"Five now, all under the age of eight," Nancy replied.

"Wow."

"I'll say. How she gets any writing done is beyond me," Anne added.

Gil cleared his throat. "I understand you've all been talking to people about Ms. Radcliff's death. Find out anything I might like to hear?"

"Enough to know half the people here hated her guts," Jen said.

"How so? And who specifically?"

Jen gave him the details of her conversations while he wrote names in a notebook as the waiter brought the drinks, and then left.

"So your own chapter president had a complaint, as did someone from a publishing house?"

"Howard Wright." Jen explained Howard and his position in the publishing world. "Not sure if he hated her, but he certainly wouldn't put up with any nonsense. Howard is the head man at the largest romance publisher in the world and can pick and choose who to contract. My guess is Carmella knew she wasn't going to sell to him, but liked to bug him anyway. And here's another little tidbit. I talked to Terry Whiting a few minutes ago. Fran was nowhere to be found after the dust-up between Carmella and Susan.

No one could find her. She and Terry finally made contact around quarter to six."

Gil shot Jen a keen glance. "Now that's interesting. Ms. Harrison told me she was trying to soothe ruffled Radcliff feathers."

"Terry was trying to soothe, not Fran," Anne said sitting back and sipping from her glass.

So Fran wasn't around and had lied about it? Where had she been? It was out of character for her not to be in control of the situation. Maybe Terry, tired of Fran's interference, hadn't informed her of the fight right away. Yet they had met later. Had the conference chair mentioned it then? And what was Fran's reaction?

A sudden thought flashed through her mind. She set her glass back on the table and focused her attention on Gil.

"You know, what Terry told you about not mentioning the argument between Carmella and Susan isn't quite true. Both Terry and Fran were in the bar before I found the body. They stopped by our table and Terry discussed the fracas openly."

"That's right," Jen said with a thoughtful expression. "Fran made a snide comment about you stopping Susan."

"Which means she knew about it a lot earlier than Terry suggested to you," Nancy told Gil.

He looked at her with raised eyebrows. "I'll look into it. How about you? Did you find anything of interest?"

"Maybe. I'm not sure. I found a seat near the head table. I was kind of surprised to see Linda Frakes there. She's an editor with a small press, but was here on her own, not taking pitches or anything. She also used to work at the Summers Agency. Left about three years ago. When I brought up Carmella's name, she flatly refused to discuss the woman. I had the feeling Carmella may have been the reason Linda left."

"Really?" Anne murmured. She vaguely recalled Linda had once been an agent, but hadn't seen the woman in several years.

"I also chatted with another author and she told me Linda and Carmella once got into a heated argument at a staff meeting. All about poaching authors."

"That seems to be a recurring theme," Jen suggested.

"How would she know about a heated argument?" Gil asked, writing again.

"She's signed with the Summers Agency. Her agent was there and told her about it."

"Anything else?" he inquired.

Anne nodded. "I had a chat with Jackie Simmons. She's an agent with Coyne and Company Literary Agents in New York. She told me Carmella was also an author and the rumor mill suggested she might be going out on her own."

"Ah, the rumor mill," Gil said with a sigh.

"Just because its gossip doesn't mean it isn't based in truth," Jen told him.

"And I also learned that Joan Quaylen had a tiff with Carmella not so long ago, too."

Gil resumed writing. "And who told you this?"

She gave him the details of all Beth had told her.

"Is that all?" Gil's pen was poised above the notebook.

"Actually, no," Anne said. She related her conversation with Wendy Travers the previous night.

"Ms. Harrison confirmed she received a phone call from the hotel manager asking her to help," Gil added. "I think I need to talk with this Alan Grayson. Any idea where I can find him?"

"In the pitch room, I imagine," Jen told him.

"I'll check on it. Now, is there anything else?"

"Not from me," Nancy said.

"I think that's it," Anne replied.

"You guys have been busy."

"And Rose is home making phone calls to various people trying to get information you can use," Anne added. "I really don't understand why Carmella was even invited to the conference. From what I heard, she wasn't actively acquiring."

Jen frowned. "That's odd. I talked with a couple of authors who pitched to her. One said Carmella requested a partial and a synopsis."

"And didn't Susan say something about pitching to her and Carmella rescinding the request for material after their altercation?" Nancy added.

Jen nodded. "That's right, she did. And the other woman I talked to told me Carmella made a request, too, but—and this is what's odd—she never gave them a business card with the e-mail address of where to send it. The first writer then said, come to think of it, Carmella never even took any notes about her pitch."

"An editor or an agent who doesn't take notes during a pitch? That's crazy. They could hear dozens of hopeful authors in a day. How would she keep them all straight?" Nancy said.

"Unless, she wasn't planning on accepting any," Anne suggested.

"And yet that's out of character, too. If Carmella

Radcliff wasn't acquiring, she wouldn't bother asking for anything," Jen replied.

"It doesn't make any sense," Anne muttered. A lot of people were acting out of character lately.

"Unless the rumors are true and she was starting her own agency. Then the requests make perfect sense. The Summers Agency wouldn't see any of them," Jen told her.

"If that's the case, why not hand out business cards with an e-mail address on where to send it?" Nancy asked.

"Like I said, it doesn't make sense," Anne repeated.

Gil smiled as he replaced the notebook and pen in his pocket. "Murder only makes sense to the murderer. Thanks for helping. I'll see what these people have to say."

Nancy fiddled with the stem of her wine glass. "I assume you've checked out the surveillance tapes? See anything?"

"Not a whole lot. They show several people coming and going from the mezzanine elevator lobby, including Ms. Radcliff and your friend, Susan. Unfortunately, the restroom area isn't covered, so we have no idea who entered."

"What about the stairs?" Jen asked.

"The main stairs from the lobby to the mezzanine, the ones Anne used, are just out of camera range. Impossible to ID anybody on the upper level. All we can see is a vague shadow of movement. Another stairwell is located around the corner from the elevators. Once again, not a good shot of anyone."

"It would have made your investigation a whole lot

easier if the hotel had more working cameras," Anne said.

"If only all investigations were easy," he replied.

"And why tapes?" Nancy asked. "I thought damned near everything was digital these days."

Gil shook his head. "That's an expensive upgrade for a place that needs to count nickels and dimes."

Anne explained about the non-working, just-there-to-make-guests-feel-good cameras throughout the hotel.

"Swell. Hello, San Sebastian Inn, the eighties called and want their surveillance system back," Nancy muttered.

Jen turned to Anne. "Sounds like Wendy isn't a happy camper either."

Anne related the rest of Wendy's woes. "What I can't understand is why conferences comp editors and agents everything."

"They come here for free?" Gil asked.

"It didn't used to be that way," Nancy replied. "Then some conference with money decided to do it to entice top-notch people and the precedent was set."

"Given all the work, I'm surprised conferences aren't a thing of the past," Jen said.

"I remember the chapter voting on whether or not to hold this one," Anne replied. "It was given the green light by a narrow margin."

"May I join you?"

Anne looked up to see Susan standing behind one of the chairs.

"Uh, yeah, sure, why not?"

Susan sat and eyed Gil Collins. "What are you doing here?"

"My job—investigating a murder." He rose. "And

now it's time I left. Nice chatting with you ladies again. Thanks for the information. Anne, I'll pick you up around seven-thirty. All right?"

"Yes, that's fine."

"Pick you up?" Jen asked with a twinkle in her eye when he was out of earshot.

"We're going out to dinner. Just the two of us. No murder and mayhem allowed."

"I knew it!" her friend crowed.

"Good luck," Nancy added with a smile.

"Information?" Susan asked.

Her question pulled Anne out of her dinner thoughts. "Oh, he just wanted to know more about some of the people here, that's all."

"You were talking about me, weren't you?"

"No, not really."

"Of course, you were. I'm not stupid. He thinks I killed her and so do you all." Susan's tone turned sharp and accusatory.

Anne shifted in her chair. If she thought that, why bother to sit with them?

"We think nothing of the kind," Nancy replied in a testy tone. "Not all of our conversations are about *you*."

"I did discover that the nook near the business center where you said you sat is only about twenty feet from the restroom door," Anne said.

"So what? I didn't see anyone enter while I was there!"

"And so far no one has come forward to say they saw you anywhere either," Jen added.

Susan glared. "You're all against me. You never liked me from day one. I don't think you could handle the competition. You're all scared of my talent."

"You're delusional!" Nancy snapped. "And I for one think it's time you found yourself new critique partners to unimpress."

"So, I'm history?"

"I'm afraid so, Susan," Anne said in a gentler tone. "The dynamic just isn't working. It happens. Don't take it personally."

Susan shoved her chair back and rose. "Of course, it's personal. Well, I don't need you either. I had a long talk with an editor and picked the brain of an indy-pubbed author. I can do this on my own. Goodbye!"

"Well, that didn't take long," Jen remarked as their former critiquer stalked from the bar.

"At least it was a clean break—if abrupt. No misunderstandings," Nancy replied.

"I suppose," Anne said. "The question is do we replace her?"

"I say let's just go with the four of us for a while," Nancy added. "Maybe we can pick up someone who really wants to learn later on."

"You know, we need a name," Jen said.

Nancy stared at her with a confused expression. "A what?"

"A name for whom? Susan? I can think of several and none are flattering," Anne said.

"No, no, not her. A name. For us. We need a name. Like a professional would have."

"A professional what?" Nancy demanded.

Anne sighed with impatience. "Jen, what are you talking about?"

"Like a private investigator or something. If we're going to solve crimes, then we need a name. How about Sleuthbusters?"

Nancy looked at Anne, and then back to Jen. "You've got to be kidding."

"No, I'm serious!" She snapped her fingers. "I've got it—The Snoop Group! Get it? We're a critique group who solves murders."

"Call us whatever you want, but can we get on with what we're doing now?" Anne asked, her tone exasperated. Only Jen would stop to pin a name on them.

"You mean waiting a while before finding a new partner? Sounds good to me," Jen told her, and then turned her gaze on Anne. "So do tell about this dinner tonight. Obviously, you're skipping ptomaine poisoning central here."

Anne, her good humor restored, laughed. "Yes! We are going to a place called Corey's over on Park."

"I've heard of it," Nancy said. "The reviews have been excellent. It's also rather pricey, so he must be serious."

"I'm more interested in what you plan to wear," Jen inquired. "I suggest something low cut and slinky."

"Low cut and slinky? I'm not sure…"

"You should be. You've got a great figure. Show it off. I'm sure Gil will be appreciative."

"Jen's got something here. If he's going to splurge on an expensive meal, then the least you can do is make him forget his credit card will smoke."

Anne almost giggled. "Okay, you win. I'll dig into my closet and see what I have."

"Just be sure to make the best of it," Jen added with a wink.

Anne glanced at her watch. "I guess I should get home and get the process started."

She deposited a couple of tens on the table and left. As she entered the lobby, she ran into Gil.

"I was on my way back to the bar."

"Why?"

"Would you like to see some of the surveillance tapes?"

"Sure. What's up?"

"I just finished the last one and want your input."

He led her down a hallway to the security control room. Banks of monitors, some in use, others blacked out encircled the area. Two guards sat and watched. Whether this was routine or something new since Carmella's murder was anybody's guess.

Gil pulled out a chair and indicated Anne do the same. She lowered herself onto the padded seat and stared at the screen. He pushed a button. The image of an elevator lobby popped up complete with a timer in the lower right hand corner.

"This is the lobby elevator. As you can see, the time is four thirty-five."

A lot of people came and went, some conference attendees, some not.

"Oh, there's Susan!"

The timer on the bottom of the screen read four-forty as she watched the woman jam her finger on the call button and hold it there, then stomp into the car when it arrived.

"She looks pissed," Gil said.

"She was."

He paused the tape. "Where were you at this time?"

"Watching Carmella flounder and yell, I guess. Not sure about the time. I was only there a few minutes, and then left to find Susan. I finally gave up and returned to the bar. Thought she'd gone home. It never occurred to me to look on the mezzanine."

"Why were you there in the first place—the hallway, not the bar?"

"Susan put on a big show of demanding an apology from Carmella. We didn't really think she'd go through with it, but I was concerned enough to follow a few minutes later. Carmella would slice and dice her. And Susan tends to get emotional."

"How emotional?"

She shrugged. "Just emotional. Sometimes she cries."

"Does she also get angry?"

Knowing what Gil was suggesting, she replied carefully, keeping Susan's outburst of a few minutes ago to herself for now. "I don't know about angry, but defensive is a good term."

He pushed the button again and the tape resumed. Once again, people came and went on a regular basis.

"See anyone who had a problem with the victim?" he asked.

"Not yet, but then I suppose some who pitched to her may have been upset. Oh! There's Fran!" The timer showed four-fifty.

Over the next several minutes, the crowd thinned as some people headed for either the bookstore or the bar. Finally, Carmella appeared a few minutes after five. She rang for the elevator and stood tapping her toe as she waited.

"Looks like she's impatient," Anne said.

The elevator came and Carmella walked in. A second later another woman wearing a large floppy hat, sunglasses, flip-flops, a full length swim suit cover up, and carrying an enormous beach bag hurried up, but the doors closed before she could get on.

He stopped the tape, ejected it, and replaced it with another. "This is the tape from the mezzanine elevator area."

Gil fast-forwarded it to show Susan exiting a few seconds after entering on the main level. She turned and walked with a sure stride down the corridor before leaving the picture.

"That's the direction of the ladies room and the business center," she said.

Several minutes afterward, Fran emerged and also turned left.

About fifteen minutes later, Carmella stepped out of the elevator and also disappeared down the hallway. Less than two minutes after that, the woman in beach garb exited from the elevator.

"Not a whole lot to go on is there?" she said.

"Not yet, at any rate."

Fran appeared again on tape at five-twenty-five apparently leaving the mezzanine. After that, there was nothing until the security men arrived.

The camera had caught several shadows toward the stairs from the main floor and near the stairwell, but nothing identifiable. Anne assumed she was one of the shadows.

"See anything unusual?" Gil asked.

"Not offhand." She paused and thought. "Why would the woman in the beach outfit go to the mezzanine? There's nothing up there for a tourist. We held a couple of workshops in some of the smaller rooms."

"And she never got back on the elevator. Look closer."

He rewound the tape. Ten minutes after exiting the car, a shadow wearing what looked like a long gown swept toward the stairwell.

"Good heavens! Could that be…?"

"The killer? Maybe. We talked to several witnesses in the main lobby restroom. Apparently, Ms. Radcliff was impatient with waiting and announced she'd go upstairs."

"So a lot of people, including the killer, may have overheard and followed, and not necessarily in the elevator, but via the stairs."

"Possible."

"Gil, I remember seeing the knife stuck in her chest, but not sure what kind."

"It was a steak knife—easily obtained from either the restaurant or room service. We're checking now to see who ordered room service last night and if a steak was involved." He turned off the VCR and helped her up.

"This mystery woman intrigues me."

"I don't suppose you recognized her, did you?"

Anne shook her head. "Not in that get up. Do you think it was a disguise?"

"Possibly. Plus the tape quality is poor. They always are. I'll let you go for now. I want to talk to Ms. Lynch and Ms. Harrison." He leaned over and gave her a light brush along the cheek with his lips. "See you later."

Anne left the room, her mind busy with Fran, Susan, tourists, and most prominently, his light kiss. And of course, with what she'd wear to dinner.

According to Jen and Nancy, that was of vital importance.

****

"Have I told you how nice you look tonight?" Gil said as they took their seats in an intimate booth at the restaurant.

"Yes, three times, but keep it up. I can take it," Anne replied with a laugh.

To her consternation, when she arrived home and searched her closet, nothing of the low-cut, slinky variety presented itself. So she made do with a sleeveless, scooped-necked little black dress. So what if it was five years old? A pair of high heels, a silver chain link belt, and jewelry dressed it up, although she did have to raid her daughter's jewelry box to find long dangling earrings.

Gil's cheeks turned a light pink. "Sorry. Guess I'm a little nervous. I feel like this is a first date."

"So do I." She heaved a sigh. "Starting over is tough. Is that what we're doing? Starting over?"

"Could be. I've missed you, Anne. Missed you a lot."

"I've missed you, too."

He smiled, reached across the candlelit table and squeezed her hand, then released it when the server arrived.

Just that simple contact sent her heart racing. Her skin burned where he'd touched it and breathing suddenly became difficult. *Please God, don't let me screw this up again.*

They both ordered red wine and opened the menus. Corey's ambiance lived up to its reputation. The high backed booths and the discreet shades on the windows along the front wall provided a feeling of closeness, as did the muted lighting. Black tablecloths helped muffle the sound of glasses and china being presented. Customers tended to talk in low tones. The menu was eclectic with everything from steak to seafood to pasta.

The waiter brought their wine. "Are you ready to order or do you need some more time?"

"Give us another ten or fifteen minutes," Gil answered. "Is there anything you'd recommend?"

"As an appetizer, the goat cheese crouton is wonderful. It's three slices of thickly sliced Texas-sized toast covered with a wild mushroom wine sauce and melted goat cheese. For a main course, might I suggest the duck with a red wine reduction? It also comes with roasted red potatoes and grilled asparagus. The Mediterranean seafood pasta is also very good."

"Thank you," Gil said. "Check back in a few minutes."

Anne closed her menu, laid it aside, and sipped from her glass. The Pinot Noir was perfect, but then she'd expected it to be that way. Corey's didn't leave anything to chance.

Gil followed her actions and smiled. "So, how and what have you been doing lately?"

"The best I can, I suppose." She sighed and told of her struggles with her writing. "I just hope what I sent in is acceptable this time."

"It will be. You're a good writer. I actually read one of your books. Liked it, although as a cop it's hard for me to suspend my imagination to vampires and werewolves. Guess I'm too logical."

Anne laughed lightly. "Sometimes it's a good thing to let go of logic and expand the mind."

"Perhaps."

She hesitated for a moment. "I also visit Candace every two weeks."

Gil's eyebrows rose. "No kidding? She tried to kill you, for crying out loud."

"I know, but she was drop dead drunk at the time and scared to death. She didn't really want to hurt me."

He frowned. "I'd say trying to bash your head in with a champagne bottle counts as wanting to hurt you."

Anne sighed. "I could never blame Candace for what happened. What Dorie did to her was worse than low."

"But she killed her just the same."

"I know. At any rate, Candace is now sober and trying to get on with her life, even if it is in prison. Dorie's obnoxious sister filed a wrongful death suit, but Candace had the sense to put all of her assets in her son's name just prior to her arrest, so I'm not sure how or if anything's been settled. I think she suspected she'd made mistakes and it was only a matter of time before you solved the case."

"Actually, you solved the case. Thank God I showed up when I did. I can't believe you confronted her alone."

"I can't either. Probably not the smartest move I ever made." She sipped again from her glass. "How's everything with you?"

For the next several minutes they discussed children, his work load, which was heavy since he sometimes doubled up in assault cases, and the past holiday season. The server returned and took their orders—the duck for him and the pasta for her. They decided to split the goat cheese crouton. They also ordered another round of wine with Anne switching to Pinot Grigio for dinner.

The food surpassed expectations. The appetizer was incredibly rich and probably the best thing she'd ever tasted. Gil declared the duck fabulous and her pasta was beyond delicious. Scallops, shrimp, and chunks of lobster along with crabmeat in delicate garlic and wine cream sauce with penne had her scraping the bowl. They both declined dessert, but opted for coffee.

Conversation throughout dinner had been sparse with both of them concentrating on the food. Now, adding cream and sugar to her coffee, Anne realized she knew little about him.

"I was so involved with self-preservation during Dorie's murder investigation that I never got around to learning more about you."

"What do you want to know? Seems to me we discussed my ex-wives."

"Are you a native Floridian?"

"Nope. Born and raised in Pennsylvania. My father was head of the geology department at a small university. Every summer he packed up my mother, two sisters, little brother, and me and dragged us around the country in a camper to explore various geological phenomena. I'll bet I chipped away at more rocks than any kid in the universe," he said with a chuckle.

So Gil was one of four children. "Where did you fall in the birth order?"

"Second. My sister Catherine is two years older. My sister Meredith is three years younger, and my baby brother Brad is a year younger than her."

"Sounds like you led a rather nomadic life."

"Only during the summer. I loved those expeditions. Never realized until years after that they were one massive educational tool. When we weren't looking at rocks and rock formations, my mother took us bird watching. Funny, in those days all I wanted to do was follow in my father's footsteps, only out of the classroom. I wanted to be in the field finding and discovering new things."

She leaned her elbow on the table and rested her chin on her fist. "So how did you end up a cop?"

He laughed softly. "It was my sophomore year in college at Penn State. Law enforcement always fascinated me—must have been all those cop shows on TV. I took an elective titled, Law Enforcement and the Criminal Mind. I was hooked. Changed my major and never looked back."

"Was your father disappointed?"

"A little at first, but in the end as long as I was happy, he didn't care."

"Are your parents still alive?"

"Yep. Retired to Arizona five years ago. Lots of rocks to chip out there."

"And your brother and sisters, where are they?"

"Cathy and her family are living in Odessa, Texas. Her husband is in the oil business. Merry is divorced, no kids, and a lawyer in Philadelphia. Brad took up where I left off. He's a geologist with a bent toward volcanoes. He's never in one place long enough to call it home."

"What brought you to the Sunshine State?"

"A job. I'd been driving a patrol car in Pittsburgh for five years when I heard that Florida State was looking for someone to head up their security department. I applied, got the job, and held it for three years. Unfortunately, I soon got bored with busting drunken frat boys. A friend suggested I contact the San Sebastian PD. I did and have been here ever since."

She reached across the table and squeezed his hand. "And I, for one, am glad you're here."

He smiled and covered her hand with his and returned the gesture. "So am I."

The now familiar heat raced along her nerves before he released his grip.

Anne sipped from her cup. As much as she wanted to talk about more personal matters, Carmella's murder refused to leave her mind.

"So, did you talk to Susan and Fran after I left?"

He nodded. "Ms. Lynch claimed to have been in that little alcove for a while—she's not sure how long, and then left to walk around. She saw no one and no one seems to have seen her either. As for Ms. Harrison, she says she went to the mezzanine to check on the meeting rooms. She also said she didn't see Ms. Lynch anywhere. Both denied entering the ladies room."

"Why would Fran check on the meeting rooms? The workshops were over. And how come we didn't see Susan getting back on the elevator? That would be the logical way to leave the mezzanine—for an innocent person, that is. Go the way you came."

Gil shrugged. "For what it's worth, I think they're both leaving out some information. I also talked to Ms. Whiting again. She admits she mentioned the argument to Ms. Harrison before they entered the bar around five-thirty, but didn't give her the details until later."

"Anything on the mystery lady?"

"Nothing. Took a still and showed it to the desk

clerk and security, but no one recognized her."

She cleared her throat. "Do you have a copy of the photo? I could take another look."

He stared at her with a frown. "I have a couple in a folder in the car. Not sure if I should share though."

"I can understand that. But maybe I can see something new."

"Let me think on it."

Anne didn't want to push the situation. The fact he was even considering her request boded well.

"That may have been the best meal I ever ate," she said on the drive home. "Thank you for taking me."

"The pleasure was mine. The company was lovely and the conversation good. I had a good time."

"So did I." They pulled into her driveway. "Nightcap?"

He hesitated, and then nodded. "I could use a little brandy."

As he exited the car, she was pleased to note he also took a photo from the folder on the back seat. He smiled and handed it to her.

"Guess it can't hurt for you to look."

She unlocked the door. "Thank you."

They had barely entered the foyer when a happy little dog rushed to greet her, his nails clicking on the porcelain tiles. Anne bent over, picked him up, and cuddled the shih-tzu.

"Hello, baby, are you happy to see me?" she crooned.

"Is that…" Gil asked.

"Yes. This is Bruno, Candace's dog. He's still with me. He's a nice companion during the day and the kids love him."

She hugged the dog one more time before setting him back on the floor. Apparently satisfied with the attention, Bruno trotted back down the hallway.

Now it was Anne's turn to hesitate. Her nerves jumped. It had been so long since he'd been here, yet it felt so right. She led the way into the living room and tossed their coats and the photo on a chair.

"I'll go see if I have that brandy," she murmured.

He took her hand. "Don't bother. I really don't want any."

She stared at him, her heart rate accelerating. Without another word, Gil pulled her into his arms and brought his lips down on hers.

Chapter Seven

Anne's heart pounded and her knees turned to jelly. Instinctively, she wound her arms around his neck and parted her lips. Oh, this was so right. This was where she belonged. In Gil's arms again. The kiss went on and on, deep, wet, and thoroughly satisfying. She tried to remember when she last changed the sheets—and did it really matter?

Finally, he broke contact and rested his forehead against hers.

"I wanted to do that so badly last night. When I walked into the lobby and saw you I knew I couldn't resist," he said in a husky voice.

She heaved a sigh. "Me, too. I was scared and upset, but the instant you entered, I knew everything would be all right. Would you like to stay the night?"

He stepped back. "Yes, I would, but I won't."

Anne ran her hand up and down his chest fingering the buttons on his shirt, tempted to undo them. "Why not?"

"I'm not quite there yet, honey. I want you, but the trust isn't completely back. Plus, we're both involved in another murder. Maybe it is a good idea for you to find that brandy."

She backed up and bit her lip. "Sure. Have a seat. Won't be a minute."

Disappointment lay heavily on her shoulders as she

made her way to the kitchen and the liquor cabinet. How long would she have to pay for her gaffes of months ago? *As long as it takes, I guess.*

She poured two snifters of brandy and returned to the living room. Gil sat in the corner of the sofa, looking at the photo from the surveillance camera. When she handed him the glass, he patted the cushion next to him. She curled up by his side and also gazed at the picture of the mystery woman.

"You know, that cover-up is pretty shapeless." The image of Alan Grayson swam through her mind. "I wonder if it's a man."

"The feet in the flip-flops look feminine to me."

"True, but with the grainy tape, it's not the world's best image. Besides, who really looks at feet? And while a woman could bundle her hair up under the hat, a man wouldn't have to bother."

"I take it you have a male candidate in mind."

"Rumor is hot and heavy that Carmella poached several of Alan Grayson's clients, and Howard Wright had words with her a few months ago about procedures regarding submissions."

"Ah, the rumor mill. Seems to me that was mentioned earlier in the bar."

"And I believe we replied that not all gossip is crap. Sometimes, it's founded in truth."

"That may be, but I also talked to people who say the late Ms. Radcliff had issues with other women, too."

"Like Susan and Fran."

"And Beth Hardaway *and* an editor named Iona Smalls. I tracked both of them down late in the afternoon. Smalls has an alibi. She was with two other editors in the lobby restroom at the time of the murder. Hardaway isn't sure where she was."

"What about that obnoxious Quaylen woman?"

Gil shook his head. "She's a pain in the ass, but I doubt she stabbed Carmella Radcliff, and then put on an act of hysteria."

"She did have issues with Carmella, though. Did you find out where the knife came from?"

"The hotel was almost full and several conference guests who got into town early ordered in room service on Thursday night. We're still sorting out who ordered steak."

Anne shrugged and sipped the brandy. The fiery liquor slipped down her throat and settled in her stomach with a warm glow.

"Steak knives are probably *de rigueur*. The kitchen would send one up with all trays. I wonder if whoever picked the trays up noticed a knife was missing."

"I doubt it. Someone picks up the tray and that's that. So far, no one's come forward with any information about a missing knife."

She stared at the photo. "Wish I had paid closer attention to the camera footage."

"Why?"

"To see how this person walked. Men and women walk differently."

"She—or he—wasn't on camera very long. The lobby camera has her for only a few seconds and there's little walking involved. The mezzanine shot has maybe five or six steps before she disappears."

Gil's phone rang. He handed her the photo and answered. "Collins here...I suspected as much. Anything else to report along those lines...I see...It's only ten. Have someone pick him up for questioning again. I'll be there in a few minutes."

"Questioning?" Anne asked as he hung up.

"Uh-huh. One of my other cases. But I did get news that concerns this case. Seems Ms. Lynch and Ms. Harrison were not exactly truthful when they talked to me earlier. Forensics found both their prints in the mezzanine ladies room—Ms. Lynch's on the stall door where the body was found, and Ms. Harrison's on the countertop by the end sink."

"That doesn't sound good."

"Only if you're Ms. Lynch or Ms. Harrison. They also found traces of blood in the same washbowl, probably the victim's. We took a sample, but the water most likely diluted it, which may render it useless. And the prints on the knife were smudged. Nothing to ID."

"The killer had the knife concealed, probably in a large purse or tote bag. She or he stabs Carmella. Maybe they wrap a paper towel around the hilt so as not to leave fingerprints, flush the towel, which most likely has blood on it, and then washes his or her hands before exiting."

"Maybe." He put aside his remaining brandy and rose. "At any rate, I've got a few hours of work ahead of me tonight."

She walked him to the door where he leaned down and brushed his lips against hers.

"If you get any more ideas, my number is still the same. Do you remember it?"

"I have it." She stretched and kissed his chin. "Glad to have you back."

He smiled and left.

She closed the door and sighed. Maybe he was

back after all, but not willing to admit it yet.

And this time I won't mess things up!

****

After Gil had left, she'd finished the brandy and studied the photo again. The grainy texture didn't help. No facial features had come through. Neither had she seen much along the lines of shape under the cover-up. Giving up, she contemplated watching television, and then going to bed. *Alone, dammit!*

It was barely ten-thirty, but she knew nervous energy would keep her awake. Then she remembered her conversation the night before with Wendy.

I should talk with that bartender. Maybe he can ID the person Carmella had the argument with.

Without stopping to think, Anne grabbed her purse and car keys along with the photo, then drove back to the hotel. For a Saturday night, the lounge was almost deserted. Only four tables were occupied and a lone man sat at the end of the bar. She assumed conference goers were still in the ballroom. Sometimes the thank you speeches from the winners of the writing contest could drag on forever. She hoped to ask her questions and leave.

The man at the bar eyed her as she sidled onto a stool. The bartender placed a coaster in front of her.

"What can I get for you?"

"Oh, I don't think I want anything to drink. Were you on duty Thursday night when the manager was called about an argument?"

"Yeah, that was me."

"I was wondering if you could tell me who the heavyset woman argued with," Anne said.

"Which time?"

"What?"

"I said, which time?"

"I'm confused. Why don't you start at the beginning?"

"It was around ten when this kinda large woman staggered in and plopped herself on a stool. She ordered a martini, and when I hesitated, she told me not to worry, she was staying in the hotel. So I gave her a drink. I assumed she had been in the dining room."

"So she was tipsy when she got here?"

"More or less."

"What happened next? Were you busy?"

"Not really. Kinda like tonight. I went in the back for a moment and when I came out, this guy had joined her. He didn't look happy and finally, the woman told him to take a flying leap. He called her a few choice names and left."

"What did he look like?"

The bartender shrugged. "I don't know. Medium height, medium weight, brown hair. Nothing much to remember."

"And later, I understand there was an altercation."

"Yeah, it was almost midnight, nearly closing, when this woman walked in and said, 'We gotta talk,' so they moved to a table. I was busy cleaning up and didn't pay too much attention to them. At first, they talked in low tones, but that soon gave way to louder voices. Finally, both were on their feet and shouting. I told them to keep it down and that perhaps they should leave. The fat one told me what I could do with myself. It was the end of a long shift. I was tired and in no mood to deal with a couple of drunks, so I called the manager. While I was on the phone, the other woman left. Eventually, someone came and got the customer out of here."

"Can you describe the second woman?" Anne asked in a hopeful tone.

"Taller than the first woman, thinner, had her hair piled up on top of her head. Can't remember what she wore. All I knew was that I was due to go home."

"Could it have been the person in this picture?" She showed him the surveillance photo.

He shrugged. "Maybe, maybe not. Can't tell."

"You made the comment that you thought the tall woman was connected with the conference. What made you think that?"

"She carried one of those big bags with writing on the side. It's fairly dark in here, so I'm not sure what it said. Why all the questions?"

Anne didn't answer, but fished in her purse and laid a twenty on the bar.

"Here, this is for you. Thanks."

Without another word, she left. The ballroom doors opened as she reached the lobby gushing out a crowd of conference goers.

She hurried out the front doors of the hotel. The woman could have been anybody—an attendee with a goodie bag or the tourist in the picture, but the man the bartender described bore a strong resemblance to Alan Grayson.

****

Anne stared at her bedroom ceiling as the clock in the foyer downstairs chimed two o'clock. Rolling over to her tummy, she burrowed her head into the pillow and closed her eyes. Sleep. She needed sleep.

Her mind, however, refused to turn off. Her chat

with the bartender had been productive, but not conclusive. If Alan Grayson had words with Carmella in the bar, then Gil needed to know. Did the surveillance tapes run on a loop or were they changed out and stored? If the latter, then the camera covering the front desk might show him coming and going. Same with the woman involved in the second argument. *I wonder if Gil would let me see the video again—this time including the one in the lobby area. Maybe I can see something or someone I'd overlooked before. Can't hurt to ask.*

Ten minutes later, she once again shifted onto her back. Both Susan and Fran had denied being in the mezzanine ladies room, yet their fingerprints had shown up.

Each woman had a motive, although flimsy. And who's to say when they were in that john? She assumed housekeeping cleaned either late at night or early in the morning. So if they used the restroom anytime during the day, the fingerprints would be there.

She closed her eyes and tried to recall as much of the tapes as possible—Susan angrily jamming her finger on the elevator call button in the lobby, and then stomping off when exiting on the mezzanine.

But stomping off to where?

Her actions indicated she had a specific place to go. Did she know the location of the business center and the little alcove near it? If so, then how could she not have known where the john was? And the chair was positioned in such a way that Susan could have seen Carmella entering the restroom.

Fran had appeared approximately ten minutes later. If she'd continued on, as she said, how did she miss seeing Susan?

If *Susan was there. And* if *Fran had gone past the ladies room.*

And then there was the mystery lady—or man. She'd practically followed on Carmella's heels. She had to fit into this—unless she was going to the business center. And if she did, how come there's no tape of her leaving via the elevator? *Plus, she certainly wasn't there when I found the body or she'd have made herself known to security.*

Anne groaned. She was missing something. She knew it. She needed to see those tapes again and considered a quick call to Gil, but stopped when she saw the time. He probably wouldn't appreciate his phone ringing at two-thirty in the morning. She'd do it before leaving for the conference in the morning.

She rose and padded into the bathroom, rummaging in the medicine chest until finding an over-the-counter sleep aid. Back in bed, she pulled the covers up to her chin. Maybe tomorrow would bring a few of the answers to her questions. Sleep had almost claimed her when a thought brought her eyes open again.

How did Gil know the prints found on the countertop belonged to Fran?

****

Anne pulled into the parking lot of the San Sebastian Inn shortly before seven. Her early morning call to Gil had gone well.

"Gil, do you suppose I can look at those surveillance tapes again?"

"Which ones?"

"The ones in the elevator lobbies and maybe the

one from the front desk area. I'm not sure what I expect to find, but there could be something I'm missing. Some face in the crowd or a face that's there and shouldn't be or maybe one that should be but isn't. I hope I'm making sense. It's only six o'clock. I didn't wake you, did I?"

"No, and I understand what you're saying. They're at the police station. When can you come down?"

She hesitated. "Could we maybe view them at the hotel? That way, if I do see something I can go straight to the area for a better look."

A long pause followed her request. "I shouldn't take them from the evidence room, but I don't suppose it'll do any harm. Plus, you can hit me up for breakfast, right?"

Anne chuckled. "Well, now that you mention it…"

"Meet me in the lobby in an hour. We'll look at the tapes, and then eat."

"Let's reverse the order. I'm hungry."

Gil laughed. "All right. See you soon."

A quick shower, scrupulous attention to her make-up, and a careful selection from her closet didn't take long. Sunday morning traffic was light and she made the usual twenty-minute trip in fifteen.

This was the last day of the conference. After a continental breakfast from seven until eight, a Sunday speaker was scheduled. Between nine and ten, an auction would be held of everything from autographed copies of books by bestselling authors to a three-chapter critique offered by a publishing house that normally didn't accept un-agented material. Following was a panel of editors and agents for an open discussion on the state of the industry. Succeeding *that* were the obligatory thank you speeches and pats on the back for the volunteers. A lot of people left after the breakfast, so time was crucial. If the killer took off, he or she might never be found.

Gil rose from a chair in the lobby as she entered. He smiled and lightly kissed her cheek. A package was in his hand.

"Good morning. You look lovely for so early in the day," he said casting a glance up and down her figure.

Heat flooded her face. She was glad she'd chosen the turquoise cotton skirt and the long-sleeved white silk blouse. The large lapels and deep "v" of the neckline made her feel sexy without shouting. A pair of multicolored ballet slippers graced her feet.

"Thank you."

He leaned forward and whispered, "I love it when you blush."

Her face flamed hotter. "You'd think that after thirty-eight years I'd learn some self-control."

Gil chuckled as he steered her toward the dining room. "I find it charming."

"Are those the tapes?" she asked eyeing the package.

"I have the two we viewed yesterday plus the one covering the front desk as you requested. Who knows? We might find something of interest."

Good, they were both thinking along the same lines.

The hostess showed them to a booth along the wall. Within seconds, a waitress arrived to fill their coffee cups.

"Will you be ordering off the menu or do you prefer the buffet?" she asked.

"I'll take the buffet," Anne said.

"Me, too," Gil added. "So tell me what goes on here today?"

She gave him the agenda. "It'll all be over by noon. Then everyone who's still left will scatter. How will you find the killer if that happens?"

"Ninety-nine-point-nine percent of the people here are not suspects. I'm here today to re-question three or four people whose statements have holes in them."

"Like who? Other than Fran and Susan, I mean."

He shook his head. "Can't tell you, but I'm sure you've got a good idea."

"Okay, I get it." She gazed toward the buffet. "Shall we?"

Anne had a theory that hotels deliberately set up buffets to encourage people to eat more. The fact she had a terrible time making decisions added to the problem. The meats consisted of bacon, sausage, ham, and even chicken fried steak. Scrambled eggs, hash brown potatoes, biscuits with gravy on the side, filled the warming trays to the brim. A hot station had a set-up for pancakes, waffles, and made-to-order omelets. Farther down the line, a diner could grab toast, bagels, fruit cups, yogurt, and numerous fruit juices.

Bagels were her downfall. She loved them.

By the time they returned to the table, her plate was loaded with sausages, a mushroom omelet, fruit, tomato juice, and a bagel, each half with its own spread—one cream cheese and one peanut butter.

"I don't know why I do this," she said with a groan. "I'll never be able to eat it all."

"I'll bet you do. You did say you were hungry, although how you eat so much and still stay slim is beyond me."

For the next several minutes they ate. Anne had worked her way through half of her omelet when someone stopped next to their table. She looked up and stopped chewing.

"Oh, good morning, Fran," she mumbled.

"I see you're indulging here instead of at the free continental breakfast in the ballroom. What kind of a statement does that make?"

"That the continental breakfast is using yesterday's bagels and whatever else is leftover?"

"You are *not* funny."

"For God's sake, Fran, chill out. Here, have a good bagel. Hope you like peanut butter." She extended the bagel toward the chapter president who stepped back with a scowl.

"Get that away from me. I'm allergic to peanuts. Even the smell can make me swell up like a toad."

Personally, Anne thought that would be something to see.

"Sorry. How about cream cheese, then?"

Fran shot a glance at Gil, and then back to her. "And I thought we had a discussion yesterday about interference with a police investigation."

"You had the discussion. I didn't. And Detective Collins and I are friends. I can have breakfast with any friend I want," she replied taking a huge bite of the peanut butter bagel. She contemplated breathing heavily on Fran who now turned her attention to Gil.

"Sorry, I couldn't take your call last night. But I'm here now. What did you want?"

"I'd just like to talk to you again." He checked his watch. "How about eight o'clock in that small room next to the where the bookstore is set up?"

She cast a wary look at him. "Talk? About what?"

"Oh, just getting a few loose ends tied up, that's all."

Fran bit her lip and shifted her weight from foot to foot. "Very well."

She turned abruptly and walked out of the dining room.

"What about Susan? Are you going to talk to her, too?"

Gil resumed eating. "Probably. Like I said, just a few loose ends."

Anne sipped from her coffee cup and told him about her conversation with the bartender.

"An officer talked to him late last night. He told us he'd already had a discussion with a woman. I figured it was you."

"That reminds me. I had a question. How did you know the fingerprints on the countertop in the ladies room belonged to Fran? Susan I can understand. I'm sure you printed her when she gave her statement, plus she may be a suspect. I remember you did that to me eight months ago. But Fran?"

"Her prints were on file."

"What?"

"It seems your esteemed chapter president was arrested and booked for DUI three years ago."

"DUI!"

"And resisting arrest, disorderly conduct, along with assault for spitting on an officer. The latter charge was dropped. Since it was her first offense, the judge let her off with probation, a suspended driver's license for a year, and lots of community service."

"For a first offense, she sure made the most of it."

Anne resumed eating. So Fran had a temper. Well, she knew that already. But apparently, she also had a problem with alcohol—at least once. Candace's image floated through her mind. No, Fran never exhibited behavior like her former critique partner.

"Gil, suppose Fran had a couple of drinks yesterday, went to the ladies room on the mezzanine, saw Carmella, confronted her, and in a semi-drunken rage, killed her?"

"Like Candace Warren?"

"Why not?"

"And she got the knife where?"

Her shoulders slumped. "Oh, I forgot about that. Wait! She could have had it in her purse."

"On the off chance she might have an opportunity to use it? I doubt it."

"Then why do you want to talk to her?"

"Annie, finish your breakfast. We've got to look at these tapes again, and I have to meet Ms. Harrison shortly."

She knew better than to push it, and cleaned her plate. Besides, Gil calling her Annie gave her a warm feeling.

After settling the bill, they once again entered the surveillance room. It was empty and all but two of the monitors were dark. Gil inserted the tape from the main elevator lobby fast-forwarding it to four-ten.

The images hadn't changed. The area was crowded. A workshop had ended not long before. Some people carried tote bags, no doubt filled with books from the bookstore and material handed out during the meetings. Now they were headed to their rooms to dump them and perhaps relax until dinner.

For the life of her, Anne saw nothing suspicious. She fast-forwarded a few minutes. The crowd was thinner now. Alan Grayson joined them, nodded to a few of the women, and entered a car.

"I wonder where he got off?" she murmured.

"Sixth floor. His room number is six-oh-seven. Tape shows he came back down around seven o'clock and left the hotel. He says to eat dinner at a real restaurant." He glanced at his watch. "Anne, I've got to go. When you're finished, put the tapes in the envelope, and leave them here."

"Oh, are the tapes on a time loop?"

"Yes, they rerecord every twenty-fours hours starting at six in the morning."

She nodded and continued viewing as he left. Nuts. Surveillance in places like hotels often used a time loop. It was cost effective. The tapes didn't have to be changed every day and the previous day's action was taped over. That, too, saved money—fewer tapes to buy. The woman who argued with Carmella in the bar wasn't likely to be shown. To keep things straight in her head, she grabbed a notebook and pen from her purse, then jotted down times and names.

Grayson had gotten on the elevator at four-twenty. *I suppose he could have put on a female disguise and taken the stairs back down.*

And if it was Grayson, how would he know Carmella was heading for the ladies room on the mezzanine? Dumb luck? Or maybe he stayed out of sight waiting until Carmella appeared, and then followed.

After killing her, he could have used the stairs to

return to the sixth floor and his room. Anne shook her head. It was flimsy, but not beyond the realm of possible.

Little occurred for the next few minutes. Impatient, she fast-forwarded again until Susan came into view. She paused the tape. Scrutinizing every detail, she came to the conclusion that her former critique partner was not only angry, but still crying as well.

Fran showed up at four-fifty and entered an elevator. Then several people came and went. At five o'clock Carmella entered the elevator lobby. She was alone and the only person in the car. As the doors closed, the tourist appeared. She watched the indicator as if to determine where it stopped, then pushed the button. Another elevator opened immediately. She entered. Both Susan and Fran had carried large purses. Certainly big enough to hide a knife. And the tourist had a huge beach bag slung over her shoulder.

Anne ejected the tape and slid in the one from the mezzanine. Susan still stomped off as if she knew where she was going. Fran emerged and headed in the same direction. Next Carmella exited. The tourist followed. She replayed the tape several times to determine the walk, however, couldn't tell if it was a man or a woman. The strides were sure and strong, an indication of determination perhaps. The biggest tell was the sunglasses. Why wear sunglasses inside? *To hide your identity, of course.* The tourist did not reenter the elevator.

The last person to leave was Fran at five twenty-five. *Wait—five twenty-five? That's over half an hour from when she got off the elevator. It wouldn't take that long to check out two meeting rooms. And why check them out at all? What was she doing for thirty minutes?* She'd mention this to Gil, if he didn't already know about it. Maybe this was one of the loose ends he wanted to tie up.

Once again, she switched tapes, inserting the new one taken from the front desk. The film clearly showed people arriving and others walking past. Anne identified Susan, Fran, Terry, and numerous others. All had headed to and from the elevators. Most carried large purses or tote bags.

Then something new appeared. Carmella was passing through the lobby when Fran followed and grabbed her arm. What looked like a heated discussion followed. Carmella then jerked away before striding toward the ladies room. Fran balled her fists, whirled and headed back toward the elevators. The time showed four forty-eight.

What the hell was that all about? Fran stated she'd never spoken to her, yet this looks like a major league argument. Anne compared her notes on times. Depending on when Carmella had left the goodie table area, a large chunk of time had passed—close to ten minutes. Where had she gone? Had she been with Fran, and did the camera catch the tail end of something?

All was relatively quiet for a while until Anne appeared at six-oh-four. She gazed at herself as she reported finding Carmella's body, and then stopped the tape. No need to relive that.

Replacing the tapes in the envelope, but unwilling to leave them in an empty room, she stuffed the package into her tote bag and left.

In the lobby, she met Nancy and Jen coming through the hotel doors.

"So, how did your dinner date go?" Jen asked immediately.

"Wonderful, thank you."

"Do anything you'd be embarrassed to write about?"

"No! This is a re-do. We're taking it slowly."

"Anything new in the investigation?" Nancy asked.

She hesitated. Should she tell them about the fingerprints? Gil hadn't said not to, but she didn't want to take any chances of screwing up again.

"Not much. He's unimpressed with both Susan and Fran's reasons for being on the mezzanine around the time of the murder. Um, I heard an interesting piece of gossip. I understand Fran was arrested a couple of years ago for DUI."

"Oh, really? I guess it can happen to anyone," Nancy said in a calm tone.

"I knew that," Jen added.

"You did? How?" Anne exclaimed. Jen always seemed to know stuff.

"You remember Brenda Renquist? She was a member several years ago. She moved last spring after a divorce. At any rate, her husband of the moment was a San Sebastian cop and apparently, he told her. From what I heard, she was a handful at the station—uh, Fran, not Brenda—screaming, kicking, cursing up a storm. Must have been a sight to see and hear. Well, Brenda told me about it during the last election cycle. Said she'd never vote for Fran Harrison. She was too volatile and hated being told she was wrong about anything, *and* that she wanted everyone to do as she said. Her way or the highway, but then we knew that from yesterday. Imagine telling us to butt out investigating! And the look on her face when we told her to cram it was priceless."

"Sounds like a candidate for anger management," Nancy said when Jen stopped to breathe. "I could probably give her the name of a good therapist."

"I haven't seen you angry since you and Dorie's worthless sister got into it that one day," Anne told her.

"I'm surprised I haven't killed someone since I quit smoking three months ago. There were times when I was really on the edge."

"You should be proud. It's not easy to go cold turkey. My husband did that about ten years ago. He was a bear for months," Jen said.

Nancy turned to Anne. "So are you going to the auction and editor/agent panel? They start at nine and ten."

Anne tapped her finger against her lips. "I don't know. Are you guys going to eat? There's still time. I certainly don't want to hear another long-winded speaker so soon after breakfast."

"Me neither," both ladies said simultaneously.

"Care to come with me and do a bit of snooping?"

"Absolutely!" Jen said clapping her hands.

"Where?"

"The mezzanine. I think a little reenactment is in order."

Chapter Eight

The three women stepped off the elevator and paused in the mezzanine lobby area. On the way up, Anne told them what the surveillance tapes had revealed.

"Sounds like Gil has a timeline as to when the murder happened," Jen said. "But with only parts of the hotel covered, it'll be hard to pick a suspect."

"That's why I want to try this. Okay, Nancy, you be Susan. Walk from the elevator, go to the balcony, and turn left. Walk fast, like you're angry, until you find the business center alcove and take a seat. I'll be Fran. Jen, you be Carmella. After I leave count to twenty, then follow and go to, but not in, the bathroom," Anne instructed.

"Whatever you say, Sherlock," Nancy said with a shrug and walked quickly across the space to the balcony overlooking the lobby, then turned and disappeared.

Anne took a deep breath and counted to twenty.

"Okay, Jen, as soon as I disappear start counting."

She moved off down the hallway. Nancy's legs and lap were clearly visible sitting in the chair. She turned and waited for Jen who appeared and stood outside the restroom door.

"Nancy, did you hear either Jen or I arrive?"

"I heard muffled footsteps due to the carpet, but

that's all."

Anne chewed her lip for a moment as she thought. "Lean forward a bit. What do you see?"

"I see Jen standing at the door."

"So, Susan could have seen Carmella going into the ladies room and followed."

"Why would she lean forward?" Nancy asked. "If she was that upset, it seems to me she'd lean back to make herself less noticeable."

"What if Carmella was noisy about her approach?" Jen suggested.

"Noisy?" Nancy said.

"Yeah, you know, like maybe she was stomping her way down the hall or perhaps talking to herself. Susan might have leaned forward then."

"That's possible, I suppose." Anne paused again. "But why would she have a knife? She came up before Carmella announced she was going to use the bathroom on this floor. Let's say she did see Carmella. Would Susan have gotten up and confronted her again?" Anne asked as Jen joined them.

"Hard to say, but if she saw Carmella, she also must have seen Fran, and vice versa."

"Assuming Susan was even here," Jen added.

"So where was she? If she'd gone back downstairs by way of either the main staircase or the stairwell, she'd have had to pass the front desk. The only thing on the other side of the lobby is the entrance to the parking lot."

"Well, she could have planned to go home, and then changed her mind," Nancy said.

"I suppose. She did say she'd gone for a walk in that little garden, and then sat out by the pool. Both are just off the parking lot." Anne turned. "Let's go into the john and take a look."

"At what?" Jen asked.

"The scene of the crime."

Nancy rolled her eyes and rose. "Exactly what is this exercise accomplishing?"

"I don't know yet, but I just know the answer is in those surveillance tapes," Anne replied pushing the door open.

"When I came in, the light was off. I flipped it on, entered the first stall, and was washing my hands when I noticed someone in the last stall. I thought it odd about the lights and called out asking if whoever was there was all right. Then I knocked on the door. It swung open and there was a very dead Carmella Radcliff."

"Yes, yes, we know. You've told us this before," Nancy said in an impatient tone.

"I am simply going over things in my mind to make sure I've got it all straight, especially if I have to testify in open court. After all, I was a bit upset. Humor me," she shot back. Honestly, sometimes Nancy could be a royal pain.

Her friend shrugged and had a look on her face suggesting *Anne* was the royal pain.

"When you think about it, it's the perfect place to commit a crime," Jen said. "She's sitting on the john and can't defend herself."

"Oh thanks, I'll remember that the next time I use a public restroom," Nancy drawled.

Anne closed her eyes and concentrated on what she'd seen in those few panic-filled seconds before fleeing.

Slowly, she reopened them. "Only she wasn't using the toilet."

"What do you mean?" Nancy asked.

"Well, her skirt wasn't pulled up and her panties weren't pulled down. She just sat there. Jen, come here. Stand in front of the stall like you'd just come out."

"In other words, she used the facilities, emerged, and found the killer waiting for her?" Nancy said as Jen complied with Anne's request.

"Correct. So, pretend I'm the killer. Maybe we'd had words with Carmella earlier like Susan. The argument resumes. I've put my purse or tote bag on the counter. I now reach in, grab the knife, and charge." Anne put her words into action. "Now, as Carmella, Jen, what do you do?"

"I try to get away." Jen backed up several steps, entered the stall, and then tried shutting it, but the narrow confines prohibited her from doing so quickly.

Anne followed, pushed hard, and also entered. "She doesn't have time to shut, let alone lock, the door. I shove the knife into her chest. She falls backward and collapses on the seat. That's gotta be how it happened." She and Jen emerged from the stall.

"Then, the killer washes his or her hands and calmly leaves," Jen added.

"Why turn off the light?" Anne mused.

"To discourage anyone from entering and finding the body too soon," Nancy answered. "Gives them a chance to establish an alibi or get away completely."

"And how does the tourist fit in to all of this?" Anne asked.

"Maybe she doesn't," Nancy said.

"Go over those times and who was where again,"

Jen suggested.

Anne fished the notebook from her tote bag. "Susan called for the elevator in the lobby at four-forty. She exited here and walked off toward the alcove. Fran followed about ten minutes later. Carmella did the same around five. The tourist showed up less than two minutes after that."

"Never to be seen again," Jen added.

"And then there's Carmella and Fran on tape arguing."

"Wonder what about?" Jen said.

"I have no idea, but I doubt Fran's going to tell us squat."

"Come on, let's get out of here. Discussing murder in the bathroom is giving me the creeps," Nancy said.

They left and found an empty meeting room further down the hall, giving Anne time to think. Gil said he wanted to tie up loose ends with Susan and Fran. He had to have seen the tape of Fran and Carmella. Maybe he wanted answers to the obvious altercation.

Inside, each grabbed a chair and sat.

"Now, let's get logical about this," Anne said.

"Start with the times," Nancy suggested.

"All right, Susan is the first at four-forty."

"Any idea where Carmella was then?" Jen asked.

Anne shrugged. "Thrashing around in the remains of the goodie table."

"Do we have a time line for when Carmella announced she wasn't going to wait in line for the bathroom and would go upstairs?" Nancy inquired.

"Not that I know of," Anne replied. "And if Susan came directly up here after the fight, then she couldn't have known Carmella was coming."

"So if she killed her, then it was bad timing on Carmella's part," Jen said.

Anne ran her hand through her hair. "If Susan was in that alcove and the tourist went to the business center, then how could either of them have not seen each other? And if they did see each other, why hasn't the tourist corroborated Susan's story?"

"And why didn't Susan speak up when asked if anyone had seen her? The alcove is only a few feet further down the corridor from the business center. The door was likely open. It's second nature to glance at someone going in. Same as you'd automatically look at someone sitting there.

"Especially if that someone is upset or crying," Anne said.

"Has Gil found and talked to this person?" Nancy added.

"I don't know if he's made a connection with the tourist yet," Anne said.

"And you said this mystery person definitely saw Carmella get on the elevator, and then watched the indicator to see where it stopped?" Jen asked.

"Definitely."

Nancy ran a finger over her lips. "And followed her to the mezzanine a couple of minutes later."

"I don't know about anybody else, but this is confusing the hell out of me," Jen said. "We have no proof that either Susan or Fran went into the john."

Anne took a deep breath. "Actually, we do." She told them about the fingerprints.

"Oh brother, this doesn't look good for either of them," Nancy stated. "And this tourist bothers me."

"I know. Why take the elevator up, but the stairs

down?" Anne demanded. Jen was right. This was confusing the hell out of her, too.

"Maybe she didn't go down, but up," Jen suggested. "Maybe her room was on the third or fourth floor. She finished her business and rather than wait on the elevator, she used the stairs, especially if she's the killer and had blood on her clothes."

"That makes as much sense as anything else," Nancy agreed. "And if she *was* just a tourist and not connected to the conference or Carmella, she could have checked out anytime and gone home."

"It still bugs me that Fran and Susan didn't see each other," Anne stated.

"Which tells me that one of them is lying her ass off," Jen said. "Possibly both."

"According to your notes and the tapes, all the coming and going went down between four-forty and a little after five," Nancy claimed. "The last workshop ended at five. The first place I go after a workshop is the restroom. The second choice is the bar. The last is the bookstore."

Anne nodded. "So let's assume Carmella arrived at the main floor ladies room around five, didn't want to wait, announced she was going upstairs, and left."

"And the elevator lobby was empty because people hadn't yet gotten around to going up to their rooms," Jen added. "Did you look at the tapes any later than when Carmella and the beach lady appeared?"

"No, but when I went to wash up before we left for dinner, both the ladies room and the elevator area were packed, and that was a little before six," she replied, then paused. "Terry said that Carmella stomped off. I wonder when? I mean, where was she between then and when she got on the elevator a little after five?"

"You said one of the tapes showed her arguing with Fran," Nancy said.

"Yeah, but that took less than twenty seconds. Where the hell was she? I need to talk to Gil, and maybe Terry, again."

"And I need to get something to eat," Jen announced checking her watch. "It's a little after eight. Think maybe I'll hit the ballroom for breakfast after all. If I wait much longer, the conference leftovers will be non-existent."

"I'll go with you," Nancy said. "How about you, Anne?"

"What? Oh, no thanks, I already ate. I'll see you for the panel discussion."

As her friends left the meeting room, Anne called Terry.

"This is Terry."

"Terry, it's Anne. I wonder if you can clear something up for me."

"I'll try. What's up?"

"How soon after I left, did Carmella stomp off from the goodie table?"

"Oh Lord, I don't know, but it couldn't have been any more than seven or eight, possibly ten minutes. She ranted and raved about suing us for a bit."

"Was Fran around during this time?"

"No. I didn't tell her about the confrontation until I saw her later. She said she was dealing with some disgruntled attendees. We were going over conference numbers when Detective Collins called."

"Disgruntled attendees?"

"There's always somebody bitching about the food,

the accommodations, the temps in the meeting rooms, and of course, editors and agents in general—especially Carmella. I guess she wasn't exactly pleasant, even when requesting material."

"I see. Thanks, Terry, and hang in there. It's almost over."

"Yeah, well right now, I'm a disgruntled conference chair. Fran isn't here and I have to introduce Kay Watson. Should have done it ten minutes ago. Now we're running a little late."

Anne was tempted to tell her Fran was likely explaining a few things caught on tape to Gil, but instead said, "You'll be fine. Don't wait for Fran."

She hung up and tapped a finger against her lips. *Disgruntled attendees, editors, and agents in general.* How many people complained about Carmella? Anne needed to talk to Fran, although she doubted the chapter president would part with any information. Still, it was worth a shot. Maybe Gil was done getting those loose ends tied up.

She walked slowly down the hallway, turning over the speculations she, Nancy, and Jen had espoused earlier in her mind. Passing an unused room, she glanced inside. Tables were set up as if for a small informal luncheon. Could Susan have walked past the alcove, perhaps seen the remains of a previous event complete with steak knives? Could she have picked one up with the sole purpose of finding Carmella and exacting revenge? Maybe she saw the agent enter the ladies room and not wanting further confrontation, decided to leave—or hide out in an empty room until the coast was clear, then had seen the lunch things, grabbed a knife, and returned to the john? It was certainly something to think about.

Anne headed for the ballroom where the breakfast hour was coming to an end and caught a break. Fran was on the phone just outside the doors. She approached as the chapter president hung up.

"Fran, could I talk to you for a second?"

"About what? And make it snappy. Thanks to Detective Collins, we're running late."

"This won't take but a minute. Look, I know we have our differences, and I'm sorry if I've irritated you, but I just want you to know, I think you and Terry have done a wonderful job with this conference."

Fran stared with a wary expression. "Okay, thank you."

"I mean, it can't be easy dealing with people carping about every little nitpicking thing. Especially when it involves personalities. I suppose Carmella's behavior gave you the most headaches."

Her eyes narrowed slightly. "Carmella had her moments, but then some people just can't take straight forward comments or criticism. Still, it's something that needs to be addressed sooner or later."

"That's very true."

"Is this conversation going somewhere or are you just trying to dig information out of me about something?"

Anne backed off a step, raising her hands as if in surrender. "No, no, I wanted to give credit where credit is due."

The chapter president nodded, and then glanced at her watch. "Well, thank you. Now if you'll excuse me, I have to get back inside, talk to a few people, and introduce our speaker. Terry should have done it ages ago. Are you coming?"

"Sure. I'll be in as soon as I visit the ladies room."

Anne walked away. She had no intention of wasting her time listening to yet another author relating a feel-good story. Instead, she returned to the dining room for a cup of coffee. It galled her to praise Fran, especially since she didn't get much information in return.

After ordering, she called Gil.

"Gil, I was wondering…"

"Where are you and where are my tapes?" His voice had a testy tone.

"In my tote bag. I didn't want to leave them in an empty room. Don't worry, they're safe. And I'm in the dining room having another cup of coffee."

He sighed, and she could almost see him running a hand through his hair.

"Sorry I snapped. Can I call you back? I'm in the middle of something."

"Uh, yeah, sure, no problem."

He hung up without saying goodbye. *Wow, must be important.*

The waiter brought her coffee. She took a cautious sip as she tried to make sense of her crime reenactment.

Obviously, Carmella and her killer had words in the restroom, but was it Susan, Fran, the tourist—who might not be a tourist—or someone else? Someone who took the stairs both up and down and wasn't caught on tape at all?

And the details of Susan's story aren't holding up. Same with Fran now that I know she had an argument with Carmella, too. Plus, she lied. She said she'd never talked to Carmella at any time during the conference.

She sighed. Nancy was right. The reenactment hadn't solved much of anything.

And why was Fran checking on meeting rooms on the mezzanine? She'd asked herself that question a dozen times.

On a hunch, Anne pulled her conference program from her tote and flipped through to the Friday track schedule. Sure enough, the timeline showed the two rooms on the mezzanine had been used for workshops from one o'clock until three on Friday only.

Just as she'd thought. The workshops were over by four. Hotel staff would eventually deal with any cleanup or breakdown that had to be done. Same for any private luncheon in another room. *So why was Fran up there?*

Something nagged at the corners of her mind. It took a minute for her to remember. She sat up straight and sucked in a deep breath.

Joan Quaylen had told her she'd been at one of the workshops, had stopped to read her program to plan where she wanted to go the next day, and *then* had decided to use the restroom only to see Anne rushing out.

Except the last workshop was over at four, and she didn't find Carmella until six. Nobody takes that long to read a program and make plans. So what the hell was Joan doing for two hours and where?

If she'd stayed in a meeting room, then why didn't she see Fran? She also could have seen Susan come and go. And if Joan was in a meeting room reading the program like she said, why didn't Fran mention seeing *her*? Unless, of course, Fran never went into the meeting room, but into the restroom instead. But if Fran did check on the rooms, why didn't the woman mention seeing Fran? *Assuming Joan Quaylen was there.*

Anne ran a hand through her hair. This was driving her nuts. Mystery novels always had logical explanations. Unfortunately, this was neither a mystery novel nor logical.

None of this was helping. Instead of narrowing down the list of suspects, she'd just added to it. And even though Joan and Carmella had words in the past, that didn't mean one obnoxious woman killed the other. Still, it was something else to tell Gil when he called her back.

As if on cue, her phone rang. She snatched at it eagerly, and then slumped when she saw the caller was Rose, not Gil.

"Hi, Rose, what's up?"

"Plenty. How's the conference going?"

"So-so. By the way, we parted ways with Susan yesterday. She wasn't happy."

"I know. She called last night with a tale of woe trying to elicit pity. Luckily, the kids were a handful, so I cut her off before she could get wound up too far. Have you got a few minutes?"

"Sure. Did you uncover something?"

"Boy, I'll say. I called chapter members I knew weren't at the conference. Most had heard about Carmella and none of them expressed much regret at her death. Kelly Parker said she pitched to her at a small conference up in Ohio last summer. Carmella requested a full, but Kelly didn't feel comfortable with her and never sent it in."

"Smart girl."

"Yeah, well, get this. Carmella started calling and

pushing her to submit. Said she really wanted this story, it had potential, yadda, yadda. Kelly finally told her she didn't think they were compatible and that she wouldn't be sending. Kelly said Carmella went ape-shit. Called her a bunch of names and said she'd make sure Kelly would never sell a book anywhere."

"That's weird. Not Carmella blowing up, but that she'd pursue an unpublished author so hard. Very out of character."

"Kelly thought so, too, and did some research. She can't confirm anything, but the rumor was Carmella hadn't had a new client in months and was being pressured by the agency to acquire."

"Hence her requests for partials here. Hmmm. Interesting. Anything else?"

"Not too much from fellow members, but I got a hold of Alice Kartchman yesterday afternoon. When I told her the news about Carmella, she almost cheered. She held her in the same esteem as she did Isadora Powell. At any rate, I told her we heard she was going to start her own agency. Alice said she'd ask around and see what she could find out. Finally heard back from her this morning. Being an intelligent woman, Alice called her agent who is with Summers, too, and brother, did she ever find out."

"And?" Anne asked as Rose paused for breath. From over the phone, she heard another conversation.

"What? I'm busy, Rory." A whining voice answered in the background. "I have no idea where your shoes are. You were the last one with them. Go ask your father."

Rose came back on. "Where was I?"

"Alice Kartchman found out something about

Carmella starting her own agency," Anne prompted.

"Alice said that for once, the grapevine is tight. Nothing substantial is coming out of it. All she heard was that Carmella may or may not form her own company. I don't put too much stock in that. Neither did Alice. Alice also said something else that was interesting—she heard that due to financial problems a couple of agencies are downsizing. She seemed to think it was more than just readers and secretaries, but that agents were getting axed, too."

"I suppose I can see that happening. With the ease of self-publishing, more and more authors are just doing it on their own. They don't need an agent. These are scary times in the publishing industry. Even the major houses are delving into e-pub imprints."

"I think they may be doing that to appease the masses. There'll always be a need for real books."

"I agree," Anne replied. "Anything else?"

"I'll say. I saved the best for last. Guess what?"

"What?" Anne picked up her cup.

"Carmella was fired last Monday."

Stunned, she almost dropped the cup into the saucer. "Are you kidding me?"

"Nope. Apparently, the author poaching was getting out of hand. Alan Grayson and a couple of other agents filed a formal complaint with the American Association of Agents about her conduct. They in turn contacted Jack Summers saying they were instigating an inquiry into the Summers Agency's business practices."

"Oh my God! I'll bet Jack Summers just about went ballistic."

"According to Alice's agent, he called Carmella in

and ten minutes later she was cleaning out her desk."

"If she no longer worked for Summers, then starting her own agency makes perfect sense."

"Maybe, maybe not. Alice's guess is Carmella knew she'd have a tough time of it. All those nasty run-ins with authors, editors, and other agents took a toll. But once again, the good old rumor mill has it that she shopped herself to every major literary agency in New York. No word yet on if any of them bit on her resume."

"Whoa, whoa, wait a minute. If she was fired on Monday, then she came down here under false pretenses."

"You got it. She gets free plane fare, free food, free hotel, and good weather on our bank account."

"And, of course, no one from the chapter would have reason to call New York to confirm if she was still employed, although she took a hell of a chance that one of the other agents didn't know she'd been canned."

"Word may not have leaked out. I mean The Summers Agency might not have made it official yet."

"That's true, in spite of the rumor mill," Anne said. "They might be waiting until they have a replacement. Then they could make the big announcement about a new agent in the fold, and not say a word about Carmella."

"You'd think they'd have let the chapter know the score," Rose grumbled.

"Why should they? They probably weren't aware of Carmella's schedule. Agents come and go to these things all the time. She'd keep her own schedule and the chain of command might not know details of where she was going or when. And they certainly wouldn't think to check *after* they fired her."

A baby crying in the background made Rose groan. "Damnation, if Rory woke the baby up, I swear I'll be short a kid. I'll call you back. I want to hear all about your date last night. Talk to you later."

Rose hung up while Anne slowly sipped her coffee. So, Carmella had been fired and was freeloading on the chapter. *What a bitch!* No wonder she didn't take notes during pitches. She knew it didn't matter, so she requested something from everyone. The first thing Jack Summers would do would be to terminate her e-mail. All those submissions would bounce, the authors would complain to either Fran or Terry, and they in turn would contact the agency, which would feel obligated to accept the submissions.

Yet if she was planning on starting her own agency, why not direct those submissions to a new e-mail account? Unless, it was her way of getting even with Jack Summers.

Carmella Radcliff was some piece of work. And she might even get out of reimbursing the chapter on the theory the material did eventually get to be seen by an agent. Assuming, of course, all weren't given an immediate "thanks, but no thanks" rejection letter.

Then a thought hit her. What if the argument Fran had with the lying agent was about this? What if Fran had found out and threatened to turn her in? What if Carmella had laughed and said so what? That could explain where Carmella was between leaving the goodie table and her appearance on the lobby tape. But was that motivation enough to kill? Perhaps something else was said to prompt such rage. And Fran had been all over the hotel in the last couple of days. Maybe had even known where to score a knife. *Maybe* had seen Carmella enter the mezzanine ladies' room from the meeting room she supposedly was in.

What if?

Fran just moved to the top of her suspect list.

Chapter Nine

Anne held her head in her hands and groaned. The conference was bordering on disaster. These get-togethers were expensive to host and any profit margin was razor thin. Editors and agents, along with major speakers, expected to be comped for airfare, hotel rooms, and conference fees. The accounts payable racked up impressive numbers in those categories. She cared deeply about the chapter, and Carmella had just screwed them for at least a thousand dollars—probably more.

And then she went and got herself killed.

Anne finished her coffee and signaled the waiter for a refill. He complied immediately. She added sugar and cream and blew on the steaming liquid, the smell of the fresh brew tickling her nose.

No doubt about it, this conference was going in the hole financially. Terry had said yesterday that several attendees wanted their conference fees back. And the really cheap ones might even demand reimbursement for hotel accommodations. But was the chapter liable? Several chapter members had law degrees. Perhaps one of them might work *pro bono* for the group if lawsuits ensued.

Can anything else go wrong?

Anne had just taken another sip when her phone rang again. Her agent's name popped up on caller ID.

Swallowing, she took a deep breath and picked up the phone. A large part of her was scared to hit the accept button.

She tried to keep her tone upbeat. "Hi, Dave, what's up?"

"Good morning, Anne. Sorry to call you so early on a Sunday morning, but I need to talk to you. Have you got a minute?"

This didn't sound encouraging. "Sure. I'm at a conference, but not busy at the moment. I suppose you've heard about Carmella Radcliff."

As a defense mechanism, she'd rather talk about anything, even murder, than her revision. Her agent had bad news. She just knew it.

"Yes, the news is all over the literary world." He paused. "Uh, look, Anne, we need to talk about the revised manuscript you turned in a few weeks ago."

Here it comes. Her stomach clenched with nerves. Suddenly, the coffee didn't taste nearly as good as a minute ago.

"Sure, Dave. What about it?"

"Well, it's an improvement over the first one, but still isn't up to your usual standards."

Her heart plummeted. "I can take another crack at it. Where do you think it's lacking?"

"The plot really isn't fresh, and your heroine is a little flat."

Shit, shit, shit. "I see. Let me think on it. It sounds fixable."

A long pause didn't help her queasy stomach.

"Anne, I talked to your editor at Dark Moments Publishing on Friday afternoon trying to get her to read it. She declined. Apparently, your last two books barely made earn out."

She knew that. Her royalty checks the last year had been depressingly low. Her inner bitch had blamed Isadora Powell's death. Anne groaned and blinked tears from her eyes. This was her worst nightmare.

"However," Dave continued, "There is a bright side. If you can freshen the plot and add some life to your main character, I might be able to sell it to a smaller press. You have a good brand going and a loyal, if small, following. The downside is your advance would be severely cut, maybe three grand at the most."

"Oh, God, this is not what I needed to hear. Is Dark Moments dumping me for good?"

"I don't know about that, but they weren't interested in this work."

Of course they were dumping her. If not, they'd have worked with her to solve the problems. Dave was trying to let her down gently.

"Maybe it's time to switch genres," she said.

"Don't be hasty. Your brand is vampires and werewolves. Your fans expect them. Switching could be traumatic for them and destroy what you've gained over the years."

"How about if I used a pseudonym?"

"Then you'd have to work to brand that name. Look, I'll e-mail it back to you with some suggestions. Fix it up, but take your time. Don't rush things. You're a good writer, Anne. This is just a slump. I have every confidence you'll pull out of it."

"Okay, thanks, Dave. I'll think about how to rework it."

She hung up and sipped lukewarm coffee. Her books were single titles with no thoughts of a series or sequels. She'd never signed a multi-book contract. Over the years, her works had sold to several publishers until Dark Moments had become the go-to place. Her last seven books had been through them. Until now, they'd never rejected her.

Nancy and Jen walked up, pulled out chairs, and sat. The waiter glided up to take coffee and buffet orders.

"What are you doing here? I thought you were having breakfast and listening to the speaker," Anne asked. She couldn't bring herself to tell them her writing woes just yet.

"Breakfast sucked and it took a whole five minutes to realize I was bored beyond belief. Plus they're running really late," Nancy replied.

"Honestly, who was in charge of getting these speakers anyway?" Jen carped. "Debbie Worth was irritating and Kay Watson never changed her voice inflection. I was in danger of falling asleep."

"Come on, let's get some real food," Nancy said.

Their coffee arrived as they hit the buffet line. Within minutes, they resumed their seats.

"I never asked how the banquet went last night," Anne said, sipping from a refreshed cup.

"The food wasn't bad for a change, and we had to sit through the announcements of the contest winners and a couple of long-winded thank you speeches, but it wasn't too awful," Jen answered as she dug into a waffle.

"What have you been up to?" Nancy asked before forking scrambled eggs between her lips.

She brought her friends up to speed on her conversations over the past twenty-four hours with the bartender, Terry, and Fran. She hadn't had time earlier.

"Fran may be dodging the question, but Terry's dealing with what every conference chair deals with. No big deal," Nancy said. "I do find it interesting that Alan Grayson actually spoke to Carmella, especially in light of what he told Wendy earlier. Shame the bartender can't ID the woman from later."

"Then I got a call from Rose, and you won't believe this one." She told them about Carmella's firing from the Summers Agency and her subsequent appearance in San Sebastian.

"Holy shit," Jen said with her fork poised halfway to her mouth. "Talk about brass balls."

"I can't believe she'd take a chance on doing something that stupid," Nancy stated. "Sooner or later, the story would get out. She'd be ruined. I mean, who'd invite her to their conference knowing that?"

"You know, I never thought of that," Anne replied.

"Unless, she got a job with another agency or thought she would soon and planned on paying us back," Nancy said.

"Or was starting her own agency," Jen said.

Anne tapped her finger on the rim of her cup before taking another sip. "And in the meantime, she saw a great opportunity to screw Jack Summers by sending in a whole bunch of useless submissions."

"I wonder who may have hired her," Jen added as she resumed eating.

"I have no idea." Anne picked at her Danish as depression once again settled on her shoulders.

"Why the long face?" Jen asked.

Her eyes filled with tears and she used a napkin to blot them away.

"Anne?" Nancy prompted.

"I had a call from my agent." She told them the gist of the conversation.

"Oh God, hon, I'm so sorry," Jen said.

Nancy squeezed her arm. "I know how you feel. My agent submitted a weak story I'd sent her while we were in the midst of the Dorie business. It should never have gone any further than her desk, but she passed it on anyway. Her actions almost severed our relationship. My editor, in turn, told me to totally rewrite it. After Candace's arrest, I was finally able to concentrate and get it done. You will, too. You're too good a writer not to fix things."

"Thanks, but I'm just not sure where to begin."

"What we need is an old-fashioned plotting session," Jen declared. "Just the four of us. We'll take off for some isolated cabin in the woods or something and spend a long weekend brainstorming."

Anne sniffed. "You know, that sounds like a good idea. You guys are the best."

Gil entered the dining area and headed their way. He smiled as he pulled out a chair.

"May I join you?"

"Of course," Jen said casting a sidelong glance at Anne.

He sat and the smile turned into a grin. "What? Eating again?"

"Just coffee."

His eyes narrowed. "You look down. What's wrong?"

She relayed her woes with the latest manuscript.

His hand covered hers. "Aw, don't worry about it, honey. Things will be all right. You're a great writer."

The endearment and physical contact made Anne's heart race. She blinked the gathering wetness from her eyes.

"Thank you. I'll get by somehow. I always do." She placed her free hand over his and squeezed.

Jen and Nancy looked at each other and pushed their half-eaten plates back.

"You know, I think this might be a good time to visit the…the, ah, bookstore," Jen said.

"Good idea. We can check out those last minute items before the crowd builds," Nancy concurred.

"You guys don't have to leave just because Gil and I are here," she said.

"No, but you're holding hands and he called you 'honey.' That's a cue for us to vamoose for a while." Jen grinned, rose, and picked up her purse.

Nancy chuckled and did the same. "We'll be back."

"They're pretty good gals," Gil said as the women walked away.

"They're wonderful."

The waiter came by, but Gil shook his head. "Nothing for me." As the man left, he gazed at Anne. "Last night I gave you the life story of Gilbert Collins. Your turn. What about you?"

Anne sighed. She assumed he asked to take her mind off her literary problems—or to keep her from asking questions about his talk with Fran. Either way, she decided to humor him.

"I probably have the most boring, predictable childhood on the face of the earth. I'm an only child. Mom liked order, so when she told me to clean my room, I cleaned my room. Daddy was a salesman and traveled a lot. Whenever he came back from a trip, he brought me something—a stuffed animal or a book. I can still remember my first Nancy Drew mystery. After that, I haunted the library, especially during the summer."

"Where did you live?"

"Carmel, Indiana, a small town just north of Indianapolis. It was an idyllic kind of place where everyone knew everybody else, nobody bothered to lock their doors, and the people trusted one another. I miss that, in spite of everyone knowing everyone else's business." She sighed. "It's grown a lot since then. I hear the original Carnegie library I went to is now a restaurant."

"How did you end up in Florida?

She laughed. "I was a student at Indiana University and came down to Fort Lauderdale one year for the spring break experience. I met a charming man named Ken Jamieson on the beach. He was from Vermont and for a week, we were inseparable. One thing led to another and two years later, we were married. His job brought him here about fifteen years ago."

"Are your parents still in Indiana?"

"My dad died of a heart attack two years ago. Mother sold the house in Indiana and moved to Scottsdale. Said she was tired of shoveling snow."

"No kidding? My folks are in Flagstaff. They liked the combination of seasons. Made it feel more like home without the extreme winters. Maybe they can get together sometime."

She sipped more coffee, while thinking that the two of them could make a trip out west together. The possibility was intriguing when she stopped to consider the fringe benefits along the way—not an unpleasant image at all.

Finally, Anne cleared her throat. "So, how did your talk with Fran go?"

"She claims to have used the restroom earlier in the day, just as I suspected she would. As chapter president, she was on the mezzanine several times between ten and two in the afternoon."

"And of course, there's no way to prove otherwise. I suppose you saw the video of Fran and Carmella near the front desk on Friday afternoon. Didn't look like a pleasant exchange."

"I saw it. Said she simply asked the woman to be less abrasive with the authors pitching to her."

"Yet it looked like she and Carmella were arguing. Did she say what Carmella said?"

"It wasn't too nice. And here's something else. She also says she never saw Susan Lynch anywhere near the alcove."

"Did you talk to Susan, too?"

"Yes. She claims not to remember how long she sat in the alcove, but thinks it may have only been a few minutes before she left."

"Considerably less time than her first statement indicated. And the fingerprints on the stall door?" Anne questioned.

"Says she used the facilities when she first came up, then sat in the alcove. She saw no one, and no one saw her."

"Did she say where she'd gone?"

"Said she needed air and returned downstairs to walk in the garden. She used the stairs because she didn't want to see or talk to anybody at the moment."

"Awfully convenient."

"But once again, not implausible. That's why I was so annoyed when you called. I was still talking to her. Her story keeps changing, but not enough to warrant an arrest yet."

"I guess it's second nature to protect yourself with a little white lie when you're a suspect. It's a lesson I learned the hard way." Anne also brought up the time discrepancy on the mezzanine tape. "What the hell was Fran doing for thirty minutes?" Anne asked.

"Killing Carmella Radcliff?"

"And cleaning up afterward? I suppose she could have done that, but did she? At the same time, it doesn't take that long to take a peek in a couple of meeting rooms. Gil, maybe she met someone in one of them—someone who used the stairs on the way up."

"Then that someone also used the stairs to leave. No one shows up in the elevator area until the security guard. And why wouldn't she tell me?"

"This isn't looking good for Susan or Fran is it?"

"I'll talk to them again. If one or both are lying, sooner or later they'll trip themselves up."

"Oh, and I noticed something while I was on the mezzanine." She told him of her about the meeting room that looked like it had been set up for dining.

"I saw that, too. The hotel says a small group of businessmen has lunch there once a month. Friday was their day."

"So Susan could have been in the alcove, seen Carmella, been upset, gotten up to leave, walked by the room, *maybe* noticed a steak knife on a table that hadn't been completely cleared, taken it, and done the deed. Same with Fran." Anne paused to take a deep breath after her thoughts.

"Anything's possible, but we have no proof she did any of that."

"I also had another thought a while ago." She related her suspicions about Joan Quaylen. "The time frame just doesn't make sense. Two hours is a long time to read a program. And there's that old 'why didn't anybody see anybody else' angle."

"Maybe that's who Ms. Harrison was talking to for thirty minutes. If so, why didn't she say so?" he said with a frown.

"Could be she had no idea who the woman was."

"I'll find her again and ask. I also need to find Alan Grayson. Someone saw him in the ballroom for breakfast, but not since. He hasn't answered either his cell or room phones. I want to know what he and Ms. Radcliff argued about in the bar."

"They probably had a stern discussion regarding mutual authors. I can see Grayson telling Carmella to back off his clients."

"Oh, and one other thing. On a hunch, I checked with the hotel. It seems Mr. Grayson ordered from room service Thursday night—steak."

"And we still can't confirm if the tourist was female or a male in disguise. I have other blockbuster news for you. Rose called and told me that Carmella Radcliff was fired from the Summers Literary Agency last Monday."

Gil sat back and stared. "So what was she doing here?"

"My question, too. Other than she wanted a free Florida vacation." She relayed the details as per Rose along with hers, Jen's, and Nancy's speculations. "You know, just because we didn't see anyone other than the tourist, getting on the elevator after Carmella, doesn't mean someone wasn't standing just outside of camera range, and then took the stairs."

"I'll get a hold of the agency immediately."

"It's Sunday," she reminded him. Apparently, her agent was the only one who doled out bad news on a weekend.

"Then I'll get the head honcho—what's his name?"

"Jack Summers."

"I'll get a hold of him to confirm ASAP."

"I have to confess, I'm running out of people to talk to about this. Fran's not going to answer any more of *my* questions, and Terry Whiting can't wait for noon and this whole conference to be over. I suppose I could tackle more attendees who talked with Carmella."

"We've been over her list of appointments on Friday. No one, other than Susan Lynch, had much of a motive since she was requesting they send something in," Gil said.

Anne sat back and sighed. "It seems this murder may not be solved."

"Even if we don't make an arrest today, any evidence surfacing later can help make a case against someone from out of the area."

"Why is it I have the uneasy feeling I know the killer again this time? I mean, look at the major suspects—Alan Grayson, Fran, Susan, and the tourist who could be anybody in a disguise."

"I left a couple of messages in Grayson's voicemail, but he hasn't returned the calls. I also went up to his room a while ago, but he didn't answer the door."

She glanced at her watch. "Don't know why he wouldn't return your calls. As for not being in his room, Grayson is scheduled to be part of the editor/agent panel after the auction. He may be in the ballroom listening to the speaker or off somewhere with a potential client."

"Perhaps, but I don't like being ignored, especially when it concerns police business." Gil frowned and rose. "Think I'll head for the ballroom and see if I can corner him."

Anne joined him. "Mind if I come along?"

"And how would I stop you?"

"You can't."

He shook his head. "Come on."

She wanted to chuckle, but refrained as she followed him from the dining room. She liked a man who knew when to admit defeat.

They opened the doors to the conference hall and stood against the wall. Up on the dais, the speaker, Kay Watson, droned on. Many in the audience of a hundred or so fidgeted and yawned.

"See him anywhere?" Gil whispered in her ear.

"Not offhand." She moved further down the wall. Her gaze scanned the room. It should be easy to spot a man amongst all the women in the place.

"Don't see him," she reported as she rejoined him.

Gil clasped her hand, quietly opened the door, and pulled her from the room. In the hallway, he yanked his cell from his pocket, scrolled down the screen with a scowl, then punched in some numbers, and waited. The look of frustration on his face told Anne, the agent wasn't answering.

"Mr. Grayson, this is Detective Gil Collins. I have

left several messages. This is official police business. Please return my call as soon as possible. Thank you." He jammed the end call button and scowled.

"Like I said, he could be with a potential client," she offered.

"Well, let's go see if we can find him. I'm getting pissed. Where would be the most obvious place to look?"

"If he wanted a quiet conversation, an unused meeting room."

They checked the rooms on the main floor, but saw no one.

"Maybe the pitch room?" Anne suggested. But it, too, was empty. "I suppose they could be in the bar."

"At this hour?"

She shrugged. "Even if it's not open, it still makes for a quiet place to talk uninterrupted."

The bar, however, yielded only a maintenance man working on a beer tap.

"We're running out of places to look," he said.

"Let's try the pool deck and the garden area."

The pool had a family playing in the shallow end and a few people sunning on chaises. Alan Grayson was not among them. The only inhabitants in the garden were birds.

"What about those rooms on the mezzanine?" he asked with a scowl.

"I suppose. It's the only place we haven't looked, but he wasn't anywhere around when the group and I were here earlier."

In a strange moment of déjà vu, Anne shivered as they climbed the stairs from the lobby. Had it really been less than forty-eight hours since she'd found

Suzanne Rossi

Carmella's body? And now, Alan Grayson was in hiding. She didn't like the feel of this. The man had to be somewhere.

The mezzanine rooms were empty.

"Gil, I just can't think of where else he could be."

"You say he's supposed to take part in some kind of discussion later?"

"Yes, a panel of editors and agents. The subject is the changes in the industry and new trends in publishing."

He waved his hand as though not interested in the subject matter. "I wonder if either Ms. Harrison or Ms. Whiting has heard from him."

"I could call Terry and ask," she said, pulling her phone from the carryall. She scrolled until finding Terry's number, then pressed the select button.

"Hello?"

"Terry, I'm sorry to interrupt, but have you seen Alan Grayson?"

"I saw him a while ago at breakfast. He was talking to some woman in the hallway. I think it may have been Jackie Simmons, but I'm not sure. Why?"

"Oh, no reason. Someone wanted to talk to him, but he seems to have left."

"Left?" Terry's voice raised several decibels.

"No, no, not the hotel. Perhaps he's in his room. Thanks."

Anne hung up and relayed Terry's information.

"Try Ms. Harrison."

"She'll probably tell me to go to hell."

"Yeah, but she'll be a lot more curious about why I want to talk to him."

Sighing, she did as requested. The phone rang

168

several times before the chapter president answered.

"Hello?"

"Hi, Fran, it's Anne Jamieson."

"What do you want now?"

"Have you seen Alan Grayson?"

"It's not my turn to watch him, and no I haven't seen him."

"He wasn't at breakfast?"

"No, and I have to get back to the dais."

"I know, and I'm sorry to have…" Fran hung up.

"Nothing."

They returned to the lobby. Gil walked up to the front desk.

"Has Alan Grayson checked out?" he asked the clerk.

The man scrolled on the computer. "No, sir."

Gil heaved a sigh. "I see, thank you."

They moved on toward the ballroom.

"Do you think he could have just left without saying anything, like he was on the run?"

"That's my first thought." Gil punched a button on his cell phone. "Rogers, have security at the airport check and see if an Alan Grayson has passed through TSA yet. Call me when you find out."

"This is weird. If Grayson killed Carmella, why run now? He's been safe for over twenty-four hours."

"Could have gotten cold feet and decided to bug out. But why skip out on the hotel bill?"

"Because he wasn't paying. The chapter was, and he could always reimburse if someone mentioned extra room charges like room service. But he didn't seem like the type to leave the conference without telling someone. I mean, a call to Terry saying something has come up is so simple. It's bad professional form to just not show. And if nothing else, Grayson is a professional."

"And still missing."

"I'm getting a bad feeling about this," Anne said.

His cell rang again. While he talked, Anne looked around the lobby. A familiar figure emerged from the souvenir shop.

"Jackie, wait up," she called hurrying after the woman.

Jackie Simmons turned, held up a plastic bag, and smiled. "Hi. Had to get a souvenir of the Sunshine State. Ducked out on that last speaker. Sorry, but she was so boring. Is the panel about to begin?"

"Not for another hour or so. We have an auction first."

"Sounds like fun. Shame I'm flying. Can't get the stuff packed. No room left in my suitcase."

"Jackie, did you see Alan Grayson this morning?"

"Yeah, we were both early birds to the breakfast."

"Did he say anything?"

"About what?"

"About leaving early or something?"

"No, not really. He just said he'd had a gander at the buffet in the ballroom and decided to eat somewhere else. Why?"

"Oh, one of the conference volunteers was looking for him, that's all. I suppose you're all set to go, too."

"As soon as the panel ends. I'm already checked out. All I have to do is grab my bags from the secure room at the front desk and head for the airport."

"By the way, did you see him talking to anyone else?"

"Yeah, as he left he had a word with that woman who dumped Carmella into the goodie table and your chapter president—can't remember her name. Guess she was verifying his presence for the panel. Will you be at the panel discussion?"

"Sure, wouldn't miss it. Any idea when all this happened?"

"I'd say around six forty-five or so. Maybe a little later." She gave Anne a strange look. "Why?"

"Like I said, someone wanted to have a word with him before the panel. I'll talk to you later."

She walked back to Gil who was still on the phone. When he hung up, she relayed what Jackie had said.

"So, he could just be out having a leisurely breakfast at an IHOP," he muttered.

"Alan Grayson doesn't strike me as an IHOP kind of guy. He's much more upscale." She paused. "And he certainly wasn't in the restaurant at that time or we'd have seen him. Or he ordered from room service."

Gil made another call. "Can you confirm if Alan Grayson in room six-oh-seven ordered room service this morning...I see thank you."

He hung up. "No room service order from Alan Grayson. Nor has he shown up at the San Sebastian Airport yet."

"What if he didn't go to our airport? What if he took a very expensive cab ride to either the Fort Lauderdale or West Palm Beach airports?"

"To maybe throw us off the track? It's possible, but not probable. Most people would head for the quickest way out of town."

Gil's phone rang yet again. "Collins...I'll be right there."

"Something wrong?" she asked. His face had a deep scowl.

"Security caught a guy slim jimmying a car in the parking lot. They ran a check on his driver's license, found his car parked nearby, and discovered he'd been very busy in the hotel. The trunk of the car was jammed with stolen goods, one of which was a business card case with the initials CR engraved on it."

"As in Carmella Radcliff?"

"Possibly. I'm going to check it out. I'll be back soon."

So, a thief could have followed Carmella into the john and killed her, she mused as Gil left. Or most likely, he heard she'd died and took advantage of the situation to root through her things in the room. *He either knew the cameras didn't work or didn't care.*

Anne headed for the elevators. Maybe she could help by knocking on Alan Grayson's door and telling him Detective Collins wanted to see him immediately.

The sixth floor hall was empty save for a housekeeping cart down a ways. She stopped in front of room 607 and knocked. No one answered. Where the hell was he? He has to be somewhere. A strange chill swept down her arms. Unless he wasn't able to reply.

Anne hammered harder on the door and called out in a loud voice. "Mr. Grayson, are you in there? Are you all right? You're needed downstairs immediately. Please answer."

Silence greeted her request. She repeated her actions and words. A maid exited one of the rooms and stared.

"Excuse me, but could you please open this door for me?"

The woman advanced. "Is this your room?"

"No, it's a friend of mine who's registered here. He didn't answer and nobody can find him. I'm worried something's happened."

The woman hesitated. "I'm not allowed to do this."

"I understand, but he might have a medical emergency. Please. If no one's inside, I'll leave. You can come with me to make sure I don't take anything. Please?"

The woman still stared, then abruptly reached for the swipe card hanging from a lanyard around her neck. She inserted it into the slot and turned the handle.

Anne pushed the door open and entered. Alan Grayson lay on the floor at the foot of the bed. His bludgeoned head a gory mess.

Chapter Ten

Anne gasped. The maid screamed and ran from the room as Anne slowly retreated backwards out the door. Doors up and down the corridor popped open. Heads poked out. The maid was in total hysteria, running up and down the hall shrieking.

"What the hell's all that noise?" a man hiding behind his door demanded.

"Hey, knock it off," a woman in a flannel nightgown shouted. "I'm trying to sleep here."

"What's going on?" yet another guest asked.

More people rushed into the hallway with questions.

Anne ignored all of the comments and the maid as she dug in her carryall for her cell. *Holy shit, I've stumbled across another one! Why me?*

She finally found it and quickly dialed Gil. A man zipping his slacks rushed up. He paused beside Anne and looked inside Grayson's room.

"Oh my God," he exclaimed as he started to enter.

Anne held him back. "No, don't go in. I'm calling the cops."

Finally, Gil answered. "Anne?"

"Gil, you need to get up to room six-oh-seven now!" Her voice shook.

"What's wrong?"

"It's Alan Grayson. He's dead. There's blood all

over the place."

"Don't touch anything. I'm on my way."

She clutched her phone still staring at Grayson's body. The man next to her was silent as another couple joined them. They each took one look and backed away.

"What the hell is going on with this hotel?" the woman asked in a scared tone.

"I don't know," her companion replied. "But we're getting out of here now. Go finish packing. I'll check out. I'd rather spend four hours at the airport than another minute in this hell hole."

The maid had finally stopped screaming. Someone had cornered her and was now talking to the woman in calm tones.

Gil strode around the corner from the elevator lobby with two uniformed patrolmen.

"Okay, everybody, back to your rooms," he ordered the bystanders. Some actually complied. Others hung around a few feet away. He turned to Anne. "Give it to me, what happened?"

She told him in a few terse sentences. He went inside the room leaving the uniformed men outside to shoo the bystanders away. Gil returned a few moments later with a deep frown.

"Go downstairs and wait for me. Don't talk to anyone about this. I'll need you to give a formal statement later." He peered at her closely. "Are you all right?"

She nodded. "As good as can be expected, I guess. I'll sit in the lobby."

"Where's the maid?"

"Down the hall," she said indicating the direction

with her chin.

"Okay, I'll see you later." He kissed her cheek and moved off quickly.

Anne left the scene of the crime and returned to the lobby. One of the people from upstairs was at the front desk, no doubt the man who'd said he'd be checking out as fast as possible. Finished, he walked past where she sat and stared. Feeling exposed, she moved to the back corridor near the ballroom. The only seating available was a leftover banquet chair. She sat and took several deep breaths.

Who the hell would want to kill Alan Grayson?

She could understand someone killing Carmella, especially in light of the things she'd learned about the woman. But Alan Grayson? It made no sense. According to Jackie, both Susan and Fran had spoken to him earlier. And she hadn't seen Susan since the dust up about the critique group yesterday.

Nancy and Jen turned the corner from where the bookstore was located, then walked toward her.

"Good God, what's wrong now? You look like death warmed over," Jen blurted.

Anne shivered at her friend's choice of words.

"Did your agent call with more bad news?" Nancy asked with a frown.

Before she could reply, one of the ballroom doors opened and two women came out, glancing at the three of them as they passed by.

"Not here. Let's go find someplace more private," she said rising and shivering. A moment of lightheadedness had her pausing to inhale another deep breath. "Someplace warm."

"The pool deck? Are you sure you're all right?"

Jen asked, her forehead furrowing.

Anne nodded and swallowed. "I'll be fine. Let's get out of here."

They hurried through the doors to the pool. The swimmers and sunbathers were still present, but the women located a table well away from them.

"Okay, what's going on?" Nancy demanded.

"Alan Grayson's dead." Too late, she remembered Gil's warning not to discuss the matter, but she couldn't keep this to herself. Maybe Nancy and Jen didn't count.

Jen's eyes opened wide as shock registered on her face. Nancy simply stared as if unable to comprehend.

"Dead?" Jen croaked.

"Like a heart attack?" Nancy asked.

Anne shivered in the warm sunshine and shook her head. "No. He was definitely murdered. I found the body—again. And for God's sake don't say anything to anybody. Gil will have my head on a platter for telling you guys."

"But... but why would someone kill Alan Grayson?" Jen's voice raised several octaves.

"Shhh... keep your voice down. Your guess is as good as mine."

"Sounds like it's open season on agents. It has to be the same person who killed Carmella," Nancy said. "Could we have a crazy person running around offing agents because one or more of them rejected him or her?"

The doors from the hotel to the pool deck opened disgorging several women.

"Looks like the speaker is done," Anne remarked.

Jen glanced at her watch. "They're running way late. Kay Watson bored everyone to death for over an hour. I guess the auction will start in a few minutes."

"Who cares?" Nancy snapped. "Do either Fran or Terry know about Alan?"

"Not to my knowledge," Anne replied. "I'm sure Gil will get around to telling them soon."

"Well, they'll find out soon enough when he doesn't show for the editor/agent panel discussion," Jen said.

More people surged into the pool area.

"Let's get out of here," Nancy said. "We'll grab a cup of coffee and find someplace isolated."

They gravitated toward the lobby and the free coffee set up in the corner, then found the only place devoid of patrons—the bar. Choosing a table in the far corner, they sat and sipped quietly. Sunlight streamed through the window next to them, warming Anne's chilled bones.

"Was he stabbed, too?" Jen asked in a hushed voice.

Anne raised a cup of coffee to her lips with a trembling hand and sipped. Even with the sugar and cream, it tasted like the cardboard container. The coffee had been sitting in the urn for quite a while.

"I have no idea, but his head was a bloody mess—just like Dorie's when we found her," she replied after swallowing the dull brew. "I wish I knew what Alan and Carmella argued about the other night. And who possibly overheard—other than the bartender who didn't admit to hearing much."

"Had to have been about the authors she'd poached," Nancy suggested.

She lowered the cup and bit her lip. "Let's get logical. Gil told me Alan Grayson ordered room service on Thursday night."

"That makes sense. He'd been traveling most of the day and was too tired to mess with either going out or to the dining room," Jen answered.

"So what made him enter the bar around ten? A nightcap, maybe?" Anne mused.

Nancy shrugged. "Those mini-fridges contain bottled water or soft drinks. Some guests bring their own. I've done it on several occasions. We all have. Why pay inflated prices for using the contents? A quick stop at a nearby liquor store and a bottle of wine lasts the entire conference."

"So Alan goes into the bar around ten, sees Carmella, maybe warns her to stay away from his authors, and she in turn because she's more than half drunk, picks a fight. But who on earth would want to kill him?" Jen questioned, drumming her fingers on the table.

A sudden thought made Anne straighten. "Holy cow, what if Alan Grayson knew something about the murder? Something he saw or heard, but didn't connect right away."

Nancy stared, her eyes wide. "And he let something slip in casual conversation, not realizing someone could take it the wrong way."

"As in a threat, maybe?" Jen said.

"A threat?" Anne replied.

"Yeah, you know, like he's talking to someone and says, 'by the way, I saw you with Carmella right before she was killed. Too bad you didn't go into the john with her'—or something along those lines."

"I don't know about that," Nancy claimed. "Alan Grayson doesn't—didn't—strike me as the kind to make such a mistake. I'd think he'd mull it over, and then go the police."

"On the other hand, Grayson hated Carmella. He could have flat out decided not to say anything. She was dead and wouldn't be a problem anymore," Anne told them.

Terry Whiting poked her head around the corner of the lounge door, saw them, and hurried over.

"Have any of you seen Alan Grayson? He didn't answer either his room or cell phones nor did he answer the door when I went up an hour or so ago," she asked with a harried expression.

Anne glanced at her companions, then back at Terry. "No, can't say that I have. Why?"

"With Carmella dead, I wanted to ask him to head up the panel discussion. Should have done it yesterday, but totally forgot. And I can't find Fran, either."

Jen cleared her throat. "I take it Fran isn't overseeing the auction."

"Fran isn't overseeing jack shit. She finally showed up to introduce Kay Watson, and then bugged out. I haven't seen her since." Her phone rang. "Oh crap! Not another crisis. On the other hand, maybe it's Grayson."

She answered and exited the room. Anne didn't tell her Alan Grayson wouldn't be calling anyone ever again.

"So where the hell is Fran?" Nancy asked.

"I have no clue. Saw her much earlier in the dining room. She and Gil met a bit later. He had a few more questions to ask her," Anne said.

Jen's eyebrows rose. "What kind of questions?"

"I don't know. He didn't say. He also wanted to talk to Susan again. And Jackie Simmons told me she saw both women talking to Grayson about the time breakfast started."

"I haven't seen Susan since yesterday," Nancy said.

"She called me last night," Jen offered. "She was still upset at us dumping her."

Nancy rolled her eyes. "What did she say? I assume it involved a lot of whimpering and sniveling."

Anne sent her friend a quick glance. "I don't like hurting other people's feelings, and the whole thing *was* rather abrupt."

"Don't feel sorry for her. It plays right into her agenda," Jen said.

"I suppose you're right. Susan isn't worth getting upset about."

"Well, I have no intention of apologizing for my comments." Nancy turned her attention back to Jen. "So what did she have to say?"

"She said the two of you were bitches who skated on past performances. Then, she stated that she was going to tackle an agent in the morning for a private reading."

"Good luck with that," Nancy murmured.

"But she was seen chatting with Grayson in the hallway this morning," Anne reminded them. A bitch? She was tired of people calling her that.

"Go on, what else did she say?"

"You're gonna love this—she suggested that Rose and I join her and form a new critique group effectively cutting you two out of contact with us."

"I never realized how sneaky she was," Nancy said with a frown.

Anne heaved a sigh. "Stop and think about it. She's

a master manipulator. Always on the verge of tears if we didn't like her work, snide comments masked with an innocent look, and constantly trying to make us feel guilty. She craves sympathy. What did you tell her?"

Jen shrugged. "I said we'd all been partners for a long time and I was happy with the current arrangement. She got a little huffy, and swore she'd nail down an agent before the conference was over. I guess Alan Grayson must have been her attempt this morning."

Nancy finished her coffee and rose. "I don't know about the rest of you, but we can speculate until forever and not come up with the answer. I'm tired of playing amateur sleuth. I think I'll take a peek in on the auction. If we raise enough money, we may actually break even on this conference."

"I think I'll join you. Might even bid on a couple of things," Jen said also rising. "How about you, Anne?"

"No thanks. I think I'll just sit here or in the lobby. Maybe wait for Gil to see if he has any information on Alan's death."

"Why? You're not a suspect this time around. Let the cops handle it," Nancy said.

She shook her head. "Go on. I'll see you later. Are you going to the panel discussion?"

"Haven't decided yet. You going, Jen?"

"Might as well. Nancy's right. Don't dwell on things, Anne. I think we've gone about as far as we can go on who killed whom. My mind is tapped out."

Her friends left. As she sipped the last lukewarm sludge from her cup, she thought about Nancy's comment. Why was she so involved in this case? Because she'd found Carmella's body and been accused by a moron of killing her?

Perhaps. And now she could add Alan Grayson to the list. Maybe she had a natural curiosity about who did it and why. Maybe she didn't like the idea of someone getting killed in general. Or she could be just plain nosy.

She sighed. Nosy—a word that described amateur sleuths in fiction to a "t," from Nancy Drew to Miss Marple to Jessica Fletcher. None had any business investigating anything and putting themselves in danger, yet that is exactly what they did.

It's what I did, too, the last time with Candace. I suspected she had killed Dorie, but showed up at her house—alone like a dumb ass—to confront her. I'm thinking amateurs just don't stop to consider the consequences of their actions.

On the other hand, that might be what made them so believable in fiction. They acted instinctively. People related to that.

Anne rose and slowly walked toward the lobby. Settling in a chair, she noticed several women enter the small room near the front desk and retrieve their luggage, then head out the doors. Even now, possible suspects were leaving the hotel. How would Gil ever unravel this one? And had her information helped him at all? This detective business was hard work.

Good thing I don't write romantic suspense. I'd be exhausted by the final page.

As much as she hated to admit it, her sleuthing abilities had hit a dead end. Unable to help herself, her thoughts returned to her agent's call. In spite of the encouraging words from Nancy, Jen, and Gil, she blinked tears from her eyes. Given her ability to thrust herself into murders, maybe romantic suspense or straight mystery might be the way to go from now on. Forget vampires and werewolves. Forget her agent's advice about branding. Start over with a pen name in a new genre. Other romance writers had done it, why couldn't she?

The only other alternative—giving up writing— was not a pleasant idea. She dismissed it immediately. Once a writer, always a writer. What on earth would she do without a plot, characters, and a setting to escape reality on a daily basis? And the royalty checks helped with those little expenses that always seemed to crop up, especially with the kids.

Gil walked up, sat on the sofa, and leaned back with a sigh. He closed his eyes and massaged the bridge of his nose between his thumb and index finger.

"Gil?"

His eyes opened. "What a mess."

"Care to tell me about it?"

"It was gruesome. Blood everywhere—on the walls, the ceiling, the furniture. Coroner's with him now, along with the forensic team."

The visual image made her gag. "Yeah, I know. And he wasn't stabbed, but bludgeoned, wasn't he?"

"Yep. Only this time the murderer took the weapon with them."

"A lot of anger was spent on his death. What kind of weapon could it have been? Any ideas?"

"The hair dryer and the iron were still in the room. No lamps or telephones had been moved."

"Which means the killer brought it with him and this was not a spur of the moment thing," she said. "No ideas at all? Could it have been a robbery? You know, someone knocks on the door, he opens it and is attacked?"

"I have no idea, but whoever did it had to be covered with blood. Lots and lots of small wounds all over his head. Preliminary exam has the doctor thinking enough force was used to crack his skull several times. Won't know until he gets him on the table for autopsy. And even superficial head wounds can bleed like a son of a gun. He could have been rendered unconscious and slowly bled to death. The carpet was saturated."

Her mind pictured the brief look she had at the scene. It was not pleasant. "Small wounds? How small?"

"Less than half an inch. Odd shape, too."

"What did they look like?"

He drew a diagram of the injuries.

"The indentations kind of reminded me of a ball-peen hammer," Gil said.

"A what?"

"It's a hammer used by metal workers. One end is rounded into a knob, while the other is shaped a bit like a regular hammer only much shorter. It's also smaller than a claw hammer, but larger than one say, a geologist would use. The wounds also brought a geologist's hammer to mind. In fact, that was my first thought. I grew up with those hammers."

"Who the hell would have access to any type of hammer at a romance writers conference? Other than a maintenance man or janitor? You don't suppose…"

"I said the marks reminded me of those hammers, not that they were made with one. If a ball-peen was used, then the indentations would have been square or more rounded depending on which end was used. A geologist's hammer doesn't usually have a curved edge."

Anne looked closer at the drawing, a straight line at the bottom with a curved line covering it.

"Hmm. Dome shaped, looks kinda like an igloo. Were the marks that clear?"

He nodded. "Several were superficial, but left a clear pattern on the skin."

"Other than your hammer thing, what would leave this type of depression?"

Gil shook his head. "I don't know, but whatever it was had to be innocuous. Something Grayson didn't notice. Couldn't have been too large. Anything else would have put him on guard. As it was, he may have answered the door and turned his back on the person."

"Not real smart."

"Maybe he knew the person and wasn't expecting to be attacked. The first blow probably incapacitated him, maybe knocking him to his knees, allowing the killer to strike again and again."

"Which means the killer either had the weapon well-hidden—perhaps in his pocket—or completely disguised. And you're right, the perpetrator would be drenched in blood himself." She ran a hand through her hair. "This is confusing as hell. Makes a steak knife look downright ordinary."

A hotel security man walked up. "Detective Collins? We pulled that surveillance tape you requested from the sixth floor elevator lobby. Could you please take a look at it? There's something you should see."

"Yeah, be right there." He rose and looked at Anne. "Stay here. I'll be back shortly."

He left while her imagination ran wild for several

minutes. Surveillance tape from the sixth floor? Did someone follow Alan Grayson and this time, did the camera have a clear picture of the person? Most surveillance tape was just grainy enough to distort images, but she'd had no trouble identifying people from the ones she had viewed earlier. But then again, she knew those people. Strangers would make it harder. She'd love to take a look along with Gil, but he hadn't invited her. By now, she knew enough to keep quiet about things like that. If he'd wanted her to see them, he'd have asked her.

Which means he doesn't want me to see who's coming and going on the sixth floor. Then it dawned on her she was probably on the tape when she'd gone up and found the body.

Nancy and Jen entered the lobby each carrying the ugliest identical vases she'd ever seen.

"Good God, what are those?" she exclaimed.

"They're hers, not mine," Nancy declared.

Anne eyed the almost two-foot-high, day-glow orange monstrosities. Wide at the bottom and narrowing toward the top, only a very large single stemmed flower, like a sunflower, would fit.

"I hope you can get your money back. What did you pay for them—and why?"

Jen giggled. "I paid fifty dollars. Beat out two other bidders for them, too."

"I repeat—why?"

"Lamps, of course. I'll sand down the surfaces, spray paint them black, drill a hole in the bottom for wiring and such, get some nifty shades, then voila, new lamps for the living room."

"Didn't you buy some beat up footstools a few

months ago at a yard sale?"

"She did, and they're still sitting in her garage," Nancy informed her.

Jen waved her hand. "So I'm a little behind with my projects. Eventually, I'll get them done, and then you can all be pea green with envy when you see how spectacular they all look."

"Since when did you start quoting Scarlett O'Hara from *Gone with the Wind*?" Anne said.

"Oh, you know what I mean," she replied while Nancy chuckled.

"Can we please get these things to your car? They're heavier than they look. Bottoms must be weighted or something."

Gil reappeared with a serious expression on his face.

"Any word yet on who killed Alan Grayson," Jen asked.

He shot a stern look toward Anne, who shrugged.

"I thought I asked you not to mention this to anyone."

"We're not anyone," Jen said in a defensive tone.

"Just don't tell anybody else," he replied. "Now, I need to find Terry Whiting and Susan Lynch. Anybody seen them?"

"We saw Terry a while ago. She was looking for Grayson, and before you ask, no we didn't tell her he was dead," Anne answered.

"Susan's at the auction in the ballroom," Jen offered.

"I saw Terry at the back of the room as we left. She was scarfing down whatever remained on the buffet," Nancy added before turning to Jen and hefting the vase higher. "Jen, your car. Please!"

"Oh sure, come on. Be right back."

Anne gazed at Gil as the women exited the front doors.

"Did the tapes show anybody?"

He nodded. "Terry Whiting got off the elevator on the sixth floor at seven-fifty this morning and turned left toward Grayson's room."

"That makes sense. When I spoke to her, she said she'd been looking for him."

"At seven-oh-five, Susan Lynch made an appearance. She also turned left."

"Susan? Are you sure?"

"Absolutely."

"Hmmm. I wonder," she murmured.

"Wonder what?"

She told him about Susan's call to Jen the night before. "And she was seen talking to him earlier outside the ballroom."

"So you're saying she chats up Grayson, who says come up to my room in a few minutes and we'll discuss it?"

"Could be, although I don't know of any agent who would listen to a pitch in their hotel room, especially a man. Like I said earlier, too many unintended consequences."

"Maybe Ms. Lynch refused to take no for an answer."

"She could be damned determined when it suited her," Anne replied thinking of the goodie table incident. None of them had imagined Susan ever confronting Carmella.

"Well, the tape shows her getting back on the

elevator at seven-ten."

"Which means he either didn't answer or told her to take a hike."

Gil shook his head. "Excuse me. I'll be back in a few minutes."

He left the lobby, heading in the direction of the ballroom. She was certain Susan would come up with a logical explanation for being on the sixth floor, even if it was a lie.

Anne spent the next several minutes mulling over all she'd learned so far this morning. Some of it made sense. Some of it didn't. And all of it was confusing.

Nancy and Jen reentered the hotel and joined Anne.

"Where's Gil?" Jen asked.

"He went to talk to Terry and Susan." Since he hadn't told her to keep quiet about the tapes, she told them what he'd seen.

"Both make sense," Nancy added. "Terry probably went up, knocked, and when he didn't answer, left."

"And from what Susan said on the phone last night, I had the impression she was going to accost every agent that came within sight. It'd be just like her to go pounding on their doors."

"But would the front desk give up room numbers to just anyone who asked?" Nancy said.

Jen shrugged. "They might if they were busy. Or perhaps, Susan overheard someone say he was on the sixth floor, and then followed him up at some point. What do you think, Anne?"

"I suppose anything is possible. It's Sunday morning, people are checking out, so I guess it could happen." Anne glanced at her watch. "I wonder when the panel will begin. You guys going?"

"I suppose," Nancy replied. "But it won't start for a while yet. They had a ton of items to auction off and a lot of bidding. Anyone who stays for the thank-you-for-volunteering session won't get out of here until early afternoon."

"I'm here, I might as well stay and listen to what the experts have to say," Jen said.

Gil walked into the lobby.

"Did you find them?" Anne asked.

"Yes. Anne, I have to go to the station for a while. I'll try to call you later. Dinner maybe?"

"Dinner? Sure, but why do you have to leave?"

He hesitated, looked at each of them, sighed, and then gave them a stern look.

"Keep this to yourselves. Do you understand?"

"Keep what to ourselves?" Nancy inquired.

"We're taking Susan Lynch in for further questioning in the murders of Carmella Radcliff and Alan Grayson."

Chapter Eleven

Jen's eyes widened and Nancy just stared with a thoughtful look on her face.

"Good heavens, Gil, why? Is there something else on those tapes you don't want us to know?" Anne asked. She didn't like to think of yet another critique partner—okay, former critique partner—as a killer.

He cast a glance at the other two women.

"Oh, come on, Gil, Anne already told us about Terry and Susan being on the sixth floor," Nancy said.

He drew in a deep breath, and then let it out in a heavy sigh. "I don't know which is more dangerous—a killer on the loose or the three of you helping with the investigation."

"Gil! Why are you bringing in Susan for more questions?" Anne asked again.

"Not here. I don't want anyone to overhear. Follow me." He led them to a small room off the hallway and closed the door behind them. "I don't know why I'm telling you all this, but the tape shows Alan Grayson getting off the elevator a few minutes before seven. Other than that, the tapes show both Ms. Lynch and Ms. Whiting coming and going, along with a lot of other people, some with luggage."

"Makes sense. They go down, have breakfast, and then either check out and leave immediately, or check out and store their bags until later," Anne said. "I've often done that at conferences."

"You still didn't answer the question," Nancy reminded him. "Why are you taking Susan down to the station?"

"Had a chat with the maid. She was cleaning a room at the end of the hallway and saw Ms. Lynch knock on Grayson's door. It opened and she entered. A minute or so later Ms. Lynch exited and exchanged some heated words with Grayson. The maid also says Ms. Lynch came up the stairs around eight, and knocked on his door again. She was doing her job and didn't see if he answered or when Ms. Lynch left. All the maid knew was that half an hour later the two of you found Grayson dead on the floor."

"Oh Lord, Grayson could have told Susan to take a hike at seven, and then she came back at eight and killed him," Jen said with a groan.

"Wait a minute," Nancy interjected. "Why was the maid working so early?"

"Claimed to have wanted to get a head start. With check-out at eleven and the conference ending, she knew there'd be a whole lot of empty rooms to deal with in the afternoon. Plus, it's Sunday. People will be heading back to the office on Monday, so the hotel will empty out fast."

"My question is why did Susan climb six floors? Why not use the elevator?" Jen asked.

"That's one of the questions, I'm going to ask her," Gil said.

"The answer's simple—she wised up about the cameras," Nancy said.

"That's a possibility. Now, I've got to get back to the station."

"Gil, do you suppose the hotel has a list of conference attendees with rooms on the sixth floor?" Anne asked.

"They do. I requested the same thing earlier."

"Do you have any objection to me seeing it?"

"No, I guess not. I'll have them make a copy for you."

As they left the room, he pulled Anne aside leaving Nancy and Jen to exit ahead of them.

"Can I trust you not to do something stupid while I'm gone?"

"I'm insulted! I wouldn't do 'something stupid', as you call it."

"You did with Candace Warren. If you hear or see anything, I may need to know, give me a call. Okay?" He ran a finger down her cheek. "I don't want you getting hurt—or worse."

Heat radiated from the pit of her stomach to her extremities. She inhaled a shaky breath.

"I don't want to get hurt or something worse either. I'll be good. I promise. But if you have Susan at the station, what can I see or hear to put me in danger?"

He leaned down and kissed her hard. "You can always find something. And what if Ms. Lynch isn't the killer? I'm just bringing her in for more questions. Call me when the conference is over and come down to the station. I'll take your statement about Grayson then."

He left while she tried to pull her rocky nerves into line. *Maybe he'll arrest Susan. That way, we can have a very interesting dinner tonight—no murder speculation—just the two of us letting nature take its course.*

Her conscience immediately jabbed her with a

guilty prod. She didn't want Susan arrested if she was innocent, but oh, how she did want some quality time with Gil Collins. And until this case was solved, quality time was not likely to occur.

Anne didn't know why she was defending Susan so strongly. She wasn't all that fond of her, and the evidence against the woman was building.

She walked into the hallway and met Nancy and Jen lingering near the ballroom doors. "Good grief, is the auction still going on?"

"Apparently," Jen answered.

"The speaker went over time by a good ten minutes, and they had to give people a pee break before the auction, so it didn't start until close to nine thirty. Factor in another restroom break when this is over, and those editors and agents won't get out of here until close to one."

"I'll bet the panel will be missing a few of them, too," Jen suggested. "Some have planes to catch."

"And I'm sure the acknowledgments to the volunteers will be whittled down to a simple thanks a lot," Nancy added.

"Gil said he'd leave a list of which attendees had rooms on the sixth floor. I think I'll take a look. You guys interested?"

"You go ahead," Nancy told her. "Like I said, I'm all sleuthed out. I'll catch the end of the auction, and then the panel. How about you, Jen?"

"Think I'll do the same. Wanna meet here when it's all over and go out to lunch? Maybe we'll know more about Susan by that time."

Anne shrugged. "Sounds good, but I have to give my statement about finding Grayson's body. On the other hand, I don't see how an hour for lunch will make much of a difference. I might also sneak in for a little of the panel. See you in a while."

As her friends slipped into the ballroom, she heard the auctioneer crying out the bids through the briefly opened door.

Anne headed for the front desk. The same woman was on duty as the afternoon of Carmella's murder.

"Hello, my name is Anne Jamieson. I understand Detective Collins left something for me here?" she asked.

"Yes, he did. Just a moment." She disappeared into a back room, then came out with a sheet of paper and handed it to her with a cold stare.

"Thank you." Anne moved off. Obviously, the clerk's suspicions from a few days ago still occupied her thoughts. *Oh, who cares what she thinks anyway? I know I didn't do it.*

Anne sat in a chair in the lobby and read. Six names were on the list with the rooms listed in order. Alan Grayson had room six-oh-seven. Jackie Simmons was in room six-ten just down the hall. Several other people at the conference also had rooms in this area, but the names were unfamiliar to Anne.

The rest of the rooms listed were toward the right of the elevators. Four were allocated to attendees from out of town. Anne had no idea who they were either.

But the last two rooms' occupants' names jumped out at her. Terry Whiting was in room six-fifteen and Beth Hardaway in room six-twenty-two.

She hadn't seen Beth since yesterday. Could she and Carmella have gotten into an argument that escalated? She rose and headed back to the front desk.

"Excuse me, sorry to bother you again, but would you happen to know when the people on this list checked in to the hotel?"

The clerk worked on the computer for a minute, and then reported, "They all checked in on Thursday after three o'clock."

"Could you please print out the exact times for each for me?"

"Yes, I suppose. That Detective Collins said to give you whatever you wanted." Her tone suggested she wasn't happy about the prospect. Anne didn't really care.

With the new information in her hands, she returned to her chair.

Terry had checked in first at three forty-five. That made sense. As conference chair, she needed to be there early to head off any small problems before they became large problems.

The women Anne didn't know had checked in anywhere from four-ten to six-thirty. She dismissed them as unlikely killers. She recognized none of the names as having pitched to either Carmella or Alan. Alan Grayson showed up at four-thirty.

I suppose one of the women I don't know could have had previous issues with Carmella and nailed her. Maybe even saw her checking in. But discovering who had issues would take a miracle of time she didn't have, not to mention effort. Given a few days, she supposed Gil could make inroads into any possible connections.

But Alan Grayson's death felt more personal. Like maybe, he knew whoever had knocked on his door and had nothing to fear. She was certain that he'd go to the police if he had any suspicions of who had killed

Carmella. *Unless, of course, he sympathized with the killer.*

Anne read on. Jackie Simmons had checked in at five-fifty, while Beth Hardaway was a late entry at seven-forty.

She needed to see the layout of the rooms—to see how close they were to the stairs and the elevators. Rising, she walked to the elevator and rode it to the sixth floor. Grayson's room was being guarded by a uniformed officer.

The room was halfway down the corridor from a stairwell at the end. The door was open, so she assumed the forensic team was still doing their job. She stopped in front of six-ten, Jackie's room and nodded to the policeman who stared back. She didn't bother to knock since Jackie had told her she'd already checked out. She also made a note that Grayson's room was not that far away from the elevator lobby.

Not sure of the significance of that, but it might make it easy for a killer to come and go if they used the elevator, not the stairs.

On the other hand, the stairs at the end of the hallway were perfect for transportation. This was undoubtedly the stairwell the maid said she'd seen Susan use. The other was a country mile away at the opposite end of the corridor.

Anne retraced her steps, walked past the elevators and stopped at Terry's room. Once again, she didn't bother to knock. Terry was busy in the ballroom.

She did knock randomly on the doors of two rooms allocated to the strangers. No answer. They had either checked out already or were downstairs.

That left Beth Hardaway's room, six twenty-two.

She rapped sharply, but as with the others, received no answer. As she turned to leave, she noticed the stairwell for this wing of the floor was only a few dozen feet away.

Not certain what she had accomplished, Anne returned to the lobby and resumed her seat.

So the stairwells are at corresponding ends of the corridor. That's perfectly normal. They probably had both an indoor and outdoor egress on the main level. Still it made for some interesting movement possibilities. Anyone could avoid the non-working cameras by using the stairs, likely the one closest to Grayson's room.

And who said the killer came from the sixth floor? He or she could be on any level, used the stairs to kill Grayson, and leave again.

Anne sighed, clutched her head in her hands, and finger massaged her scalp. This case had way too many holes and unanswered questions. On impulse, she pulled out her cell and punched in Rose's speed dial.

"Hi, Anne, how's the conference? Any word yet on who killed Carmella?"

Anne brought her friend up to date on the latest developments.

"Alan Grayson was murdered, too?" Rose said in a shocked tone. "And Gil's arrested Susan for both killings? Good God, what's going on?"

"Not arrested, just taken down to police headquarters for more questioning."

"Poor Susan. Remember when we were all hauled in for the third degree in Dorie's murder? I cried all the way home, more with relief I hadn't been arrested than anything else. For as much of a pain as Susan is, Fran is worse. Shame Gil didn't haul her in."

"I'd have no remorse over that. Susan can't be having a good time. I have the feeling she's either out-and-out lying or not telling all she knows. Wish I'd seen her this morning. I could have told her honesty is the best policy when dealing with the police."

"I know Susan was angry, but I just don't see her sticking a knife in Carmella Radcliff."

"Me neither, but then you never know," she replied thinking of Candace. "Rose, when you spoke with Alice, did she say anything about Carmella and Alan Grayson or Beth Hardaway? And what about Jackie Simmons? Any information on her? I met her for the first time yesterday."

"The only thing Alice said about Grayson was the poaching of authors that brought about the letter from the agents association regarding disciplinary action. I do know that Beth and Carmella weren't the best of chums. Carmella dropped Beth as a client, and when Beth's career revitalized tried to get her back into the fold."

"Beth never mentioned that when I spoke with her," Anne replied.

"My information is second hand, but supposedly it happened at the national conference last summer. I think Carmella was on the skids. She wasn't bringing in new clients and was losing old ones. Apparently Beth was having none of it."

"Could be. What about Jackie Simmons?"

"I've never heard of Jackie Simmons."

"Just a minute." Anne held the phone in place with her shoulder while she rummaged in her carryall for the conference program. Finding it, she flipped through until coming to the editor/agent bios. "It says here she's with Coyne and Company Literary Agents."

"Haven't really heard of them either. Let me give Alice a call. She'll know."

"I'd appreciate it."

Anne hung up. So Carmella had tried to get Beth Hardaway to re-sign with her. At least, that was the word on the street. But if Beth told her former agent to sit on it and rotate, then that gave Carmella more of a motive for killing Beth. Not the other way around.

That was the problem with rumors. Some were true, some were false, and some a mix of both. Still, no doubt about it, Carmella Radcliff had given most of the publishing world a motive for murder.

The sound of voices from the wide corridor leading to the ballroom told her the auction must finally be over. She glanced at her watch. About time, it was almost eleven thirty.

Attendees gushed through the lobby on their way to the restroom or elevators. Nancy and Jen sauntered up.

"You know if you sit there much longer, you're going to take root," Jen said with a grin.

She told them about her trip to the sixth floor.

"And how did that help?" Nancy asked.

"It didn't, not really." She also told them about her phone call to Rose, and the new information, little that it was. "I've spent the last few minutes thinking what an asshole Carmella Radcliff was."

"That she was," Jen agreed.

"I mean, seriously, she's fired, shows up anyway, and gets offed in the ladies john where I just happen to find her. And then Alan Grayson gets killed, and I have the bad luck of finding him, too. No doubt about it, this conference will go down in history as the worst ever—anywhere. I'll also bet it's our last. Much as it pains me to admit it, Fran was right—nobody will want to come to another one."

"I feel sorry for Terry. I talked to her a while ago," Nancy said. "She was almost in tears. She tried to shorten the auction by half an hour, but many of the items donated were done so with the proviso the company name or the individual donating was mentioned during the process. She had to go on with it. Plus, she had an argument with the catering manager about the food quality. She demanded a reduction in cost and was refused."

"Damn those contracts," Anne murmured.

"And the hotel is threatening to charge an extra day for the ballroom fee if we aren't out by noon," Nancy continued. "As you said, 'Damn those contracts.' I came close to telling her about Alan Grayson."

"Oh God, you didn't, did you?" Anne replied. Gil would kill them all if word got out before the police released the information.

"No, but she's going nuts trying to find him. I finally told her to choose another person to head up the panel."

"Plus, some of the panel members are backing out due to travel issues," Jen added. "Those who had early afternoon flights will now barely have time to clear security at the airport before the plane takes off."

"Terry has every reason to be stressed," Anne said. "I noticed on the pitch sheet that she was supposed to pitch to Carmella on Saturday morning. She's a good writer and since Carmella was requesting submissions for a change, Terry had every hope of getting her foot in the door."

"I know. She told me yesterday that she pitched with Alan Grayson instead, but he told her he wasn't looking for what she wrote," Jen replied. "Even if Carmella wasn't with the agency, someone would have read it."

Anne shook her head. "Maybe, maybe not. With all those submissions, Jack Summers may just reject all of them out of hand without having ever looked at them."

Nancy's forehead furrowed. "I'd like to know how Carmella Radcliff got away with so much crap for so many years. She was rude, abrasive, and worse than nasty to a lot of people. Why did Jack Summers put up with it for so long? Makes no sense."

"Old times' sake, maybe," Anne said. "I heard she and Jack were an item at one time. Can't remember who told me."

"Old times' sake until Grayson complained to the agents' association," Jen replied.

"She had chutzpah, I'll say that," Nancy commented shaking her head. "I still can't believe no one noticed she didn't hand out a business card or bothered to take notes during the pitches."

Jen shrugged. "Remember how it was when you used to pitch? You're nervous, concentrating on what to say and making sense in a ten minute time frame, and so relieved when it's over, you just leave and hope for the best."

"Jen has a point," Anne said. "By the time you realize you don't have a card or an e-mail address, the agent is talking with someone else. So, the next thing you do is look in the program under the bio section.

Sometimes the contact point is listed."

"And if it's not, you can always go to the website," Jen added. "Or corner the agent later and request a card, although knowing Carmella, she probably had an excuse for not having one handy."

"Maybe she gave whoever asked her old email at the agency," Anne finished.

"I still say she was taking a hell of a chance. Suppose someone submitted immediately," Nancy muttered.

"For all we know, Carmella may have told people to give it a week or two, that she'd be out of the office or something," Anne explained.

"Most authors would do that anyway," Jen said. "You know, make any last minute edits for the best possible outcome."

"I still can't help feeling that Alan Grayson was involved in some way. Maybe he did disguise himself and follow Carmella to the mezzanine where he killed her," Anne mused.

"Yeah, but then who killed Grayson and why?" Nancy asked.

"I don't know. Maybe we're looking at two different killers. Alan offs Carmella, and a rejected author who pitched offs Alan."

"A rejection isn't grounds for murder," Nancy reminded her.

"It might be, if the person pitching had been pinning their hopes on Carmella Radcliff," Jen stated. "Like you said, she was requesting material, and for all we know some of those requests were for full manuscripts. Instead, they get Alan Grayson who doesn't sound like he liked a whole lot."

"In fact, I heard him say that exact thing over the phone when I cornered him yesterday after lunch. So, when Carmella died, Alan took over some of her schedule. An unpubbed author gets a no from him and goes up to his room to beg or demand, and kills him?" Anne speculated.

"Way too far-fetched," Nancy said.

"Not if the author was one of those oh-so-close-but-no-cigar types who figured they had it in the bag with Carmella," Jen replied.

Nancy waved her hand sharply in the air. "Oh, all of this is pure supposition. We don't have an ounce of proof against anyone. Besides, no one ever had anything in the bag when it came to a submission to Carmella Radcliff."

"You're absolutely right," Anne said with a sigh. "By the way, have either of you seen Beth Hardaway today?"

Both women shook their heads.

"Jen, do me a favor and ask the desk clerk if she's checked out. I'd like to talk to her about this business with Carmella again."

Jen hustled up to the desk, spoke with the clerk, and returned a minute later.

"Checked out at seven-forty and climbed into a cab."

"Nuts. Oh well, I'm not sure how much credence to put into whether or not Carmella wanted Beth back," Anne said as her phone rang. She pulled it out of her bag and glanced at the caller ID. "Oh, it's Rose...Hey, Rose, that was quick."

"Got a hold of Alice right away."

"What did she have to say?"

"Elizabeth Coyne was an agent with the Peek Agency until about four years ago when she went out on her own."

"Peek! That's Alan Grayson's employer."

"I know. At any rate, Alice says Coyne is a smart cookie. In the first couple of years, it was just her and another woman. Kept the costs down as much as possible. Then she started showing up at conferences out of pocket."

"So, if no one invited her, she paid her own freight."

"Exactly. She handed out business cards and took pitches in the bar. Eventually, the agency landed several decent authors and the works were sold to small presses. She wasn't making a whole lot of money, but Alice says her clients were happy with the representation. Elizabeth added two more agents about a year ago."

"Was one of them Jackie Simmons?"

"I don't know. Alice had never heard of her."

"Obviously, the agency handles romance, but what about other genres?"

"Didn't think to ask. You'll have to go to the website for more information."

"Okay. Thanks a lot for your help, Rose. I'll call you tomorrow."

She hung up and relayed Rose's conversation to Nancy and Jen.

"I remember seeing something on them when I was scouting out agents a couple of years ago," Jen said.

"Just a minute," Nancy said pulling out her phone. "Let me look up the Coyne & Company website." She was silent for a few minutes while reading, and then clicked the phone off. "Coyne & Company represents all genres except horror and erotic romance."

"That's quite a spread," Anne said. "You need several agents with specialized expertise to cover everything."

Nancy rose. "Well, I don't know about you, but the panel discussion will be starting soon. I think I'll hit the restroom first. You guys coming?"

"Yeah," Jen said also standing. "Anne?"

"In a while. I'm hoping Gil will call with news about Susan. If I don't hear in fifteen or twenty minutes, I'll join you."

"Suit yourself, but I think you're taking this to the extreme. You're not a suspect, and you don't really like Susan. Let Gil do his job," Nancy jabbed.

Anne sighed as her friends walked away. Maybe Nancy was right. Maybe she should just forget about who killed the two people and concentrate on her dinner tonight with Gil.

She agreed with Jen that visualizing Susan knocking off Carmella Radcliff was hard to believe. *But then we didn't think Candace could kill either. Given the circumstances, I suppose anybody could kill if provoked.*

And try as she might, she couldn't just ignore Susan's plight—even though she didn't care for the woman. *If she's innocent, then someone else is guilty. But who?*

The likelihood of a second killer loomed larger. *And if so, then who offed whom?*

Chapter Twelve

Anne glanced at her watch. Nancy and Jen were right. The sessions this morning were dragging on way past the time limits. The way she saw it, Terry had two ways to go—shorten the editor/agent panel discussion, the most popular event, or cough up the extra money the hotel demanded for going over the contracted hour of noon. The hotel might grant them an extra twenty or thirty minutes, but that was all, especially if the ballroom was rented for an evening event.

Neither was much of an option. Attendees wanted to hear the latest about the industry from insiders, not to mention those people's assessment of the conference, so to truncate it to a half hour or less would not go over well. Perhaps a little negotiation with the hotel was in order. After all, it *was* Sunday and the ballroom might not be needed for an event this afternoon or even tonight. And hotels were always aware of good public relations. Why piss off a group who may return for an event?

Iona Smalls walked past toward the front desk rolling a suitcase behind her.

"Iona! Are you leaving?"

The editor turned, smiled, and made her way over to where Anne sat.

"In a while. My plane leaves at one thirty and if I don't want to chase it down the runway, I have to get out of here no later than noon. I canceled out on the panel discussion."

"Oh, that's a shame, but I totally understand."

Iona glanced at her watch and lowered herself into one of the chairs. "I've got a few minutes before checking out. You guys put on a wonderful conference, in spite of Carmella getting killed."

"Thanks. I'll pass that along to Terry Whiting, the chairperson, and Fran Harrison, our chapter president. They'll be happy to hear it."

"The food was sucky, but that's not unusual anymore.

Since she had an insider sitting next to her, she decided to ask a few questions.

"Iona, did you see or talk to Alan Grayson either yesterday or today?"

"Talked to him last night after the banquet. We had a drink together in the bar. He said he'd never worked so hard for so little in his life."

"Meaning he didn't get much in the line of publishable stories?" This coincided with her gut feeling.

"He said most of them were not very good. He hated telling aspiring authors their work just wasn't up to industry standards yet. One woman got hot under the collar about it and said he was being shortsighted. He told me he tried to let her down gently, but she got demanding, so he finally blurted out the truth—her story was awful. She replied he'd be sorry when she made it to the big time or words to that effect." Iona shook her head. "Some people just can't take no for an answer."

Anne straightened and focused on the editor's face,

sincerely hoping the woman wasn't Susan. "Any idea who the woman was?"

"Yeah, Alan said it was the drama queen from the day before. You know; the one who found Carmella after you. He said she actually began her pitch with that information. Can you believe it?"

Anne snorted. *Joan Quaylen? I might have known.* "I can believe it. She accused me of the murder. The woman is a royal pain. Did you see Alan this morning?"

"This morning? No, oh wait a minute, yes I did. He was waiting for the elevator when I came down. He advised me to skip the buffet and order room service. He was right. It was pretty bad."

"Was he alone in the elevator area?"

"Yeah, although I did pass some woman heading that way just after he got into the elevator." Iona shot her a strange look. "Why?"

"Oh, no reason. Terry's been looking for him, along with a couple of other people."

"Maybe he's in hiding until the panel starts. In fact, if it hasn't begun already, it soon will. He's probably already in place on the dais. To tell you the truth, Alan is a bit of a prick, if you get my drift. A horrible stuffed shirt kind of guy. He might be a crackerjack agent, but as a person, he isn't well liked. Only mingles because he has to. Personally, I don't like him much myself. But not nearly as much as I loathed old Carmella. I won't miss her at all." She cast another look at her watch and rose. "It's that time. Gotta go. Have a good day, Anne. Hope to see you again at Nationals in July."

"Have a safe flight, Iona," she replied in an absent tone as the editor walked away with her luggage.

So, Joan Quaylen had words with Alan Grayson. Could his brutal assessment of her work have turned the woman into a killer? And who was the woman Iona saw following Grayson this morning? If indeed, she was following him. Susan? Joan? The time frame suggested Susan, yet Joan Quaylen could just as easily have taken the stairs. But Anne doubted the slightly tubby woman would haul her butt up six flights of stairs. On the other hand, she could have been one of the people in the surveillance tape coming and going on the sixth floor. Who knows? Maybe she took the elevator to the fifth floor and used the stairs for the last flight. According to the maid, Susan had used the stairs later in the morning.

Or could the woman Iona saw have been Susan on her first visit to Grayson? Oh crap, what's the use of speculating? It's too confusing and becoming more so every minute. Logic is breaking down big time.

Plus, Iona didn't like either Alan or Carmella. She may have had an alibi for the time of Carmella's death, but what about Alan's? And Carmella could have been stabbed later than supposed. The tapes showed her getting off the elevator around five. Anne had found her a little after six. Iona could have come out of the downstairs ladies' room just in time to see Carmella walking away and followed. And for all anybody knew, Iona was the second person in the bar that night.

Tired of sitting around, Anne got up and wandered into the small boutique down the corridor to the ballroom. A bored clerk barely looked up from her magazine spread open on the counter. The place was a typical hotel specialty store—nice stuff, but overpriced as hell. A purse hanging on a wall peg caught her eye, but no way would she shell out a hundred and twenty-five bucks for it.

"Lovely purse, isn't it?" the clerk said, finally taking an interest in a potential customer.

"Very nice, but way out of my budget. Have you had a lot of business from the conference goers?"

"Some," the clerk said with a shrug. "Most come in to just browse or talk on their phones. Had one woman come in late yesterday afternoon practically frothing at the mouth to someone about how no one had even asked her to submit a partial—whatever that means. She tried on every bracelet and necklace we had before settling for a pair of earrings."

Frothing at the mouth? "I don't suppose you have the woman's name, do you? I'm with the conference. A woman showed off some earrings last night, but I can't remember her name. Should have written it down, I guess. When we talked I promised to send her some information she requested."

She held her breath. Would the bored clerk buy her bullshit story?

"I may if she charged them. Some people pay cash." The clerk pulled out a box full of receipts and pawed through the scraps of paper. "This is a consignment store. If the buyer is staying in the hotel, we always get a name whenever possible so the owner of whatever is sold has a record—you know, name, address, e-mail. Just about everyone gives that information when they check in. Yeah, here it is. I remember now, she was the only one to buy earrings. The woman's name was Joan Quaylen."

She wasn't so sure anyone staying at the hotel would appreciate the disbursement of personal information to a shop owner. For that matter, they probably wouldn't approve of the clerk giving her the information on who bought what.

Thank goodness for boredom. Some people will say anything to anybody just to talk.

"Oh, that's right, I remember now, too, Joan Quaylen. Thanks."

Anne left and mulled over what the clerk had said. But would the woman still be frothing the next morning? *She might if she'd spoken with Grayson this morning again and he told her to kiss off.*

Her thoughts were cut short when her phone rang. Seeing Gil's ID, she answered eagerly.

"Gil? How's Susan? Did you arrest her?"

"According to the officer who talked with her at the hotel, she was on the phone immediately to her lawyer and her husband. Neither has arrived here at the station as of yet, so we haven't had a chance to ask her anything."

"Well, I think you need to talk to Joan Quaylen again, too." She relayed the information given to her by both Iona and the boutique clerk. She also mentioned Iona's comments on Grayson and Carmella.

"Anne, you have a woman who was angry, but that's all. Nobody saw her with Grayson this morning and nobody can place her on the sixth floor at any time. I saw the tape. She wasn't on it. As for that editor, there's nothing to suggest she was anywhere close to either of them."

"She could have used the stairs."

"Honey, I know you're trying to help, but there's nothing more you can do. Besides I talked with Ms. Quaylen earlier about why she was on the mezzanine two hours after the last workshop ended."

"And what did she have to say?"

"Ms. Quaylen claims to have gone out to the pool deck, had a couple of drinks, and chatted with some people. When she got up to go to her room realized she'd left her bag of stuff you guys hand out…"

"A goodie bag," Anne offered.

"A goodie bag—she realized she'd left it in the last meeting room she was in up on the mezzanine. She walked up the stairs, found it, sat down to plan the next day's activities, decided to stop in the ladies' room, and the rest is history as they say. Naturally, the woman can't pinpoint the time exactly."

"Naturally."

"And the only person she saw running from the restroom was you," Gil said.

Anne heaved a sigh. "*Naturally*. What about Fran?"

"I also asked her about the time discrepancy."

"And?"

"Ms. Harrison said she wanted a few minutes of peace and quiet, so she slipped upstairs to one of the mezzanine rooms, made a few private phone calls, and just relaxed."

"Yet never saw Susan, and believe me if Fran had seen her, she'd have told you."

"Which means Ms. Lynch was not in the alcove when Ms. Harrison passed at four-fifty."

"Ten minutes after the tapes show Susan getting on the elevator, which means Susan could have been in the restroom like she said. Maybe she was still there when Carmella entered. *Maybe* the argument resumed."

"It's logical with the exception of the knife," Gil said. "The knife makes it premeditated, and so far,

Susan Lynch's actions seemed spur of the moment. And before you say anything, we have no knowledge of a steak knife missing from a room where a lunch had taken place."

"So why have you got her at the station?"

"Because she was present at the scene of both crimes at approximately the time the murders were committed—once by her own admission, and again via the maid's observations. And by the way, the maid positively identified Susan Lynch as the woman knocking on Grayson's door and later emerging from the stairwell."

"But you just said her actions were spur of the moment," Anne protested.

"I said they *seemed* spur of the moment."

"Then why would she have a knife?"

"For all I know, she collects steak knives from hotel restaurants," Gil answered in a testy tone.

"Okay, okay, I'm sorry to be so…so…"

"At the moment, aggravating?"

"Gil!"

"I'm sorry, too. I know you're trying to help, but like I said, I'm not sure you can do any more."

Anne swallowed and took a deep breath. "You may be right, but a thought crossed my mind a few minutes ago—what if we're dealing with two killers? Suppose Alan Grayson killed Carmella, but a different person had a beef with him that escalated into a fatal argument? I mean, the maid said she was in and out of rooms. Susan could have left, and this other person came while she was running the vacuum or something."

"I've thought of that, too. We're gathering fingerprints along with forensic evidence like possible hairs and fibers from his room."

Of course, they were. She had seen the team herself when she went to the sixth floor.

"I guess it's time for me to hang up my Sherlock Holmes hat and join the real world again," she said with a plaintive sigh.

"Honey, you and your friends have given me some good insight and information. Now, let me run with it."

She could almost hear him smiling. "All right, the ball's in your court."

"Oh, one last thing. I heard back from Jack Summers. He confirms that Carmella Radcliff was let go on Monday. According to him, she was furious and threatened to form her own agency taking her clients— a couple big producers—with her."

"Hmmm. I wonder how that would work out legally."

"Legally? How?"

"I guess it depends on whether the author's contract is with the agent or the agency—or both. An author signs with an agent who works for an agency, and everybody gets a cut from the commission. Sometimes the contract is written for a specific agent. That way if the agent and the agency part ways, the author doesn't have to change agents. With others, it could state the author is signing with the agency. If the agent leaves, the author is handed off to a new agent. Am I making sense?"

"More or less. So if Ms. Radcliff decided to start her own agency, she may or may not retain her clients?"

"I don't know how the Summers Agency works. Might be easier to find employment with a new agency."

"Summers also confirmed he ran into the head of a rival agency in a restaurant on Friday night who claimed Ms. Radcliff had contacted him about joining them. As far as he knew, no offer has been put on the table as of yet."

"Did he say which agency?" Anne asked.

She heard the sound of paper being riffled and assumed Gil was consulting his notebook and flipping through the pages.

"Just a second, ah, here it is—The Peek Agency."

"Alan Grayson worked for them. I wonder if that's what he and Carmella had words about in the bar on Thursday night. Oh, wouldn't that have been an interesting conversation? Still, I can't see The Peek Agency hiring Carmella after filing a complaint with the American Association of Agents just a few days before. Carmella had guts even applying."

"We'll never know what the argument was about, but I sure wish I'd been able to talk to Grayson."

"If you had, the case might have been solved by now and he might still be alive." Anne paused. Gil was right about everything. It was time to move on. To her, moving on meant seeing Gil without a murder investigation muddying the romantic waters. "Are we still on for dinner tonight?"

"I'm not sure. I don't think this will take too long once Ms. Lynch's attorney arrives. Where do you want to go?"

"How about a great little place not far from here?"

"Fine with me. What's its name?"

"Chez Jamieson. I believe we dined there once several months ago," she said in a teasing tone.

217

Gil chuckled. "If I'm not mistaken, the food was delicious, the atmosphere spellbinding, and the company charming and beautiful."

Anne laughed with him. "And not to mention fascinating."

"But of course!"

"How about seven thirty? Any preference on what you'd like to eat?"

"None whatsoever. I leave that up to the chef. Mr. Lynch and the lawyer are here. I've gotta run. I'll talk to you later."

He hung up before she could wish him good luck.

As she walked slowly back to the lobby, Anne remembered the last time she'd cooked dinner for Gil. New York strips, baked potatoes with all the trimmings, and salad with homemade dressing. *Do I duplicate it or try something new?*

She opted for a new approach. *Let him know I'm not a one trick pony in the kitchen.*

Recipes floated in and out of her mind as she flipped through her mental menu list. Shrimp Scampi? She made a mean one, but all that garlic? She had hopes of a little extracurricular activity later in the evening. The last time she'd done this, Gil had left soon after eating.

Beef Wellington? Too tricky for a date night. A Mexican themed dinner? She loved spicy food, but had no clue as to Gil's preferences. *Don't want to cook a kicking hot meal if he doesn't like a lot of spice.* French cuisine? No, too time consuming. Then it hit her.

Stroganoff! Simple and it didn't take forever to make. *Add noodles, asparagus, a fruit salad, along with some hot buttered bread, and dinner is served.*

Relieved, she made a quick list of things to get at the grocery on her way home. The temptation to leave now was strong, but she'd promised to meet Nancy and Jen here in the lobby when the conference finally ended.

A glance at her watch and the lack of traffic in the lobby told her the editor/agent panel discussion had begun. Tired of sitting and with nothing better to do, she made her way into the ballroom.

The tables from breakfast had been left in place. Less than half were occupied. She estimated no more than forty or fifty people were present. Anne spotted Nancy and Jen at a full table near the front. With nothing available near them, she took a seat in the back of the audience with three other women, none of whom she recognized.

Up on the dais, what was usually a dazzling star-studded cast of presenters was but a dim light. She counted only two agents and three editors. The head table, able to seat a dozen, stretched a long way on either side of them, the gleaming white tablecloth resembling a snow bank. With Carmella and Alan Grayson not there, the turnout wasn't what they expected either.

What a shame. I feel sorry for Terry. She worked so hard to make this a success.

Though the crowd was small, the questions came at a rapid clip with the panel each taking a turn answering. Anne checked her watch again—twelve-twenty. At this pace, no one would get out of here before sundown.

Craning her neck, she scanned the room. As moderator, Terry stood at a podium off to the side of the dais. She was also checking her watch every few minutes, probably wondering how to shorten this without pissing off the attendees.

Fran sat on a lone chair against the wall midway between Terry and one of the ballroom doors. She fidgeted, crossing and then uncrossing her legs, patting her hair, and fiddling with something in her lap. She was either bored or just wanting this conference nightmare to be over, too.

One of the women at her table leaned over to ask Anne in a hushed tone, "Is it true Alan Grayson had a heart attack and died?"

Startled by the question, she could only stare for a moment while thinking up an answer.

"I really don't know. Where did you hear that?"

Gil certainly wouldn't want any more information than necessary about this being bandied about. Keeping it quiet, however, was an exercise in futility. The maid, the couple who called it in to the front desk, the guests in the corridor, hotel personnel, and even security could have leaked the news.

"In the restroom during the last break. Someone said a maid found him."

"I heard he fell and hit his head hard enough to kill him," another lady told her. "And he sure as hell ain't here."

The third woman also chimed in. "Well, this is one conference I won't be attending again. One person murdered and another missing, perhaps dead? I'm just hoping I can get out of the lobby with my life."

Anne cringed inwardly. This was exactly what she'd feared would happen. Editors and agents would come to another—that was their job, but would speakers and attendees? Even though she'd chided Fran for her cold comment about attendance on Friday, the woman did have a point. They needed to get out of the conference business. These events just weren't cost efficient.

Meanwhile, the discussion on the dais continued. She wasn't really interested and had a problem keeping her mind focused. It kept slipping back to Gil and Susan.

What's happening? Is Gil being gentle with Susan like he was with Candace? Or is he giving her a hard time with pointed, persistent questions—like he did with me?

Is Susan crying or stubbornly refusing to answer anything? Is her attorney advising her with whispered conversation at every question? Maybe she's confessed?

In spite of all she'd learned in the past forty-eight hours, Anne didn't think Gil had much of anything on which to warrant an arrest. She and the Snoop Group, as Jen had christened them, had done all they could.

Applause and Terry's voice at the microphone brought her back to the ballroom.

"I want to thank you all for your participation today," the conference chair said to the agents and editors. "And now, I'll turn the mike over to our chapter president, Fran Harrison. Fran, you have the con."

Her attempt at humor fell flat. Unsmiling, Fran hurried to the podium.

"First of all, I want to thank all of you for attending this year. I hope you had a good time and learned something along the way. Now, I'd also like to thank our volunteers without whom this conference would not have been possible."

Another apathetic smattering of applause rippled through the room. Anne tuned out the rushed 'thank yous' to individuals filling the air. The editors and agents squirmed in their seats, trapped by politeness into staying and listening.

"And I hope you all have a safe trip home. Goodbye until next year!"

Finally! The slim crowd gave more weak applause and immediately pushed back chairs to leave. Those on the dais did the same. Anne lost sight of Nancy and Jen as people jammed the doorways. Oh well, they'd agreed to meet in the lobby.

Anne rose and gazed up front. At the head table, a few of the panel members were shaking hands with Terry and Fran. Most gathered their belongings in preparation for a long overdue exit. It was nearly one o'clock. As far as she knew, no one had been informed of Alan Grayson's death.

She was about to leave when something caught her eye. Shock left her rooted to the floor and her breaths came in short bursts.

Oh my God! Why didn't I see this before? I should have—a dozen times over!

Gil had the wrong person at the station. Carmella's killer was standing in front of her!

Chapter Thirteen

Oh, dear Lord! It's so obvious!

Anne stared at the head table with a growing sense of panic. Even now, the conversations were breaking up. Terry moved on to speak with someone else while Fran shook hands with Howard Wright and Jackie Simmons.

The long tablecloth hid the lower portion of their bodies. Howard's briefcase sat on the table. Jackie's large tote bag was slung over her right shoulder. Both laughed at something, then turned to pick up the rest of their belongings. Jackie stuffed a folder and a lightweight cardigan into the tote, checked her watch, and hurried away.

Another vision slapped Anne in the face keeping her frozen in place. *How many times did I see those images on the surveillance tapes? Jackie's bag looks identical to the one of the mystery tourist!*

She'd been so focused on the long beach cover-up worn by the tourist she'd ignored the tote bag. And at a conference, everyone had a tote bag. *But* Jackie's was distinctive—a wide chevron design. The bag had been hanging over the tourist's right shoulder in the tapes, but the camera angle had been from the left. Only a small portion of the bag had been visible, but now gazing at it full on jogged Anne's memory. And as the agent had turned, the words, 'Cancun, Mexico,' were written on the side. The bartender had stated the woman in the bar arguing with Carmella had a bag with writing on it, making him think about the conference.

The times I'd seen and spoken with Jackie had been face-to-face, but now I'm seeing her from a distance like with the surveillance tapes. The tablecloth reminds me of the cover-up.

Then a tiny piece of a conversation popped into her head. At the time, the significance of it had gone unnoticed. Now, it slammed into her brain like a runaway locomotive.

"Imagine walking into the restroom, flipping on the lights, and finding her. What made you open the stall door?"

Her heart raced and her palms grew damp. *My God, Jackie? I didn't tell anyone other than Gil, Nancy, Jen, and Rose about turning on the lights or about finding Carmella in a stall.*

She fumbled in her carryall for her phone and called Gil.

"Anne, honey, I can't talk right now. Susan and her attorney are in conference. Questioning can resume at any minute."

"Gil, you've got the wrong person."

"What do you mean?"

She explained about Jackie's tote and how the skirting on the table had resembled a long garment. "Meet me at the hotel front desk ASAP. I think Jackie Simmons killed Carmella—maybe Alan, too. Hurry! She's about to leave!"

"I'll call for a squad car immediately. And you get out of the way. Don't go near her."

He hung up. As Anne watched helplessly, Jackie

left the dais and headed for the door. *She's probably on the way up to her room for her luggage, and then to check-out. No wait a minute, she told me earlier she'd already done that. All she needs to do is grab her suitcase from the secure room. Maybe I can delay her a few minutes. I'll just talk and thank her for coming, yadda, yadda. No harm in that.*

Ignoring Gil's warning and not thinking about the possible danger, she rose and hurried after Jackie, catching up to the agent in the hallway outside. Several people milled about, but most headed for the lobby. What could go wrong? Safety in numbers, right?

"Jackie, wait up!" She couldn't help but stare at the orange and blue beach bag.

"Hi, Anne. I'd love to chat, but I have to leave for the airport." She brushed a lock of hair over her shoulder with a nervous gesture.

"This'll just take a moment. I want to thank you for all you've done this weekend. I mean, taking over some of Carmella's appointments must have kept you so busy. You probably didn't have time to breathe. I'm sorry you didn't get a chance to go to the beach...and you have such a lovely beach bag." Anne wondered if Jackie caught the irony of the words.

"Thanks." The agent fingered the one of the large chevron stripes. "Bought it when I went to Mexico last year. Happy to help out with the appointments, and I guess I'll go to the beach another time. Now, if you'll excuse me..." she turned to leave.

"The police made an arrest a while ago," Anne blurted hoping the lie would buy some time.

"Oh really, that's good. I'm sorry, but my time is so short."

The woman moved away with a quick step. Anne followed.

"Aren't you even interested in who they arrested?"

"No. Carmella was a bitch. No one will miss her, and Alan was a..." She stopped and slowly turned, her eyes narrowed in on Anne.

"Alan?" she repeated in a soft tone.

Before Anne could react, Jackie grasped her arm with one hand while reaching into her tote bag with the other. She withdrew a knife and drawing Anne close, pressed it against her side.

"Let's talk about this in a quiet spot."

With the knife firmly in place, she shoved her toward a small room off the hallway. Anne struggled and cast frantic glances around her, but most of the people had already left and those who remained talked amongst themselves. They paid no attention to her. With her heart pounding at an alarming rate, she opened her mouth to scream.

Jackie pressed the knife harder against Anne's ribs. "Don't even think about it. I swear I'll jam this thing in up to the hilt if you even try to scream."

Anne wasn't even sure she could emit so much as a croak. Her throat was desert dry. It was too late, anyway. Her abductor pushed her into the room and slammed the door.

"Another knife?" Anne asked in a shaky voice.

"It's a letter opener. I bought it in the souvenir shop last Thursday evening with the sole purpose of sticking it into Carmella Radcliff at the first available opportunity. Changed my mind when I saw the steak knife on the room service tray outside Grayson's room. Besides, the clerk in the shop would have remembered me buying the damned thing. How did you know? I mean, that is why you stopped me, isn't it?"

So Carmella's death was premeditated. They were right on that assumption.

"I...I don't know what you're talking about? I just wanted to thank you..."

Jackie shoved her further into the room. "Don't give me that crap. I heard from a couple of people how you and your friends were helping the cops."

Anne swallowed hard. She had to keep Jackie talking until Gil arrived.

"All right. I saw the surveillance tapes of a woman in beach attire in both the main and mezzanine elevator lobbies just after Carmella was there. I didn't connect the beach bag she carried with your tote until just a moment ago. Plus, you mentioned something about me flipping on the lights and looking in the stall. At that time, no one knew the lights had been off or that I'd found her in a stall. And of course, Alan Grayson's death hasn't been officially released yet. The fact that your room was just a few doors down from his is another sign. Why, Jackie?"

The knife still pressed against Anne's side. She had to put distance between herself and the deadly blade fast. A row of chairs lined the wall. Her knees threatened to give way. Before Jackie could respond Anne collapsed in one, her carryall clutched to her chest. The agent stood over her less than a foot away, the knife poised to strike just inches from her throat.

"The bitch. I was having dinner Thursday night when Carmella came into the restaurant. I could tell she'd had a few belts. Her gait was wobbly. She stopped by my table, gave me a smug smile, then proceeded to tell me she had resigned from The Summers Agency and had just been hired by my agency."

Was that true? Had Carmella been hired by Elizabeth Coyne? If so, then Carmella and Elizabeth were the only ones to know.

"I was stunned. Coyne and Company was overstaffed as it was. When I mentioned this to her, she laughed and said she hoped I found a job real soon, but not to worry, she'd take good care of my clients.

"When she left, I called my boss. She refused to confirm anything—merely said we'd talk when I got back on Monday. She tried to make it sound like everything was all right, but I could tell from the tone of her voice it wasn't."

"But…but murder?" Anne's said in a squeaky tone.

"We'd clashed and had words at a conference last summer. She deliberately went after an author I'd been schmoozing for weeks. Stole her right out from under my nose. This was just another brick on the load of hate I felt for Carmella. I was furious. No way would I allow that corpulent little rat take my job."

"So, you decided to kill Carmella."

"After I left the dining room, I saw the opener in the window of the souvenir shop and bought it. I waited in the lobby until I saw Carmella come out of the restaurant and go into the bar. Alan Grayson followed a few minutes later, and then left. I could tell he was angry. I poked my head in the doorway, but there were too many people about. I sat in the lobby for a while until the crowd thinned."

"Then you went in to confront Carmella."

Did anyone see Jackie forcing me into the room?

Have the police arrived? Is Gil here yet? As if on cue, her phone rang.

"Don't answer!" Jackie ordered waving the knife under Anne's nose.

"I won't. What did you say to Carmella?"

Jackie is going to kill me. She has to. I know too much. And this room is the perfect place to do it. It'll be hours before someone thinks to check in here for me.

The longer the woman talked, the quicker Gil and the cops would find them before it was too late.

"Told her I worked too hard to become a full-fledged agent to let her take it away from me. She called me a few names and said she could bring ten times the clients into the Coyne and Company than I ever would. We got loud and the bartender told us to shut up. I told Carmella I'd get even."

"So you returned to your room, saw the steak knife on the tray, and grabbed it."

Jackie nodded and smirked. "You sure are curious. Oh, well, what does it matter? You'll soon be dead and I'll be out of here. I guess it doesn't make any difference if I brag a little. I think I did a damned good job of dispatching my rival, and that asshole Grayson."

Anne swallowed again and shivered at the calm attitude her captor conveyed. Jackie's smile chilled her blood.

"Did you know where and when you'd kill her?"

"I thought about it all night. Finally decided to watch and wait. Sooner or later, I'd get her alone."

"And you had time to stalk Carmella on Friday since she had more appointments than you."

"That's right. I was in the bookstore and saw the fight between Carmella and some woman, so I hurried up to my room, slipped on my beach cover-up along with my hat and a pair of sunglasses, took the stairs all the way down to the lobby and waited just out of sight around the corner from the restrooms. I knew Carmella would appear. When she did, I'd follow her until it was just the two of us. She ended up heading for the john. The line was long and she said something about not waiting. I tailed her to the elevators and watched to see where it stopped. Her room was on the fourth floor. All the better. Knock on the door, shove her inside, and get it over with."

Keep her talking. She might get careless.

"I take it she never saw you."

"Never gave me so much as a glance."

"You got lucky. Suppose she had recognized you?"

Jackie's eyes had glazed over. She didn't answer, but continued her tale. "The elevator stopped at the mezzanine. I called for another car. I found the restroom and went in to check. Carmella was just coming out of the end stall. I pulled the knife out of my bag. She squeaked and tried to retreat into the can. I was faster. Knew just where to stick the knife where it would do the most good. I sank that sucker in as far as I could, wiped my prints off with the edge of the cover up, then washed my hands, turned out the lights, and left."

"By way of the stairs."

"Had to. I had blood on me. Figured I wouldn't see anyone that way. Went straight to my room, got out of it, and shoved it into one of those plastic laundry bags the hotel provides. I figured to dump it in a trash can at the airport."

"And Alan?"

"Apparently, Alan opened his door at the same time I opened mine. Just my lousy luck. Maybe even noticed the blood. I never saw or heard him."

Of course she never saw or heard him. She'd just committed murder. Her nerves had to have been jangled. But not half as jangled as mine right now.

Anne was terrified, yet had to remain calm. She refused to give Jackie a reason to stop talking.

"Did he know it was your room?"

"I'm not sure. After lunch on Saturday, I sat out by the pool."

"I remember—to escape that annoying woman."

Where the hell is Gil? That had to have been him on the phone or at least, Nancy or Jen. I was supposed to have met them in the lobby by now.

"He came out for a smoke and saw me. I'd put my bag on the table. This morning he pulled me aside just before breakfast. He told me he recognized it from the hallway the day before. Also said he figured out the stains he'd seen were blood and put two and two together. Said not to worry, my secret was safe with him and why didn't I drop by his room when I was done eating—we could have a drink and celebrate. I didn't believe him. I suspected he had something up his sleeve—like blackmail."

Had he? They'd never know now. Alan Grayson had been an idiot to say anything to Jackie. But not half the idiot Anne had been for ignoring Gil's orders not to get near this maniacal bitch.

Oh, Gil, I don't want to die. Please hurry.

"I followed him to the elevators and saw him get on. I ran up the stairs to my room. I waited a couple of minutes before knocking on his door. He let me in, joking about how glad he was that Carmella was dead. I closed the door behind me and as soon as his back was turned, took off my stiletto and whacked him on the side of the head. He never saw it coming, staggered, and fell. I kept hitting him. Over and over. When the heel broke off, I used the other one. Finally, he lay still. I was pretty sure if he wasn't already dead, he soon would be. Just like Carmella. I returned to my room, changed out of the bloody clothes, showered, and went back downstairs."

A stiletto! Those four-plus-inch heels could be deadly. Who on earth would suspect a shoe as the murder weapon? All she had to do was stick the shoes in the laundry bag along with the clothes, shower, wash her hair, and leave.

Jackie had said all of this in a calm voice, but her eyes blazed with fury and her nostrils flared. A muscle twitched in her cheek.

Terror clawed deep in Anne's gut, but she didn't stop talking. *Keep talking!*

"So when Susan Lynch appeared shortly after seven, he was expecting you and probably told her to hit the road. When she showed up again to pester him at eight o'clock, nobody answered since Alan was dead, but she was there long enough for a maid to see her in the hallway," Anne murmured.

"Who? Doesn't matter. I was all alone both coming and going. That's about it. No way was I going to allow anybody to shaft me out of the best job I'd ever had, especially that bitch Carmella Radcliff. Travel, excitement, making contacts with other agents and editors—it was a dream job. Worked my way up from Elizabeth Coyne's secretary to reader to agent. Now, you know everything. Felt good to confess, even if it is to someone I have to kill," Jackie said in a soft voice.

Anne's heart pounded and her breath threatened to choke her. She couldn't stop the tremors from shaking her from head to foot.

"Just turn yourself in, Jackie. I called the police. They'll be here any second. In fact, that was probably them on the phone calling to let me know they've arrived." Her voice sounded thin and reedy. She swallowed in an attempt to dislodge the lump in her throat.

Jackie laughed without mirth. "No you didn't or you wouldn't have talked to me in the first place. I heard you were a notorious busybody. Always poking into stuff that doesn't concern you. Like with that author last year."

"Take my word for it, I called. Think about what you're about to do. You won't get away with it. Not a third time."

Do something! Anything! Don't just let her control whether you live or die.

"Sure I will. As long as I can make it to the airport, I'm home free. Guess I'll have to unload this little implement of destruction there, too. Sorry, honey." She raised the letter opener. Her arm descended.

Fight or flight? Anne did both, reacting faster than she thought possible. She screamed, grasped her tote bag, and shoved it upward to meet the thrusting blade. It hit something hard inside the bag—probably a book. Jackie staggered back a few feet—just enough for Anne to shriek again and stumble to her feet, ready to make a break for the door. The bag with the knife still stuck in it, fell from her hands.

"You bitch!" Jackie pulled the opener free and rushed at her, poised for another slash.

The door burst open and slammed against the wall with a loud bang. Gil and two uniformed officers entered with guns drawn, ready to shoot. Nancy and Jen stood just outside the entryway.

"Drop the knife!" Gil ordered, his gun trained on Jackie. "Now!"

Jackie hesitated, and then complied with a sob. The letter opener bounced a couple of times on the carpet.

"Hands in the air where we can see them."

Jackie raised her arms.

"Now, on your knees."

Jackie obeyed.

"Down on the ground, on your stomach, and put your hands behind your head."

Jackie did so.

"Cuff her," Gil demanded.

One of the officers holstered his gun and moved in.

With her hands cuffed in zip ties behind her, the agent's sobs intensified. "Oh God, I'm so sorry. I didn't know what else to do. She was such a bitch and deserved to die. I didn't mean it, really I didn't. I just couldn't help it. You understand, don't you, Anne? You know I had no choice."

Jackie's words suggested she was sorry, but Anne didn't buy it. She didn't answer. There was nothing to say. *Of course, she meant to kill Carmella, just like she planned out killing Alan.*

Her attacker's eyes were wide, staring, and terror filled. But whether at the realization of what she'd done and was about to do again or at the fact she'd been caught, Anne didn't know.

The uniformed policemen bagged the letter opener and hauled the sobbing agent to her feet, frisked her, and then removed her from the room.

Gil turned to Anne, folding her into his arms. The tremors, miraculously gone at the moment of imminent death, now returned. She shook like a sapling in a storm.

"I thought I told you to stay away from her!" His voice was a cross between angry and exasperated with a hint of relief thrown in.

"But she was leaving and in a hurry. I just thought maybe I could delay her in conversation until you or the squad car arrived." She buried her head in his shoulder to stifle a fear-laced sob.

With Jackie gone, Nancy and Jen rushed in.

"Oh my God, are you all right?" Jen said with a gasp.

"Geez, Anne, you gotta quit doing stuff like this," Nancy added in a shaken tone.

"How...how did you find us?" Anne asked pulling back and looking into Gil's worried eyes.

"The officers got here and asked where to find Ms. Simmons' room. They were told she'd checked out. Not sure if there had been some mix-up, they called me as I rolled into the parking lot. I came in and ran into Nancy and Jen in the lobby. They said you were ten minutes late."

"And that's late for you," Nancy replied. "Very out of character."

"I called. When you didn't answer, I almost had a heart attack. You told me in *your* call that you were in the ballroom with Jackie, so we went there." He cast a glance at Nancy and Jen. "I told you to wait by the ballroom."

"I know. We followed anyway," Jen explained.

Gil shook his head. "I asked around until finally finding a woman who said she'd seen you and Ms. Simmons in the hallway earlier. Another woman said she'd seen the two of you going into one of the rooms, but didn't know which. I'll bet I opened every door until I heard you scream."

"She had a lot of guts literally kidnapping you in the hallway outside the ballroom," Nancy said.

"What I can't believe is nobody noticed you weren't going quietly. You didn't just do as she said, did you?" Jen asked.

"I tried to get away, but Jackie was beyond reason. And then there was that letter opener. She had it pressed just beneath my ribs. Plus, I was scared to death. Don't think I could have screamed then if I'd tired," Anne answered. "I doubt if she really thought logically at all. She just knew she was in danger of getting caught." She looked up at Gil. "Can I go home? I'm exhausted."

He smiled. "Station first for your statement—make that statements—Alan Grayson, remember? Did she tell you how and why she killed Ms. Radcliff?"

"In spades. She also killed Alan Grayson. If you search her luggage, you'll find a bloody beach cover up along with other blood-stained clothes in a plastic bag and a pair of stiletto high heels, one broken, with blood on them."

"A stiletto?" Gil asked with raised eyebrows.

"Alan Grayson's murder weapon."

"Wow. Those tiny heels can really pack a punch," Jen informed him.

Gil shifted his arm to around Anne's waist and steered them all toward the door. "Come on, let's get out of here."

Anne was only too glad to leave. This was the last damned conference she'd attend for a while.

And I certainly won't go to the ladies room alone!
****

Anne hated giving statements. They were a total drudgery of remembering facts and of what was said to whom and when. And now she had to give two of them. Nancy and Jen had driven to the police station separately for moral support if needed, while she'd ridden in with Gil.

"How long will this take?" she asked.

"Not long. I promise."

"Are we still on for a home cooked meal?"

He sighed. "I'm not sure. It depends on how quickly Ms. Simmons gets a lawyer and how long it takes them to consult. There are a lot of questions we need to ask and a ton of paperwork. Maybe we shouldn't count on tonight. But I could take a rain check for tomorrow night."

"Probably just as well. I'm not sure I can boil water right now anyway."

At the station, she'd been escorted into an interrogation room where she'd told everything that had happened. The whole process lasted close to three hours. By the time she was done, Anne felt like she'd given birth.

Both physically and emotionally exhausted, she walked into the station lobby where Nancy and Jen waited.

"Thanks for coming. I can't believe you waited all

this time."

"We thought you might appreciate it," Nancy said.

"Just in case you needed a shoulder to lean on," Jen added. "And something to eat. Never did get around to lunch."

Anne glanced at her watch. "It's only a little after four o'clock. Too early for dinner."

"Tell you what," Nancy suggested. "You have to go back to the hotel to get your car. I'll drive you there while Jen goes to a liquor store for some wine. Then we'll meet at your house, order in pizza, and dissect this conference of horrors."

"Now *that* sounds like a plan," Jen replied with enthusiasm.

"Well, I can't say that I'll be attending any conferences in the near future," Nancy said echoing Anne's thoughts of a while ago as they drove back to the hotel.

"Me neither," Anne replied. "And I'll wager the San Sebastian Inn won't be hosting a Southeast Florida chapter affair again any time soon."

"I think that's a pretty safe bet. I still can't believe Jackie Simmons killed both Carmella and Alan, and tried to kill you."

"I know. Looking back on it, the whole thing sounds like something one of us would write about."

Nancy shook her head. "Not me. Starting tomorrow, I'm working like a fiend to make my deadline at the end of the week."

"All I know is I'm going to relax tonight and all day tomorrow. The kids are spending their spring break with Ken in Orlando, so I have a whole week to try and fix that rejected manuscript. No interruptions."

Nancy chuckled. "Not even Gil?"

"Okay, maybe just a little interruption," Anne amended thinking about dinner tomorrow night, and then paused for a moment. "I wonder how Susan is doing."

"Probably still pouting that we dumped her, and trying to figure out a way to make us seem like the bad guys."

"No, no, I mean about her ordeal with the police today. It must have been scary in that interrogation room waiting for her attorney. I can relate."

"She was a suspect—and a suspect with a shaky, uncorroborated alibi. Knowing Susan, she'll probably turn it into a badly written story."

Nancy dropped Anne off in the now almost empty parking lot at the hotel.

"See you at your place," she said as she drove away.

Anne slid behind the steering wheel and took a deep breath as she thought about the day's events. Should she have done anything differently? Jackie was leaving for the airport. Gil and the police were on their way to the hotel. She had to delay Jackie, didn't she? Oh, well, what did it matter? It was over.

Her phone rang as she inserted the key into the ignition. Called ID showed it was Terry Whiting.

"Hi, Terry. I take it the conference is over. How did you hold up?"

"Yeah, this loser is finally done and I'm fine. I called Detective Collins for an update a few minutes ago. He told me about Alan Grayson and how he's arrested Jackie Simmons for the murders. I just can't believe it! And to think I was furious with the man for not showing up at the panel discussion. Imagine! Furious with a dead man. I feel awful."

"You didn't know he was dead, Terry." She told Terry what had happened between her and Jackie.

"Are you serious? Are you all right?"

"I'm fine. Just a little shaken. What else did Gil tell you?"

"Not much. I mean, why did Jackie kill two people?"

Anne told her about Carmella's subterfuge and how things played out as best she could.

"So the chapter is stuck with Carmella's fraudulent expenses and the rep of being a killer conference. Wonderful."

Anne winced at the bad, but appropriate pun. "Does Fran know any of this yet?"

"I don't know and I don't care. Fran Harrison is a royal pain in the ass. After Carmella died, she kept asking over and over if I had any profit or loss numbers yet. I kept telling her I wouldn't have them until I talked to our treasurer and had received the final bill from the hotel."

"I take it we lost money," Anne said with a sigh.

"Given Carmella's duplicity, I'd have to say we're in the red by a good three thousand dollars, maybe more. If we'd known Carmella had been fired, we might have saved a few bucks. There certainly wouldn't have been time to get a replacement." A moment of silence followed. "Anne, I want to thank you for all the support you've given to this conference and to the chapter over the years. I don't care what Fran says, you *are* a valuable member. I think you should run for chapter president. With your organizational skills, you'd be terrific. Please, give it some consideration. And now, I've got to go. My husband is taking me out to dinner at the fanciest restaurant in town as a reward for all the time I put in on this thing. It's been almost a year's worth of work. Have a good one and I'll see you at the next meeting."

Anne hung up. Run for chapter president? Most likely against Fran? That could get interesting.

She mulled over Terry's information about the profit and loss numbers and the hurried consultation.

I'll bet Fran found out that Carmella was here under false pretenses. She could have contacted the Summers Agency to complain about Carmella's drunkenness on Thursday night, her subsequent abrasiveness at the critique panel discussion, and been apprised of the situation. Maybe that's what the argument I saw on the surveillance tape was all about—Fran confronting the agent.

"She was probably furious, went upstairs to cool off, made a few phone calls to try and verify the information," Anne muttered out loud.

Anne fastened her seat belt, started the car, and headed out of the parking lot. Who cared what Fran knew or when? The killer had been caught. That's what counted. She refused to dwell on it. She'd have pizza and wine with her friends, get a good night's sleep, and plan for tomorrow.

Now that everything was over, she could concentrate on the important things again—like her relationship with Gil.

Chapter Fourteen

Anne pulled into her driveway to find Nancy pacing along the front porch with her cell phone clapped against her ear and Jen sitting on the top step with a large wine tote next to her. She blinked sudden tears from her eyes. *It's good to have friends.* What would she do without these women? Strange how the murder of Isadora Powell last year had brought them all closer.

Nancy—steady, no nonsense, and giving her opinion with clarity straight from the hip.

Jen was the antithesis of Nancy. Always chattering, she could sometimes get on a person's nerves, but her heart was pure gold.

And then there was Rose. A hectic home life left little time for much else, yet she managed to write—and write well.

Smiling to herself, she exited the car. As she approached the house, Nancy hung up.

"I just ordered two large pizzas—one pepperoni and mushroom, the other sausage and black olives—both with extra cheese. Is that okay? Delivery should be in about twenty minutes."

"It's fine with me," she replied.

"Hope that twenty minutes goes fast. I'm starving. I can probably put away three or four slices," Jen said. She rose and held the bag out. "Here, I got two bottles of red, one for us and one for you to drink later. After the day you've had, you need it."

Anne couldn't argue with her friend on that point. She unlocked the front door and they trooped into the living room. She dumped her carryall on the coffee table, retreated to the kitchen where she opened one of the wine bottles, grabbed some glasses, and then flopped into her favorite corner of the sofa. Nancy had settled into the other. Jen selected an easy chair.

"Boy, am I ever glad this day is over," Anne said with a groan.

"Boy, am I ever glad this *conference* is over," Nancy echoed.

"Amen," Jen answered.

Anne reached into her bag and withdrew her phone. "I think I'll bring Rose up to date and see if she'd like to join us."

Their missing critique partner answered on the second ring.

"Rose, it's Anne. Just wanted to let know what's happened." She gave Rose a shortened version of the events.

"You're kidding!" she replied in a shocked tone. "I know this business can be back-stabbing, but I never took the phrase literally—even though Carmella wasn't stabbed in the back. And a *stiletto*? That's just plain out and out bizarre. Are you all right?"

"I'm fine. A little shaken, but that's wearing off. And yes, the shoe thing was weird, but at the same time brilliant. Alan Grayson never saw it coming. Who would? Men don't pay any attention to shoes, much less think of them as weapons. Nancy, Jen, and I are at my place. We have lots of wine and pizzas are on the way.

Would you like to join us?"

"I'd love to, but already have dinner in the oven. For once Jack is watching a TV show—cartoons to boot—with the kids. I don't want to rock the boat. Critique meeting on Thursday?"

"As far as I know. Just a minute," she paused and asked the others, "Critique on Thursday?"

Nancy nodded as Jen replied, "Fine. It's my turn to host."

"That's a go at Jen's," she told Rose. "The usual time. See you there."

Anne hung up. Thank God for routine. Before she could say anything, the doorbell rang.

"Must be the pizza," Nancy said.

"Wow, this has to be the fastest delivery in history," Jen replied.

Anne hurried to the door expecting to see the Top Notch Pizza delivery guy. Instead, she opened up to Susan.

"Uh, Susan, hi, come on in," she said, startled at the woman's presence. *What on earth is she doing here?*

Susan entered. "I saw Nancy and Jen's cars outside. Am I interrupting?"

"No, not at all. We're just holding a little post-conference chat."

She led her new guest into the living room. Susan took a chair and stared at them.

Jen finally broke the awkward silence. "I suppose you know that Jackie Simmons killed Carmella and Alan Grayson."

"I know. That nasty Detective Collins told me."

Anne's defensive nature rose, but she bit her lip

and refrained from answering.

"Do you also know Anne put herself in danger by trying to stop Jackie from leaving the hotel?" Nancy asked.

"Oh really?" She didn't sound all that interested.

"Yes, really," Nancy replied, and then told Susan about Anne's ordeal.

"Glad it all turned out all right," Susan said with a shrug as though unconcerned or non-believing.

It's not about her, so she doesn't care. Anne ignored the tiny dart of guilt jabbing at her. She also tried to give her former critique partner the benefit of the doubt, but it was hard.

Another awkward silence ensued before Jen commented, "I guess the past few hours have been rough on you. How are you holding up?"

"As good as can be expected when my so-called friends think I killed two people and turned me in," Susan said in a sharp, accusatory tone.

Nancy straightened. "We did not turn you in! Your shaky alibi and lack of transparency concerning your whereabouts did that."

"You thought I did it, and told that detective so."

"On the contrary, Susan," Anne answered exasperated with the woman. "We told Gil we *didn't* believe you had harmed anyone."

"Over and over and over," Nancy murmured in a tired tone.

"Yeah, but he suspected me all the same. True friends wouldn't have let him take me out of a room crowded with my colleagues and be hustled down to the police station like a common criminal."

"Well, I'm damned sorry about that, but exactly

how were we supposed to stop him? It was a police decision. We did the best we could to defend you at every turn, but somehow I don't think you'd believe that regardless of how often we told you," Jen snapped in an unusually angry voice. "So why are you here? To pick a fight?"

"I'm here to let you know I forgive you for dumping me from the group."

Anne, Nancy, and Jen all gazed at each other as though to say, 'is she kidding?'

She forgives us? This woman has real problems.

"Okay, fine, Susan," Anne said.

Susan patted her hair. "You'll regret it, of course. I think you'll discover my opinions carried a lot of weight, and my talent is undeniable."

Anne sucked in a deep breath. *Oh, brother. She forgives us yet manages to insult us at the same time.*

Stunned disbelief showed on Nancy and Jen's faces. She jumped in before they could say anything.

"These things happen," Anne told her in a calm tone—one she was far from feeling. "But that's no reason why we can't all still be friends. Look, we ordered some pizza. You're welcome to join us if you want."

Susan sniffed and rose. "Is that a sincere invitation?"

Anne ground her teeth and lied. "Of course."

"No, it isn't. I can see it in all your faces. And for your information, I have already contacted several chapter members about forming a new critique group. Better writers than the bunch of you who aren't jealous or afraid of my talent! I know what I'm doing as much as you people." She did an about face and stomped toward the foyer. Pausing on the threshold, she turned to glare at them. "I will bury you with how good I am, and the reviews will be five-star!"

Anne rose and followed. "Susan…"

Susan whirled and walked to the front door. Jerking it open, she called out, "Your fucking pizza is here!"

With that parting shot, their former critique partner stalked past the bemused, waiting delivery man.

Nancy came up behind her. "Wow, I have no clue what that was all about, but am I ever glad she's out of our lives. She's delusional or maybe just plain nuts." She paid for the pizza while Anne returned to the living room.

Jen emerged from the kitchen with paper plates and a stack of napkins. "Whew, that was nasty. I just hope I never have to deal with her again on a personal level. In a way, I feel sorry for Susan. I wonder how long it'll take for her to realize she's just not any good at this."

"Probably never. She'll go on and on blaming others for her failures," Anne replied.

Ten minutes later, they were all on their second slice of pizza and refilling the wine glasses.

"I had a call from Terry Whiting earlier," Anne mumbled through a mouthful of pepperoni and mushrooms. "She suggested I run for chapter president against Fran in September. What do you guys think?"

"I think that's a super idea!" Jen replied before taking a huge bite of sausage and black olives.

Nancy broke off a stringing morsel of mozzarella and popped it into her mouth, then said, "I'll be your campaign manager. With your organizational skills and logical mind, you'll do a terrific job."

"And you won't alienate half the members like Fran does," Jen added.

Anne shrugged. "It'll be a lot of work, but I'll give it some thought. She also said something odd." She told the rest about Fran asking repeatedly for profit and loss information.

"Before the conference was even over?" Jen asked.

"She must have been damned nervous about something," Nancy added.

"I wonder if she maybe called Jack Summers to complain about Carmella and he told her the truth—that she'd been fired," Anne said. "It would sure explain the argument I saw on the tapes."

"I think you may be right, but there is no way in hell Fran would ever admit it," Nancy commented before taking a sip of wine.

Anne reached for her phone. "Just a minute, I need to talk to Terry about something that's been bugging me for a couple of days."

She dialed. Terry answered on the third ring.

"This had better be important, girl. I'm about to leave for a date with a lot of martinis and some great food for a change."

"I understand, and this will only take a moment. Terry, when you got the phone call about Carmella being dead, you said you and Fran were going over attendance totals. I take it that included some quick math on profit and loss."

"Without a doubt. Fran was using the calculator on her phone like nobody's business."

"But why were you doing it then on the first day of the conference?"

"Fran called me around five-thirty, quarter to six.

Said she wanted to keep abreast of the financial aspects or some such shit. Typical Fran. Wanting to know everything, but didn't want to do any of the work. Why?"

"Oh, no real reason." So Fran initiated the meeting after her altercation with Carmella. "Thanks, Terry. Have a martini for me. If anyone deserves to get tight it's you."

Anne hung up and relayed Terry's reply.

"Just like I thought," Nancy said. "Fran knew something."

"Anne, you simply have to run for chapter President. Fran isn't doing us any favors with her dictatorial ways and attitude," Jen declared biting into another slice of pizza.

An hour and a half later, she waved goodbye to her friends. They'd dissected the events of the last few days and their former critique partner, but had little to say about the conference itself.

Which just goes to show it couldn't have been all that great.

It was only a little after eight, so she decided to call her kids in Orlando. Yesterday's events had rammed home the importance of family. Lisa answered on the third ring.

"Hi Mom."

"Well, hello yourself. Are you enjoying spring break?"

"Yeah, it's fun. Had a big day today. Dad and Paula took us to Epcot. We did the theme park Friday and Saturday, and tomorrow we're going over to Daytona for a couple of days. Can't wait for the beach."

Anne barely heard most of what her daughter said.

Instead, she concentrated on one name.

"Paula?"

Silence reigned for a moment until Lisa replied. "She's Dad's girlfriend. She's really nice. Ken and I like her. You...are you okay with Dad having a girlfriend?"

Was she? "Sure, honey. Your dad and I are free to see other people now. In fact, I'm making dinner tomorrow night for a man I'd like to see more of, too, so don't worry."

"Oh, I didn't know. Will we get to meet him when we get back?"

"Of course. His name is Gil Collins and he's a detective with the San Sebastian Police Department."

"You're dating a cop?"

"I think you'll like him." She wasn't sure how her daughter was taking the news. Was it okay that her father could have a girlfriend, but her mother not to have a boyfriend? "Well, I was just touching base. Is your brother around?"

"No. Paula's son has his driver's license, so they went to some action-adventure-shoot-'em-up movie at the mall. They invited me, but I said no. I'd rather read."

Anne forced a laugh. "Tell him I said hi. Have a good time in Daytona. I'll see you next Sunday. Love you."

"Love you, too, Mom."

She hung up, not sure what to feel. So her ex-husband had a girlfriend. Why not? She was actively pursuing Gil. Still the reality brought home the fact the marriage was truly over. What rankled was her failure to keep it in the first place. Now with Gil in the picture again, maybe she'd been given a second chance.

Ken and I have both moved on. Her writer's mind imagined the end of one chapter of a book and the beginning of another.

Anne curled up in the corner of the sofa, polished off the last of the wine, and watched an old movie, all the while planning for tomorrow night's dinner.

Dinner with Gil. I hope this is *the beginning of a new chapter in my life—one that lasts a long time.*

****

Anne awoke the next morning energized after one of the best night's sleep she'd had in ages. Maybe it was the wine. Or perhaps the knowledge she'd helped put a killer behind bars—one she didn't know so well this time. Whatever. But she suspected part of her good mood was due to anticipation of tonight's home cooked dinner with Gil.

In the kitchen, she started the coffee, let Bruno out, and then fed him before finally getting fully awake with that first cup of French roast.

She inhaled a deep breath and looked down at Bruno nestled next to her feet. His little shih-tzu eyes sparkled and his fluffy tail wagged.

"Guess it's time to get on with routine, huh, little guy?"

Maybe now she could concentrate on fixing that rejected manuscript and move on with her life.

Gil called as she poured her second cup of coffee.

"Are we still on for tonight?" he asked.

"Absolutely. Is seven-thirty all right with you?"

"Fine."

"Any more news on Jackie?"

"Still a few loose ends to tie up, but not much.

She's scheduled to be arraigned this afternoon. I'll tell you more details when I see you."

She craved details now, but would wait until this evening. After hanging up, she made a long to-do list, and then bent to pet the little shih-tzu.

"Times a'wastin', Bruno. Let's get this show on the road." He barked as though agreeing.

She laughed as she went upstairs to dress for the day.

****

Anne stirred the simmering stroganoff. The aroma had her mouth watering. She set the spoon down and wandered into the dining room where, for the hundredth time in the last hour, she adjusted the silverware for a perfect alignment.

The doorbell rang at precisely seven-thirty. Anne opened to find a smiling Gil cradling a bottle of wine.

"Hi, right on time. Come on in."

"I believe in punctuality," he commented leaning down to kiss her cheek.

"So do I." She accepted the wine when he handed it to her.

"We obviously have a lot in common."

Lord, she hoped so.

"Come on in to the kitchen. I'll get the corkscrew and you can do the honors."

With the wine opened and the glasses filled, Gil sat at the breakfast bar and snacked on the hors d'oeuvres Anne had painstakingly made earlier in the afternoon.

"So, how did the arraignment go?" she asked, sitting next to him as he popped a bacon-wrapped shrimp into his mouth.

"She pleaded guilty. With the evidence we had and

your statement, there was no doubt she did it. Plus, after your hostage incident, we discovered a trail of blood drops on the carpet in the hallway from Grayson's room to hers. The blood was hard to see since the carpet was dark red with a navy blue pattern. We also came up with more blood on the carpet in her room. Must have transferred from her clothes when she changed.

"Her lawyer finally showed up at the station yesterday afternoon, and then huddled with her for another three hours. In the end, she decided to give us a full confession—complete with how she might not have been in her right mind at the moment for either murder, professed extreme remorse, and will throw herself on the mercy of the court for a reduced sentence."

"How much time will she do?"

"Not as much as she deserves. The only thing she's remorseful about is that she got caught."

Anne nibbled on a spinach stuffed mushroom and sipped her wine. "Well, it's over now. Did you ever talk to Elizabeth Coyne?"

He nodded. "She said Carmella contacted her about a job last Wednesday. Ms. Coyne said she was seriously contemplating it."

"I can see it now. Carmella dangled a few hot author names in front of Elizabeth like a carrot before a hungry horse."

"According to Ms. Coyne, Ms. Stewart wasn't living up to expectations as an agent."

Anne shook her head. "What a waste. And to kill over a job, of all things! If Carmella hadn't been loaded that night and taunted Jackie, Jackie wouldn't have known about any of this until she got back to New York. Jackie also probably suspected she was hanging on to her job by a slim thread. No wonder she cracked."

Gil eyed her over the rim of his glass. "Don't tell me you're feeling sorry for the killer again."

She shrugged. "In a way, I am. Jackie tried hard, but didn't quite have the stuff agents are made of, I guess. I can easily see the parallels between Candace and Jackie—nice women, but two people marginally competent at what they did being pushed too far." A timer dinged behind her. "Excuse me. My appliance is telling me it's time to put the noodles on."

"Whatever we're having smells great."

"Beef stroganoff, hot buttered bread, seasoned green beans, and a salad with homemade dressing."

Gil grinned. "Sounds wonderful."

Less than fifteen minutes later, they dug into a delicious, perfectly cooked stroganoff. He further endeared himself to her when he helped clear the table and dried the few dishes that needed to be hand washed.

They returned to the living room where Anne swirled the remains of the wine in her glass while gazing into the deep red liquid. "So, now what?"

He set his glass on the coffee table before turning toward her. "You tell me."

Her glass joined his. Anticipation made her heart beat faster.

He reached out and tugged at one of the curls framing her face.

"Redheads—I was always a sucker for redheads."

"Are your ex-wives redheads, too?"

He grinned and rose, pulling her with him. "Nope, a blonde and a brunette."

"Ah, so I round out the group. Well, they say the third time is the charm."

"I believe they do. And I, for one, couldn't be happier." He smoothed his hand down her face and rested it on her cheek.

Her heart rate increased further as heat gushed from her core to every extremity. She moved closer.

"I'm glad," she whispered.

"So am I."

"Gil…"

"Shhhhh. Don't say anything."

He leaned in and brushed his lips over hers in a gentle caress.

Anne's legs trembled and her knees wobbled. Without thinking, she clutched at his polo shirt bringing him closer. Like fire, the heat within her kindled rapidly. The kiss changed from gentle to hard and demanding. She wound her arms around his neck and kissed him back as hard as she could. He pulled her tighter into his embrace. A delightful hardness pressed against her abdomen. A low moan formed in the back of her throat.

Gil broke contact and rested his forehead against hers.

"Oh, Annie, how I want you," he said in a raspy voice.

"I want you, too." She pulled back slightly to gaze into his eyes. "Do you want to spend the night? Has the trust been restored?"

She knew her words sounded pleading, but didn't care.

He feathered little kisses along her brow and temples before returning her look. His half-lidded eyes oozed desire. Her heart thumped in heavy rhythmic beats. Anticipation of both his answer and the possible outcome made her nerves hum.

"Yes. I trust you."

His hands cupped her face as he once again lowered his mouth to hers.

A whimper, part desire, part relief escaped from between their lips. She broke the kiss and took his hand.

"Then let me lead the way," she whispered tugging him toward the stairs.

In the bedroom, Anne closed the door. Moonlight streaming through the window was all the illumination needed. Like two pieces of a puzzle, they came together.

His fingers found the buttons on her blouse and quickly undid them. The smooth silk slipped from her shoulders and fell to the floor.

Her eager hands pulled his shirt from his slacks. She ran her fingers over his smooth chest all the while pushing the material up. He helped by yanking the fabric over his head.

The rest of their clothes soon hit the carpet, too. Naked, she allowed her gaze to rake up and down his body. Her fingers followed. He was trim and the muscles firm. Not quite six-pack abs, but she didn't care. Anne ripped the bedclothes down. Without words, Gil lowered her to the sheets. He lay next to her, his lips doing wicked things to her neck and collarbone.

His lips continued the exploration of her body, sending her hormones into full overload. How long she had waited for this! Gil, his hands stroking her overheated skin with a light feathery touch, fueled the fire burning within hotter. *Forever, I want this forever.*

Then, she thought no more. She enjoyed.

Later after the heat of passion had flamed out,

Anne finally caught her breath.

"Oh my," she murmured.

"Yeah, oh my." He raised her hand and kissed it. "That was...spectacular."

"Oh yes, without a doubt. Welcome home, Gil."

"Welcome back, Annie." His arm snaked under her shoulders and pulled her close.

Anne breathed deeply and snuggled against him. Welcome home and welcome back—like they'd each been gone on a trip and now returned to where they belonged.

Thank you, God, for giving me a second chance.

****

Gil left early the next morning after breakfast with the promise to call later. Anne had awakened with a new determination to get the rest of her life back on track.

For starters, she would knuckle down and make the necessary changes to her rejected submission and send it off to her agent. He'd either sell it or he wouldn't. She refused to dither over it.

She also decided to run for chapter president. Nancy was right. Her logical decisions and organization skills were excellent and both were assets for the job. And she knew she could count on the support of Nancy, Jen, and Rose.

And with her relationship with Gil back where it belonged, she had no doubt things were looking up. She just hoped she never had to deal with him in a professional capacity again. On the other hand, she really was a body magnet.

Bruno walked up and sat in front of her, his head cocked in a plea for attention. She laughed and picked him up.

"How about it, Bruno? Think I can stay out of trouble for a while?"

Humming a tune, she refilled her coffee cup and made yet another decision. She'd take a crack at writing romantic suspense.

I'll need a pen name, of course, but that can come later. And the first story will be all about a fraudulent agent who gets murdered at a conference.

Anne stood next to the counter and sipped her coffee. A new career direction and a renewed relationship sounded like winners.

Life is good—damned good.

A word from the author...

I was born in Indianapolis, Indiana, but lived for many years in Memphis, Tennessee, which I now consider home. I have two adult children and seven grandchildren. At present, I reside in Ft. Lauderdale, Florida, with my husband, Bruce.

I've been a serious writer since 2002 and belong to Romance Writers of America, River City Romance Writers, Mystery Writers of America, and Florida Mystery Writers.

I love writing and hope readers enjoy the journey along with me.

~*~

Other Suzanne Rossi titles
available from The Wild Rose Press, Inc.

ALONG CAME QUINN
ALL IN THE FAMILY
A TANGLED WEB
NEARLY DEPARTED
HEAR NO EVIL
THE REUNION
DEADLY INHERITANCE
DEATH IS THE PITS
THROUGH MY EYES
A NOVEL DEATH (first of the Snoop Group Series)
RENDEZVOUS WITH DEATH
THE GOOD TWIN
THE ASSASSIN

Thank you for purchasing
this publication of The Wild Rose Press, Inc.

If you enjoyed the story, we would appreciate your
letting others know by leaving a review.

For other wonderful stories,
please visit our on-line bookstore at
www.thewildrosepress.com.

For questions or more information
contact us at
info@thewildrosepress.com.

The Wild Rose Press, Inc.
www.thewildrosepress.com

Stay current with The Wild Rose Press, Inc.

Like us on Facebook

https://www.facebook.com/TheWildRosePress

And Follow us on Twitter
https://twitter.com/WildRosePress

www.ingramcontent.com/pod-product-compliance
Lightning Source LLC
Chambersburg PA
CBHW070334260626
47160CB00003B/1041